I am not for you.

I belong to one man and one man alone, and he does not share. Not like you desire me, at least.

And you—you are not worthy to even think his name. You could not even begin to fathom the sophistication and the polish and the culture and the charm and the elegance and the easy power and the natural domination that man possesses. You just cannot.

I do not think his name. I do not speak his name. Not when I am alone, and not when he deigns to visit me, his chattel. And I certainly do not ever, ever mention him to you, any of you. He is the sun arcing across the horizon, and you are fireflies flitting to and fro in the night, each of you thinking your little light shines the brightest, never realizing how small and insignificant you truly are.

madame X

JASINDA WILDER

BERKLEY BOOKS, NEW YORK

BERKLEY

An imprint of Penguin Random House LLC
375 Hudson Street, New York, New York 10014

MADAME X

This book is an original publication of the Berkley Publishing Group.

Library of Congress Cataloging-in-Publication Data

Wilder, Jasinda.
Madame X / Jasinda Wilder. — Berkley trade paperback edition.
pages ; cm
ISBN 978-1-101-98688-2 (softcover)
1. Man-woman relationships—Fiction.
2. Sexual dominance and submission—Fiction.   I. Title.
PS3623.I5386M33 2015
813'.6—dc23
2015021646

PUBLISHING HISTORY
Berkley trade paperback edition / October 2015

PRINTED IN THE UNITED STATES OF AMERICA

10 9 8 7 6 5 4 3 2 1

Cover photographs: *Woman* © Mayer George / Shutterstock;
New York City Skyline © Ultima Gaina / Thinkstock.
Cover design by Sarah Hansen.
Interior text design by Laura K. Corless.

Penguin
Random
House

ONE

You are beautiful, today. Your eyes are deep-set and dark brown, with a patina of warmth that I am discovering hides a turbulent ocean of intelligence and cunning and cruelty. You are young, today. Not even twenty-five, I believe. Your youth shows in your inability to sit still on my pristine white leather couch, the way you cross your long, lean, slate-gray Armani-sheathed legs ankle-on-knee, and then stretch them out ankle-on-ankle in front of you, and the way you reach with a Rolex-braceleted wrist and delicately pick at an invisible loose thread on your black V-neck T-shirt, the way you brush at your knee with strong but fragile-seeming fingers, and then touch your jaw and then dig in your hip pocket for your sleek smartphone—which isn't there, because unshackling you from that device is an integral part of the training program. And you *definitely* need training.

Your name is Jonathan, today. Not Jon, or John, or Johnny, but Jonathan. You very subtly accentuate the first syllable, *Jon*athan. It is cute, that little accent on the first syllable of your oh-so-generic name. *Jon*athan. As if to make sure I am listening before you say the rest, as if to say "pay attention to who I am." You are so young, Jonathan. You are only a few years younger than I am, but age is so much more than how many times one has spun around the sun. Your age shows through in more than your incapacity for stillness; it is in your eyes, those layered brown eyes, how you look at me with lust and calculation and wonder and not a little fear.

You are like all the rest of you—oh, how I hate the lack of a you-plural conjugation in the English language; other languages are so much more precise and effective and elegant. Let me try this again: You (singular, *Jon*athan) are very much like all the rest of you (plural, the multitude of men-boys that have come and gone before you-singular, *Jon*athan).

You, *Jon*athan, look at me with that needy greedy hungry lusty fear, wondering how you can possess me, how you can circum-navigate the rules binding us to this contract, how you can get me to leave with you and be yours and how you can get me to loosen my top or bend over for you a little so you can catch a better glimpse down my blouse, how you can *have me* in any way at all. But like all the others, you cannot. Not any of that.

I am not for you.

I belong to one man and one man alone, and he does not share. Not what you desire of me, at least.

And you—you, *Jon*athan, and you-plural—you are not worthy to even think his name. You could not even begin to fathom the sophistication and the polish and the culture and the charm and the elegance and the easy power and the natural domination that man possesses. You just cannot.

He is the sun arcing across the horizon, and you are fireflies flitting to and fro in the night, each of you thinking your little light shines the brightest, never realizing how small and insignificant you truly are.

We are sitting on my couch right now, sipping at Harney & Sons Earl Grey tea, and I am noting your posture and the drape of your arm as you lounge, and the angle of your wrist as you sip, and the sweep of your neck and the shift of your eyes. I see all of this, I note each detail, and I adjudicate it all, make mental tallies and prepare my lesson. For now, though, I sip, and try to let you guide our conversation.

You are an abysmal conversationalist, Jonathan. You speak of sports, like a common boy squatting on a bar stool swilling beer. As if *I* could ever possibly spare a single moment of thought for such tripe. But I let you natter on about some player, and I nod and *ummmm-hmmm* at all the right pauses, and let my eyes shine as if I give one single shit. Because you need this lesson, Jonathan. I am going to let you ramble about this football of yours and pretend to care and will let you go on and on and waste my time and yours, and when you run out of words, or maybe even finally realize I am merely humoring you, I am going to gut you like a fish.

You bore me, so I will not be gentle about it, Jonathan.

". . . And he's putting up numbers like nobody's business, you know? Like, he's just a fucking *beast* on the field, no one can touch him, not once he's got the ball. Every game I'm like, I'm like *give him the fucking ball you goddamned idiot*, just feed him the ball, it's all you have to do. Obviously I picked him for my fantasy football league, and he's gonna make me a shitload of money . . ." You gesticulate with your hands, roll them in circles, and you go on and on and on, until I'm having to force myself to hear each individual word as if they're nuggets of sound without substance.

I finish my tea.

I pour another cup, and drink half of that, and you have not finished your first because you're *still talking*, and it is just interminable.

Finally, I cannot endure it any longer.

I set my teacup down on the saucer with a loud, intentional clatter, and you're startled into silence. I let the absence of noise flow through me for a moment, bathe in the silence and let my thoughts collect, and let you see my displeasure. You sweat, you shift uncomfortably on the leather, and you do not quite meet my gaze. You know you have erred.

"Madame X, I'm sorry, I—"

"That is quite enough, *Jon*athan." I say it the way you do, accentuating that first syllable, to show you how silly it sounds. "You have wasted nearly thirty minutes of my time. Remind me, *Jon*athan, how much per hour do our sessions cost your father?"

"I, um . . ."

I eye you with razors in my gaze. "Yes? Speak up, speak clearly, and do attempt to eradicate the noisome filler words."

"A thousand dollars an hour, Madame X."

"Correct. One thousand U.S. dollars per hour. And having just wasted thirty minutes babbling about *football*, how much have you wasted?"

"Five hundred dollars."

"Correct. At least you can manage simple mathematics." I sip at my tea, gathering my ire into a concentrated ball at my core. "Enlighten me, *Jon*athan, as to why you thought such ridiculous trash would be worth my time."

"I, um—"

I set my cup down with a clatter yet again, and you flinch. I stand up, smooth my dress over my hips—and I do not miss the rake of your eyes over me as I do so—and I move to the doorway. "We are done here, Mr. Cartwright."

"No, Madame X, I'm sorry, I'll do better, I promise—"

"I don't think you will, because I don't believe you are capable of better, Mr. Cartwright. You can't even stop saying 'um' and 'like' and using vulgarity. Not to mention wasting our time together to talk about football."

"I was making conversation, Madame X."

"No, *Jonathan*, you were not. You were not talking *to* me, you were talking *at* me. You were spewing excrement from your mouth, simply for the sake of hearing yourself speak. Perhaps among your . . . *friends* . . . such trash could be considered conversation. *I* am a *lady*. I am not your friend. I am not some empty-headed bar slut that can be dazzled by your white teeth and coiffured hair and expensive slacks. I don't care how much your father is worth, Mr. Cartwright. Not even remotely. So if you wish to continue these sessions, you're going to have to improve, and rather swiftly. I do not have time to waste, nor the patience to deal with nonsense."

"I'm sorry, Madame X."

I glare at you. "You're sniveling, and groveling. You act like a child. When you speak you fill your sentences with profanity and yet say nothing of value. And when I call you out on your failings, you apologize like a boy caught with his hand in the cookie jar."

You just stare at me, sitting forward with your wrists on your knees, fingers twitching and scratching and plucking restlessly. You have no dignity, no posture, no elegance. You have all the charm of a tree stump.

My work with you will be a true test of my skills. I find myself angry as I lecture you. Angry at you, for being an apish dolt. Angry at . . . *him* . . . for making me waste my time on a fumbling, stuttering, cursing man-child like you, because you, Jonathan, are all that represents the worst of my clientele. I am bored with you, and I am angry, simmering with barely veiled contempt; and Jonathan? That does not bode well for you.

"Sit up straight. Keep your hands still. Lean back on the couch and relax. Your body language must exude confidence and control, Mr. Cartwright. You must appear at ease at all times."

"I *am* at ease," you argue.

I do not bother responding, I just pace across the room toward you and stop so I am standing almost between your knees. I keep my eyes on yours, let all the weight of my bearing and training bear down on you, let my total and complete disregard for you show. You are no one. You are nothing. You are a child. A beautiful, spoiled child. And I let all this show in my gaze as I stare down at you.

You shift uncomfortably yet again, transferring your weight from one buttock to the other. You look away first, and you trace the crease of your slacks with a finger.

And I merely stand in front of you, staring you down in silence. You crack.

"What? What do you want, Madame X?"

"And *that* is why you're here. You shouldn't have to ask that. You should know. Better yet, *you* should tell *me* what I want. That would be a start."

"What would it take for you to be interested in me?" You ask this in a simpering tone, even though I can tell you meant it to sound seductive. Or something.

I laugh and turn away. "Oh, *Jonathan*. I could *never* be. You couldn't possibly interest me. Not in the slightest. You lack . . . well, there is simply too much to enumerate. Which is why you're here."

I hear you stand up, and I wait for you to make your move. You sidle up behind me, and yes, you are tall, and yes, you have spent enough time in the gym to have a well-sculpted physique. Without dominance and bearing, however . . . it is nothing. You put your hands on my waist, turn me in place, and I let you.

"Why am I here, Madame X?"

"You shouldn't have to ask that, *Jonathan*."

"Why do you keep saying my name that way?"

"It's how you say it."

"It sounds ridiculous."

"And so do you."

You lower your brows and the scrim of warmth I once saw is being skimmed away. Good. I want to pare the façade away; I want to get to your true nature.

"I do not," you insist.

I smile, and it is an amused, cruel smile. "If you want to argue, seek out your sister. Or join a high school debate team. Arguing should be beneath you."

"Why am I here, Madame X?" You ask it again, and still your hands are on my waist, but you do nothing with that.

My allowing you to touch me is currency, and yet you fail to spend it.

"You really don't know?"

You shrug. "Not really."

"Who am I?"

"You're Madame X."

"And what does that mean, do you think?"

You blink, and glance up to the right. "You're . . . you provide a service." I merely stare at you with a raised eyebrow. You clear your throat and stammer. "Well, I—um."

"If you say 'um' one more time, I shall be displeased." My voice is cold, but I let you continue to touch me, just to see what you will do.

"I don't want to say it."

"Coward." I let the word drop from my lips like a stone.

You let go, pace a few steps away, flushing, and turn back. "You're like a . . . a prostitute. Or an escort. But . . . not."

I let the razors come out of my gaze as you turn to watch my reaction. I stalk toward you, hips swaying with extra seduction, lip curled in scorn. "Oh really? You think so?"

"Well, not exactly, but . . ."

"You think this is about *sex*?" I stop a hairbreadth away from you. The tips of my breasts almost touch your T-shirt, but do not. "What gave you that impression, Mr. Cartwright?"

You blush, and then pale. "Well, I mean, your name is Madame X. Like a . . . a madam. And a thousand dollars an hour? I mean, come on."

"What about me says *prostitute*, Mr. Cartwright?" I lift my chin and keep my gaze unblinking on yours.

"Nothing . . . I mean . . ." You pause and I let the silence hang, let you hang yourself on your silence.

A minute of silence is excruciating under most circumstances; for you, this is pure torture.

"Did you read the contract, Mr. Cartwright?" I arch an eyebrow.

You shrug with insouciance. "Not really."

"And yet you hope to inherit your father's company?" I shake my head. "Pathetic."

You are getting incensed. Your tells are like telegraphs: flaring nostrils, narrowed eyes, fingers flexing into fists. "I'm getting tired of this. I'm not paying a thousand dollars an hour to be insulted."

"*You* aren't paying me anything, your *father* is. And I hope you do get tired of it. Maybe you will find the internal fortitude to stop earning my insults."

I turn away from you and retrieve our contract. It is short and simply worded, but iron-clad. You signed it, and so did I, and so did your father. I know the wording by heart, and I know your father read it, but you are simply too lazy and too entitled to be bothered.

With the contract in one hand, I use my other to shove you. The flat of my palm strikes you center-chest, and you're so surprised you fall backward and sit down hard on the couch. You are shocked into stillness. I put one foot on the gleaming dark African teak hardwood between your feet, place the stiletto of my black Louboutin on your chest, press just hard enough to cause discomfort.

"Pay attention, Jonathan. First, and most important, never *ever* sign anything without reading it all, every paragraph and subheading, every line of fine print. You'd think your father would have taught you this by now." You open your mouth to protest, but I grind my heel into your chest and you snap your teeth closed. "I'm going to read this to you, Jonathan, and you're going to listen. It's very simple, really."

I lean forward, and your eyes widen as I intensify the pain. And still, your eyes flit to the curve of my calf where the deep jade of the Valentino dress has pulled up to just beneath my knee.

"Pay *attention*, you twit. Keep your eyes on mine, not on my legs." I ease off so you can listen. "'By signing this document, the signees agree to the following stipulations as they pertain to both the contractor, hereafter referred to as Madame X, and the client, Jonathan Edward Cartwright III. Item number one: Neither Madame X nor the client shall in any way refer to or discuss with anyone this contract or the services provided, nor the stipulations or conditions contained herein. Item number two: Remuneration to Madame X shall be carried out via electronic bank transfer from the accounts of Jonathan Edward Cartwright II to the accounts of Indigo Services, LLC, the terms of which shall not be added to, enhanced, changed, or in any way amended by either Madame X or the client. Item number three: The services provided by Madame X, acting as a subcontracting agent for Indigo Services, shall not include sex acts of any kind, whether oral, manual, or penetrative, and such acts shall not be inferred, requested, or demanded by either Madame X on behalf of Indigo Services or by Jonathan Edward Cartwright III nor any representatives of the client.

Item number four: The particulars of this contract as pertain to the educational services provided shall remain under the authority of Madame X alone, and may not be challenged, defied, or protested by the client or his representatives, and to in any way seek to alter or challenge the educational program and any methods used shall result in the termination of the contract, which shall result in a termination fee equal to the total estimated billable program hours provided at inquiry, plus a grievance fee of thirty-five percent of the total. Item number five: The educational program pamphlet provided at inquiry is a licensed, copyrighted, and legally protected proprietary document. The pamphlet and its contents shall not be copied, distributed, or in any way communicated to anyone not named in this contract. Breach of this item shall result in immediate termination of the contract, resulting in all of the attendant termination fees, as well as any and all actions necessary to punish copyright infringement.'" I pause and glance at you, and see that you have indeed been listening, and that you also wish you'd read the contract, and, probably, the pamphlet. "Well, Jonathan? Any questions?"

You shake your head. "No. No. I see that I was in error by not reading the contract. I'm sorry, Madame X. I hope I didn't insult you."

I smile generously and withdraw my foot from your chest. You rub at the sore spot with a palm, and I am dismayed to see that your hand shakes as you do so. "Did you read the pamphlet, Jonathan?"

You shake your head again. "No, no, I didn't."

"Stop wasting words. Say what you mean, and only that."

"Okay."

"Not 'okay,' Jonathan; 'yes, Madame X.'" It is a test; if you actually obey me, respond with such sniveling submissiveness, then you will have failed the test, and failed it miserably.

Your eyes narrow and you take a deep breath. "You're playing games with me."

I smile at you, and this is my razor-blade smile, my predator smile. You shrink away from me as I lean in, and your eyes go to my cleavage. "Eyes on mine, Jonathan," I snap. "You don't get to look at me like that. You haven't earned it."

"Earned it?" There is hope in your voice.

Pathetic boy.

I put my hands on the back of the couch, on either side of your head. My face is inches from yours, and I can smell your putrid breath, and I can tell you didn't bother to brush your teeth this morning. I do not even know where to start with you, how I can even begin to salvage your entitled, spoiled, lazy, passive personality. I stare you down until you look away and try to bury yourself into the couch cushions.

When I know you will listen, I straighten and stand with my spine stiff and my head high, literally and figuratively looking down my nose at you. "I am not being paid to be *nice* to you, Jonathan, so I'm not going to be. I am being paid to teach you how to be a *man*. How to sit, stand, speak, eat, drink, and think like not just some rich and lazy little bastard, but like the heir to a multibillion-dollar company. I wouldn't give you the time of day otherwise, Jonathan. I wouldn't look at you twice. I wouldn't even bother to smile at you if I saw you at a bar, or on the street. You exude incompetence. Your entire bearing and attitude says you don't give a single shit how you're perceived."

"I thought I wasn't *supposed* to care?" you ask.

"Wrong. You must *always* be aware how you are perceived. Appearing as if you're so confident in yourself that the opinions of passersby don't matter is one thing, and that is what you're after: the appearance of casual confidence, the appearance of insouciance and just enough arrogance to be attractive." I gesture at you with a finger, sweeping up and down to indicate you as a whole. "Right now, Jonathan? You stink. Your breath is rancid, and you've put on far too much overpriced, low-quality cologne. That all by itself is a turn-off. No woman will ever want to be around a man who can't even remember to brush his teeth before he meets her. And that's just my olfactory impression. You're deferent and submissive, yet utterly arrogant. You didn't bother to read a contract you signed, so you don't even know what it is you agreed to. This tells me you're hopelessly lazy and totally incompetent. You have no bearing, no presence. I have no desire to spend another moment in your company, not for anything. You bored me with talk of *football*, of all things. In a word, Jonathan Cartwright, you are pathetic. We're done here."

I point at the door, and you stand up, visibly angry now.

"You can't talk to me like this—"

"I most certainly can. I do not need you. I have a client waiting list two years long. I did not seek you out; your father sought *me* out, because you are hopeless. Your father, now . . . *he* has presence. When your father enters a room, people notice. When he speaks, people listen. And yes, that is due in part to the fact that he's one of the wealthiest men in the country. But how do you think he earned his wealth? By sitting around and watching football? By coasting along on his father's coattails? No! He *demanded* that his peers take notice, and they did. He demands attention and respect simply by merit of who he is. You . . . do not." I twist the doorknob and pull the door open, gesture to the foyer and the elevator beyond. "Go away, Jonathan, and don't bother coming back unless you can learn basic hygiene at the very least, if not how to make interesting conversation."

You stare at me, anger and embarrassment and hurt in your eyes. You *hate* being compared to your father, of course, but only because you know that such comparisons find you deeply lacking.

I shut the door behind you, and when I hear the elevator door slide open and closed once more, only then do I let myself slump against the door and shake with nerves and breathe. I just insulted the son of one of the most powerful men in the world.

But then, such is my job.

A knock on the door, the silent swing of hinges, and then heat and hardness behind me, a faint but intoxicating hint of cologne, the creak of leather. Hands on my waist, lips at my neck. Breath on my skin.

I don't dare tense, don't dare suck in a sharp breath of fear. I don't dare pull away.

Strong, hard, powerful hands twist me in place, and an index finger touches my chin, lifts my face, tilts my gaze. I cannot breathe, don't dare, haven't been given permission.

"You are lovelier than ever, X." A deep, smooth, cultured voice, like the purr of a finely tuned engine.

"Thank you, Caleb." My own voice is quiet, careful, my words chosen and precise.

"Scotch." The command is a murmur, barely audible.

I know how to prepare it: a cut-crystal tumbler, a single ice cube, thick amber liquid an inch from the top. I offer the tumbler and wait, keep my eyes downcast, hands behind my back.

"You were too harsh on Jonathan."

"I must respectfully disagree."

"His father expects results."

I bristle, and it does not go unnoticed. "Have I ever failed to produce results?"

"You sent him away after less than an hour."

"He wasn't ready. He needed to be shown his faults. He needs to understand how much he has to learn."

"Perhaps you're right." Ice clinks, and I take the empty tumbler, set it aside, and force myself to remain in place, force myself to keep breathing and remind myself that I must obey. "I didn't come here to discuss Jonathan Cartwright, however."

"I suppose not." I shouldn't have said that. I regret it as soon as the words tumble free.

My wrist bones scrape together under a crushing grip. Hard dark eyes find mine, piercing and frightening. "You suppose not?"

I should beg forgiveness, but I know better. I lift my chin and meet those cold, cruel, intelligent dark eyes. "You know I will fulfill the contract. That's all I meant."

"No, that isn't all you meant." A hand passes through artfully messy black hair. "Tell me what you really meant, X."

I swallow hard. "You're here for what you always want when you visit me."

"Which is?" A warm finger touches my breastbone, slides into the valley of my cleavage. "Tell me what I want."

"Me." I whisper it, so not even the walls can hear.

"All too true." My skin burns where that strong finger with its manicured nail traces a cutting line up to my shoulder. "You test my patience, at times."

I stand stock-still, not even breathing. Breath whispers across my neck, huffs hot on my nape, and fingers toy with the zipper of my dress.

"I know," I say.

And then, just when I expect to feel the zipper slide down my spine, body heat recedes and that hot breath now laced with hints of scotch is gone, and a single word sears my soul:

"Strip."

My tongue scrapes over dry lips, and my lungs constrict, protesting my inability to breathe. My hands tremble. I know this is expected of me, and I cannot, dare not resist, or protest. And . . .

part of me doesn't want to. But I wish . . . I wish for the freedom to choose what I want.

I have hesitated too long.

"X. I said . . . *strip*." The zipper slides down to between my shoulder blades. "Show me your skin."

Reaching behind my back, I lower the zipper to its nesting place at the base of my spine. Hard, insistent hands assist me in brushing the sleeves from my shoulders, down my arms, and then the dress is floating to the floor at my feet. That's all the help I'll get. I know from long experience that I must make a show of what comes next.

I turn my head, and see tanned skin and the perpetual two-day stubble on a refined, powerful jawline, sharp cheekbones, firm, thin lips, black eyes like voids, eyes that drip desire. My hair drapes over one shoulder. I lift one knee so my now-bare toes touch the gleaming teak, curl my shoulders in, let my gaze show my vulnerability. With a deep breath, I unhook my bra, let the garment fall away.

I reach for my underwear.

"No," comes the purr, "leave them. Let me."

I let my fingers graze my thighs, wait. My underwear slides down slowly, and where fingers touch, so too do lips, hot and damp, touching my skin, and I cannot flinch, cannot pull away or express how badly I want only to be alone, to even *once* have the right to want something else.

But I do not have that right.

Hands blaze over my bared skin and ignite my desire against my will. I know all too well the heat of this touch, the fires of climax, the moments of afterglow when dark eyes drowse and powerful hands are stilled and I am allowed to let my guard down. I stand still, knees shaking, as lips scour and slide over trembling skin. My thighs are nosed open, and lightning strikes with the touch of a tongue to my slick skin.

I gasp, but a single look silences me.

"Don't breathe, don't speak, don't make a sound." I feel the whisper on my hip, feel the vibrations in my bones, and I nod my assent. "Don't come until I tell you."

I have no choice but to stand and accept silently the assault on my senses: down-soft hair against my belly, stubble on my thighs, hands cupping my backside, fury blooming within me. I hold it back, keep it tamped down, bite my tongue to silence the moans, fist my hands at my sides, because I haven't been given permission to touch.

"Good. Let go now, X. Give me your voice." A finger pierces me, curls, finds my need and sets it free, and I loose my voice, let moans and whimpers escape. "Good, very good. So beautiful, so sexy. Now show me your room."

I lead the way to my bedroom, push open the door to reveal the white bedspread, plumped black pillows, all tucked and arranged, as required. I lie down, setting aside pillows, and wait. Eyes rake over my nude form, examine me, assess me.

"I think an extra twenty minutes in the gym would do you well." This criticism is delivered clinically, meant to remind me of my place. "Trim down, just a touch."

I hide the clutch in my gut, the ache in my heart, the burn in my eyes. Hide it, bury it, because it is not allowed. I blink, nod. "Of course, Caleb."

"You are lovely, X. Don't mistake me."

"I know. And thank you."

"It's just that our clients expect perfection." A lifted eyebrow indicates that I should finish the statement.

"And so do you."

"Exactly. And you, X, I know you can deliver. You *are* perfect, or very nearly, at least." A smile now, blazing and brilliant and blinding, excruciatingly beautiful, meant to soothe. A finger touches my lips and then traces favorite locations on my anatomy: lips, throat, breasts, hips. "Roll over."

I move to my stomach.

"On your knees."

I draw my knees beneath my stomach.

"Give me your hands."

I reach back with both hands, and my wrists are pinioned in one large, brutally powerful hand. My shoulder blades touch each other as my arms are drawn together, and my face is pressed into the mattress. I swallow hard, brace, breathe.

Oh, the ache, the fierce throb as I'm penetrated. I'm rocked forward and my shoulders twinge and the grip on my wrists holds me in place.

I have no choice but to feel the burgeoning blaze, no choice but to let it push through me and make me breathless, and I want to cry, want to cry, want to cry.

But I don't.

Not yet.

I let myself go when I'm told to do so: "Come for me, X."

And then it's over, and I'm turned to lie on my back, gasping, and whispers bathe over me. "So good, X. So beautiful." A finger to my chin, lifting my gaze. "Did you enjoy that?"

"Yes." It's not a lie. Not entirely, at least.

Physically, I am rocked to trembling. Physically, aftershocks still seize me and touch makes me shiver and I am breathless. Physically, yes, I enjoyed it. I cannot help but enjoy it.

Yet . . . there is a space within me, a deep, deep, deep well where truths I do not even dare think live hidden and always buried. Down there, where those truths reside, I know I crave . . . absolution, freedom, a breath taken in privacy, a word spoken without ulterior motive.

But I cannot let those thoughts bubble up. Cannot, and do not.

I am a master of self-control, after all. I could hold off orgasm indefinitely. I could go without breathing until told to breathe or pass out. I could remain sitting motionless for hours, until told to move. I know I can do these things, because I have. I learned total control in the harshest of schools.

And so it is child's play to let my body drape loosely in the guise of intimacy on a hard, taut, muscular body until a chime from discarded slacks demands attention.

"I have to take this." A pause, a breath, a tap of finger on a cell phone screen. "This is Caleb. Yes. Yes. Sure, give me twenty minutes. Of course. No, don't let him in until I get there."

A kiss to my temple, a finger tracing my body from shoulder to hip to foot. "I have to go."

"All right." I don't ask when to expect a return, because I don't want to know, and because I wouldn't get an answer.

"Will you miss me?"

"Of course." This is a lie, and we both know it.

"Good. Your next client is in two hours, so you have time to shower, dress, and prepare. His name is William Colin Drake, and he's the heir to a technology development company worth fifty billion. Usual terms and conditions apply. The file on William will arrive in the usual manner."

"Should I expect as much trouble with William as with Jonathan?"

A quirk of a smile, amusement. "No, I should think not. William is a much different animal, from what I've observed." A pause, and a speculative glance at me. "But, X?"

"Yes, Caleb?"

"Watch yourself with William. He's got a mean streak."

"Thank you for the warning."

"He needs to learn to control it, so you'll have to draw it out of him and make him aware of it. But be careful."

Draw out his mean streak. Poke a snake, prod a sleeping bear. Risk injury. It won't be the first time, and it won't be the last. Hopefully I won't need medical attention like I did last time. That's not covered in the contract, of course, but it's understood: Never, ever harm the property of Caleb Indigo; it's just not smart business.

When the door closes behind a broad, suit-swathed back, I shower the sex-stink off. I scrub harder and longer than I have to and fight the boil of forbidden emotions. When my skin is rubbed raw, I force myself out of the shower and dress, apply makeup, remake the bed, prepare tea.

And then I seat myself on the couch and breathe, compose myself, push down the vulnerability, put away the fear and the desire. Once again, I am Madame X.

spare a single, momentary glance at the small dark dot in the ceiling, hidden in a corner, and let my eyes betray me. I imagine I see a red dot within the black depths of the camera, and I imagine I can see all the way along the trail of electrons and through the monitor to the faces on the other side.

I imagine, but that is all I can do.

There is a decisive rap on the door, and I rise, breathe out slowly, lift my chin, smooth my dress over my hips, and wiggle my foot in my shoe, breathe, breathe, let the moment linger.

And then I open the door, and I welcome you.

You are handsome, but not beautiful. You hold yourself with dignity, and your gaze betrays arrogance. And yes, as I meet your narrow gray gaze, I see ugliness, a propensity for cruelty, a viciousness.

"I see they didn't exaggerate how hot you are," you say.

I ignore your remark, and gesture to my couch. "William, welcome. Thank you for coming. Have a seat, please. Would you like some tea?"

You eye the decanter. "Scotch would be better." And then you sink down on the couch, cross your ankle over your knee, and wait to be served, and your eyes follow me hungrily. I hand you the tumbler, three ice cubes, a finger of scotch. "I read the contract, and I have to say it wasn't what I was expecting. Neither are you."

I hand you the contract, and you read it yet again, and then you sign it, and so do I. "What were you expecting, William?"

"Well, I certainly wasn't expecting item three, that's for sure. I signed it, so I'll abide by the rules, but I'm disappointed, Madame X. I'd love to get you out of that dress." Your eyes peruse me, take their time cataloging and critiquing my body.

"I'm sure you would, William."

"Call me Will, please." You sip with casual elegance.

"All right then, Will. Tell me, what do you hope to get out of our sessions together?"

"I have a better question." You lean forward, lift the contract as if about to rip it. "What do you say we tear this puppy apart and get to the good stuff? We can always sign it again later."

I must still smell faintly of sex, despite how ruthlessly I scrubbed: Your nostrils flare, and you inhale, lean closer, let your shoulder touch mine. I take the contract from you, gently but firmly, set it on the coffee table, and slide it away from you.

"I think not, William." I stand, take the tumbler from you. You don't protest, but your eyes harden. "You signed it, and you are legally bound by it now. If you do not wish to continue, you may petition to have the contract absolved. If not, then I must insist you keep any further such comments to yourself, as they are neither allowed nor desired."

You stand up, and you are right in front of me. Your eyes are hard, deep, and swirling with potent venom. "Oh, I think you lie, Madame X. I think they *are* desired. But . . . I signed the contract, and I'm a man of my word." You resume your seat on the couch and cross your ankles and grin at me. "So. Teach me. I'm ready to learn."

I walk away from the nugget of truth in your words, breathe slowly, and then turn to you, let my razor-sharp gaze rake over you, let the silence expand. You don't shift, but you begin to show signs of discomfort.

"Tell me, William. What is your deepest, darkest secret?"

You are the one to let the silence breathe, this time, and your eyes pierce, and burn. "I'm not sure you really want to know, Madame X."

"Oh, but I do, William. I wouldn't have asked if I didn't." I take two steps closer to you. "You don't really think you can shock me, do you?"

You swallow, and blink, and then you let a smile curl your lips. "Fine, but you asked for it. And . . . this is covered under the contract, yes? You can't talk about this to anyone?"

"I cannot, and I would not." I don't tell you about the cameras, or the microphones.

"I like it . . . rough," you say. "And I like them . . . unwilling." You eye me, as if to assess the effect of your words.

I nod. "Go on."

And you do go on, in ever more graphic detail.

I've never been so glad of the third stipulation as I am now.

TWO

wake abruptly; I am not alone.

Expensive cologne, just a hint of it in the air. There are other scents layered beneath the cologne, but they are too faint for me to identify. My bedroom is blackout dark, so there is nothing to see but shadows within shadows. My noise machine shushes, the soothing, gentle crash of waves on a shore.

Sleep is nearly impossible for me, because of the dreams.

"Caleb." I keep my voice low, steady.

There is no answer. I need none, however. I will wait. I sit up, tug the sheet across my chest, tuck it under my arms. The flat sheet—a thousand thread count, softest Egyptian cotton—is my only shield, and it is a thin and flimsy one at best.

Click. Low amber light washes over me, bathing the room in a dim glow. There, in the Louis XIV armchair in the corner beside my bed, next to the floor-to-ceiling window with its black-out curtain. Tailored black slacks, from a suit. Crisp white shirt, cuff links with two-carat diamond inserts. The collar is unbuttoned. Only one button, just the very uppermost; the concession to the late hour is shocking in its uncharacteristic casualness. No tie. I see it folded, the thinnest end hanging out of an inner pocket of the suit coat, which is draped over the back of the chair.

Dark eyes fixed on me. Unblinking. Piercing. Steady, cold, unreadable. Yet . . . there is something. Wariness? Something I cannot fathom.

"Lower the sheet."

Ah. A slight slur.

I release the sheet, let it pool around my waist. My nipples harden in the coolness, under the scrutiny of that dark gaze.

"Kick it away."

I bend my knee, lift my leg, push the sheet away with my toe. Red silk underwear, bikini cut. I keep my gaze level, my breathing even, do nothing to betray the hammering of my heart, the churn in my belly.

"To whom do you belong, X?"

"To you, Caleb." It is the only answer. The only answer there has ever been.

"What do I want, X?"

"Me."

One button, two, three, and then the shirt joins the suit coat, folded neatly on the back of the chair. Shoes, set aside. Socks folded, tucked into a shoe. Trousers, next. The zipper, so slowly. A torture of moments, waiting for the *zzzzzzhrip*. Waiting for the thin, stretchy cotton of black boxer-briefs to find their resting place atop the trousers, folded in department-store-precise thirds on the cushion.

I do not look away. I follow each motion, and I keep my expression neutral. The body revealed is a study in classic masculine beauty. A sculpture of perfection carved from flesh. Muscles toned, carefully and exquisitely crafted. A smattering of dark hair on the chest, a trail from flat belly to thick erection. It is a body designed to engender desire in the viewer. And it does. Oh yes, it does. I am not immune.

The bed dips. Long, thick fingers with neatly manicured nails sweep through my thick black hair, which is loose around my shoulders at the moment. It is never down, unless I am in bed. Otherwise, it is done up in a chignon, or a neat braid pinned in a coil. Never down. The curve of a woman's neck and throat is as exotic and erotic as breasts, when properly displayed; this was an early lesson. A tug of the hand, and my throat is bared, my head pulled back. This roughness is unexpected. I stifle a gasp of surprise. Not fear. I cannot, must not fear. I dare not even allow myself to feel it, much less let it show.

Lips, nipping and kissing my throat. Wet, slow, ever so slightly clumsy. Those lips, on my cheek. Sour alcohol-laced breath wafts over me. Fingers delve, dig, pierce. I am not ready, but that does not matter. Not now, not in this moment. Perhaps not ever. Momentary discomfort, and then a finger finds my most sensitive bundle of nerves, sweeps across it, and I feel wetness lubricate me, seep through my privates. A gasp, then. A male grunt, as uncharacteristic as the unbuttoned collar and the intoxicated late-night visit.

A tongue, sweeping across my nipple. Hardness nudging my softness. Penetration. Once, twice, lips on my cheek, my chin, my throat, my breastbone. I am pressed into the mattress by heavy weight, a hand on my hip, a trim waist pressing my thighs apart. I begin to wonder, deep in the recesses of my mind, how long this will last, this face-to-face encounter.

Not long.

Hands on my hips, turning me to my stomach. Drawing my hips up, my knees beneath me. A hand fisting in my hair, another on my hip. Hot, hard presence behind me, fingers searching, finding me damp and ready, guiding the thick bare member into me.

Long, slow, unhurried. Not exactly rough, but sloppy. Not with the usual efficiency and masterful pacing. No, this is a slow rhythm, lazy at first and then building and building and building. I cannot resist the burgeoning within me, the pressure of an impending climax throbbing through me. I dare not release it, however, so I clench my fists and squeeze my eyes shut and focus on containing it, holding it back.

The pace becomes punishing, then. Closest to rough as it's ever been. But still, even in intoxication, exquisitely masterful. This body was created for sex. Designed to own, to pleasure, to dominate. And I am, all of those things.

Whether I will it, or no.

"Now, X. Come for me, right now. Give me your voice." A rasping murmur, low and strong.

I finally let go with a panting moan at the base of my throat, let the climax burn through me.

Finished, I am allowed to fall forward. Absence behind me. Faucet running. I am nudged to my back, handed a damp, warm washcloth.

"Clean yourself."

I obey, and return the cloth, roll to my side, and let my eyes slide closed. Let my emotions welter, tumble, let the post-orgasmic drowsiness tug me under. Let the deep, powerful riptide of my most private thoughts and fears and desires spin me into a disoriented tumble, far beneath the tumultuous surface of the sea that is consciousness.

Blood. Sirens. Loss. Confusion. Rain in the darkness, lightning gouging the blackness, thunder throbbing in the distance. Weeping. Alone.

"X—wake up. Wake up. You're dreaming again." Hands on my waist, lips at my ear, a comforting whisper.

I bolt upright, sobbing. Hair sticks to my forehead in sweat-smeared tangles. Strands in my mouth. My back is damp with sweat. My arms shake. My heart is hammering.

"Sshh. Hush. You're okay now."

I shake my head. I'm not okay. Eyes closed, fighting for breath—I can see nothing but snatches of nightmare:

Blood, crimson and thick, swirling and mixing with rain on a sidewalk. A pair of eyes, open, vacant and unseeing. Limbs bent at unnatural angles. A stab of lightning, sudden and bright, illuminating the night for the space of a heartbeat. An all-consuming sensation of horror, terror, the kind of loss that steals your breath and sucks the marrow from your bones.

Sobs. Wracked, shaking, incapable of speech. I try to push it down, gain control, but I cannot. I can only sob and gasp and tremble, shiver and weep. My lungs ache. I cannot breathe, cannot think, can only see the blood, the blood, scarlet and thick as syrup, arterial, lifeblood leaking away and mixing with rain.

"X. Breathe. Breathe, okay? Look at me. Look at my eyes." I seek dark eyes, find them strangely warm, concerned.

"Can't—can't breathe—" I gasp.

Pulled against a firm, smooth chest. Heartbeat under my ear. I tense; comfort like this is alien. I still cannot breathe, or blink. Paralyzed with fear, with the poison of nightmares in my blood.

"How did we meet, X?"

"You—s-s-saved me."

"That's right. What did I save you from?"

"Him. Him." I feel a presence from my dream, a malevolence, a hunger for that scarlet lifeblood.

"I found you on the sidewalk, bleeding to death. You'd been badly hurt. Beaten nearly to death. Savaged almost beyond recognition. I took you in my arms and carried you to the hospital. You'd crawled, alone, dying . . . so far. A mile, almost. They think you knew where the hospital was, and you were trying to get there. But you didn't quite make it."

"You carried me to the hospital." In reciting the words, I can begin to find my breath.

"That's right." A pause, a breath. "I brought you in, and they wouldn't let me go back with you, but you had no identification and you were unconscious. I just couldn't leave you alone, not knowing what had happened to you. Not knowing if you'd be okay. So they let me stay in the triage room while they worked on you."

"You waited for six hours. I died on the table, but they brought me back." I know these words, this story. It is the only history I have.

"Your head had been badly damaged. Of your many injuries, your cranial injury was the most worrisome, they told me. You might never regain consciousness, they told me. And if you did, you might remember nothing. Or some things but not others. Or everything. Or you might be paralyzed, or have a stroke. With the damage to your brain, there was no way to know until you woke up."

"And I almost didn't wake up."

"I had to leave eventually, but I came back the next day, to check on you."

"And the next, and the next." I know all the beats, all the pauses, where to say my lines. I can breathe. I can work my lungs: inflate, deflate; inhale, exhale. Flex my fingers, blink my eyes, focus on curling my toes. Familiar exercises.

"The police found the crime scene where you'd been attacked. It was murder. You had a family, but they'd been murdered. And you'd witnessed it. Seen it all. Barely survived."

"And he's still out there."

"Waiting for you to show your face. Waiting to make sure you can't ever tell anyone what you know."

"But I don't know anything. I can't remember anything." This is true. This is a part of the ritual, but it is true.

"I know that, and *you* know that. But he doesn't. The murderer is out there, and knows you survived, and knows you saw everything."

"You'll protect me." Another truth.

One of very few. I am protected. Provided for. Kept safe.

Kept.

"I will protect you. You have to trust me, X. I'll keep you safe, but you have to trust me."

"I trust you, Caleb." Those four words, I must bite them out. Sometimes, I do not believe them; other times, I do. Tonight is the former.

It is like eating an orange, trying to separate the seeds from the flesh and spit out the seeds only. There is truth, but also lies. Trust, but something bitter as well, something foul.

"Good." Fingers in my thick black hair. Smoothing. Petting. "Sleep now."

Click. Darkness now, a blanket settling over me, the noise machine soothing me with gently crashing waves on an imaginary shore. I let the sound of the waves take me away, like floating away on a tide.

Distantly, I hear the door open, close.

I am alone.

THREE

The light of dawn brings with it shame. I am weak. I was weak. The nightmares, they sap me of my strength. Turn me into this creature, this soft, vulnerable thing, all underbelly and no armor. Starved for oxygen, starved for light, hungry for touch to remind me that the dreams are only fiction, to remind me that I am safe, I turn to the only comfort I can find.

The ritual.

The words.

The history.

But in the light of day—showered and dressed, hair braided and twisted into a knot at the back of my head, makeup carefully applied, feet sheathed in expensive heels—garbed in my armor, I am not that mewling kitten, and I despise her. If I could get my claws into that version of myself, I would shred her without mercy, tear her to bits. Shake her until her teeth clack together, give her a taste of the verbal venom I use to keep errant rich boys in line. Tell her a lady does not show fear. A lady does not cry in front of anyone. A lady does not ever show weakness. *Chin up*, I'd say. *Back straight. Find your dignity, put it on like a suit of armor.*

I do those things. Scour myself of emotion. Turn away from the mirror in my walk-in closet, away from the temptation to examine the scars on my belly, my arms, my shoulder, beneath the roots of my hair on the left side of my skull, midway up between the top of my ear and the crown of my head. There are no scars. No reminders of a lost past. No weakness, no nightmares, no need for comfort.

I am X.

It is just past five in the morning. I prepare a breakfast of free-range egg whites, hand-ground wheat toast with a thin scrim of organic butter. Slice open a grapefruit, cover half with plastic wrap and return it to the refrigerator, tap a few granules of Truvia onto each wedge of the grapefruit. Black tea, no sugar or milk. Organic vitamin supplements.

Later, between clients, I will spend an hour on the rowing machine, and then an hour doing yoga. Then there will be lunch: a salad of fresh, organically grown spinach, walnuts, dried cranberries, crumbles of bleu cheese, and a drizzle of vinaigrette, a bowl of fresh fruit sliced and mixed, a bottle of distilled, deionized water. Or, alternatively, a superfoods smoothie, green, bitter, and healthy.

An extra twenty minutes in the gym, I'd been told. Trim down, that meant. The diet and exercise instruction had come with the packet I received every morning, a large manila envelope slipped under the door, containing the dossiers on my clients for the day and the attendant contracts.

Timed correctly, there are always a few extra minutes after breakfast and before my first client of the day. I finish breakfast at 5:45 A.M., and my first client arrives at 6:15 A.M.; the earliest slot is reserved for the most difficult of clients, those most in need of a jarring lesson. If you cannot make the early time, you fail the course, and you are charged the termination and grievance fee.

In the thirty minutes to myself, before William Drake arrives, I stand at the window in the living room, staring down at the bustling streets below. This is my favorite pastime, watching the people scurry here and there, talking on their cell phones, newspapers tucked under business-suit arms, slim pencil dresses slit just so in the back and hugging stockinged legs. I imagine their stories.

That man, there, in the charcoal suit just a little too loose around the middle, shoulder pads a little too thick, slacks a little long at the heel. Balding, a tea-saucer-sized bare spot at the back of his head. Talking on a cell phone, hand gesturing frantically, angrily, forefinger stabbing the air. Red in the face. He's a struggling businessman, fighting upstream in a cutthroat business. Stocks, maybe. Or law. Corporate law. He's always behind, just barely not making it. A wife, a young son. He's older than his wife by several years, and his son is just starting school. He's old enough that taking care of a child on top of fighting to make it at the firm is a Sisyphean task. His wife married him because she thought their fortunes would improve, a promotion would put them in an easier place, and she needed a green card, maybe. There's affection, but no real love. He's too busy for love, too busy clocking sixty or eighty hours per week trying to make the exorbitant New York City rent. They live in the Bronx, maybe, so she can be nearer to her family, because she needs help. She's probably working a job on the side while her son goes to school, stashing away money unbeknownst to her husband, because she's losing faith in his ability to take care of them. Enough that she could move out and provide for her son if worse came to worst.

It is a pleasant distraction, focusing on the fictional, normal lives of random people. It allows me to safely wonder what life is like out there, for them. Safely, because to wonder what such a life out there would be like for me? That's dangerous. A threat to my sanity, which depends on a careful balancing act.

I hear the faint *ding* of the elevator arriving. I glance at the Venetian-style wall clock: 6:10 A.M.; five minutes early. But a moment or two passes and there is no knock at the door. I move across the room, keeping my heel clicks as silent as possible, and stand by the door, listening.

"Yeah, I'm almost there," you say, your voice low. "I fucking hate these early-ass appointments. No, my dad makes me go. Some kind of stupid corporate training, basically. Make me a better leader, bullshit like that. Put my ass in line. No, man, it's not like that. I can't really get into it. No, for real, I'm not allowed to talk about it. I signed a contract, and if I fuck this up my dad's going to cut me off totally. After what happened with that slut Yasmin, I'm on real thin ice with him, so I've got to toe the fucking line. . . . Or what? Or he'll basically gut the position of president out of the charter and turn all the power over to the board, which means I won't inherit dick when he retires. He's got the documents drawn up. He showed them to me. No, man, I fucking *saw* them, okay? It was after he got the judge to let me out on bail. He had to pay a shitload of money to keep the whole thing quiet. Paid Yasmin like half a mil to keep her fat mouth shut about what happened. My plan? My plan is to go along with this training program, keep my dad happy, play the game. I've got friends on the inside, on the board, certain members who are unhappy with where Dad's been taking the company. If I can string things along another year or two, I can probably work a little magic behind the scenes, steal the whole shit show from the old fucker, and I mean pull a real-deal coup d'état. And as soon as I've got my hands on the company . . . man, I'll be set. I've got

plans . . . no, I can't make it out tonight. I've got . . . other plans. . . .
No, I let that bitch go, she was a screamer. This is a new one. She's
all wrapped up like a sweet little present. She ain't wearing a damn
thing except the handcuffs, and I didn't even have to gag her. No,
you asshole, you can't *help*. Last time I let you help, you took it *way*
too fucking far, and I had to pay the slut to keep her from yapping
about what your stupid ass did to her. I've told you, there's an art to
it. Listen, dude, I'm gonna be late, I've gotta go. The bitch that runs
this show doesn't fuck around, I can tell you that much for free.
Anyway, for real, I've got to go. And Brady? Stay the fuck away from
my place, okay? I'm serious. I'll kill you for fucking real if you go
anywhere near her. All right, bye."

My heart thuds as I take a couple quick steps away from the door,
smoothing my expression into neutrality.

Deep breaths. Focus. Put on the armor. No cracks, no chinks.
Hard. Cold. Smooth. Unassailable. Imagine claws in place of fingernails. Viper eyes. Ice.

Knock-knock.

I glance at the clock: 6:17 A.M. One last deep breath, blown out
through pursed lips. Twist the knob, swing open the door. "Mr.
Drake." An arched eyebrow. "You're late."

You bring up your arm, extend your wrist, bare your extravagant
Blancpain watch. I loathe that movement: arm rises, flick the wrist
forward. It's ostentatious, vain. And that watch? Easily three hundred thousand dollars. Alligator leather, eighteen-karat gold, sapphire crystal face . . . all the fancy trappings of the insecure wealthy.
I am not impressed.

"By like, two minutes, X." You breeze past me, and I gag on your
cologne. You had to have bathed in it to stink so thickly of it. "It's
cool, man. No big deal. Two minutes, whatever. I'm here."

I remain standing by the door, hands at my sides, head high, staring down my nose at you. "No, Mr. Drake. Not whatever." I gesture at the door. "You may go. We are done here."

You have the decency to look at least a little worried. "X, come on. It's two minutes. Who the fuck cares about two little minutes? I was on the phone."

I know, I heard—I know better than to say this, however. "*I* care about two minutes, Mr. Drake. One minute, thirty seconds, a single moment. Late is *late*. You should be knocking on this door at six fourteen. Punctuality is a key trait of the successful, Mr. Drake."

"My dad is late for board meetings all the time," you point out, not moving from your position three steps into my condo.

I quirk an eyebrow. "Your father is the founder, CEO, and majority shareholder of one of the most powerful corporations on earth. He has power, which grants him the privilege of being late, to show up whenever he wishes, because he wields the control. You wield *nothing*, William. You receive an allowance. You are *tolerated*. Your lot in life is to do what you're told, to show up where you are told to show up, *when* you are told to show up, and not a single millisecond later. Your father is one of the biggest, baddest sharks in the ocean, and you are a *guppy*. Good-bye, William. Perhaps next week you will think twice about yapping on your mobile phone outside my door, thus wasting my time, which—need I remind you—is infinitely more valuable than yours will ever be."

You cross the three steps between us in a blur. Your hand is on my throat, cutting off my air supply. Leaving bruises, certainly. You are nose-to-nose with me, eyes radiating fury, panic, and hate. "What did you hear, *whore*?"

I blink, forcing myself to remain calm. My toes barely touch the floor, my high heels drooping off my feet. I cannot breathe. Stars blink and flash in my eyes. I do not fight, do not scrabble at your arms or wrists. I stare at you. Make sure you are holding my gaze. And then, deliberately, I let my gaze flick upward, to the corner of the ceiling where the camera is hidden. Your eyes follow mine, and although you cannot possibly see it as it is far too well hidden, my meaning is clear. I lift my chin, arch an eyebrow.

You drop me. I inhale a deep breath, forcing myself to do so slowly, to lock my knees and remain upright, on my feet. Instinct has me wanting to collapse to the floor, gasping, rubbing my throat. But I do not. Dignity is my armor.

Ding.

Elevator doors *whoosh* open, and you go pale. My door is still open. You back up a step, two, three. Shake your head. Four enormous men stalk through the doorway, wearing identical black suits, white shirts, and slim black ties, with earpieces in their right ears, cords trailing under their collars.

"You will come with us, please, Mr. Drake." One of them speaks, but his lips barely move so it could have come from any one of them.

It is politely phrased, of course, because you are heir to a multibillion-dollar company. But then, you put your hands on me, and Caleb does not tolerate that. Not at all. Not from anyone. If you were not such a pathetic, nasty piece of scum, I would almost pity you. I know these men, and they do not feel mercy.

But then, neither do I.

You puff out your chest. Your lip curls in a derisive sneer. "Fuck off. You can't tell me to do shit." You breeze past me.

You make it perhaps four full strides, which brings you out of my condo and into the hallway. You even round the corner. Big mistake, William. There are no cameras out there. One of the guards moves like a striking cobra, faster than thought. A single blow, jackhammer hard, to your liver. You drop like a sack of flour, moaning, writhing.

"Len," I say. One of the guards swivels his head on his thick neck, glances at me. I beckon to him, a crook of my finger.

He moves to stand in front of me, hands clasped behind his back. "Ma'am?"

"I overheard him speaking on the phone to a friend. I heard some . . . rather unsavory pieces of information." I point at the ceiling. "Are your microphones powerful enough to have caught it?"

Len's face remains impassive. "I don't know what you're—"

"Don't insult my intelligence, Len."

A pause. "I'll check the tapes, ma'am." Len glances at you. "He's a piece of shit."

"He's a predator, Len. A sick, twisted criminal. He has a woman held captive somewhere, and he's going to do something awful to her, if he hasn't already."

"You fucking bitch!" you rasp from the floor. "You can't prove shit."

One of the guards puts a large, polished-to-a-shine dress shoe on your throat. "You don't speak to Madame X that way, boy."

"My father will have all of your jobs," you threaten.

Len laughs. "There are people in this world far more dangerous than your father, kid. Our employer makes your *daddy* look like a sad little kitten."

You glance at me, curious now. "X? She's just a whore."

The shoe presses down, and you choke. Len strides over to you, kneels beside you. "Kid, you have no clue what you're talking about. My friends and I? We're just pawns on the chessboard. X? She's the queen. And you? You're not even on the board. Your precious papa? He might rank as high as a knight. *Maybe.*" Len reaches into his suit coat pocket, pulls out a copy of the contract. "And this? This is a legally binding document, signed by you and your daddy. There's a whole shitload of fine print on this thing, son. You know what that fine print says? It says that my friends and I are going to stomp the sniveling fuck out of your puny little corpse, and then you're gonna show us your little playroom, and then we're going to drag you to the nearest police precinct. And *then* . . . and then our employer is going to sue your father for every dollar and every share he's worth, and there's nothing anyone can do to stop us. Get me . . . *son?*"

You quiver. You want to bluff, you want to bluster. You have never been bullied or threatened before. I doubt you have ever even felt pain. Lily-white little pissant. But Len's eyes, they are a shade of steel-gray that brings to mind razor blades and gunmetal. They are not just cold eyes; ice is cold, winter is cold. Len's eyes? They are vacuum cold. Deep space cold. Zero Kelvin cold. They are not lifeless, because they exude threat, like those of a leopard stalking prey. They hold truths of a dripping-scarlet variety.

Len glances at me. "We can handle things from here, ma'am."

I take that as the cue it is and return inside. Close the door. But I can't resist standing with my ear to the door. There are sounds that make my gut twist. Thuds, smacks, crunches. The sounds gradually become . . . wet.

I shiver, and push away from the door.

Eventually there's the *ding* of the elevator, and I am alone once more. Forty-seven minutes until my next client.

Hands shaking, I make a mug of tea. Earl Grey, a touch of milk. By the time I'm swallowing the final mouthful, the elevator *ding*s again, and my door opens.

The figure that stalks through my door is not a client.

Fury turns dark eyes darker. Lids narrowed to slits. Chest swelling and compressing, fingers curled into fists.

"Are you okay, X?" Voice like thunder, rumbling on the horizon.

I shrug. "It was . . . unpleasant, but I will be fine." My voice is steady, but raspy from being choked.

Hands on my shoulders, gently but firmly holding me in place. Eyes sweep over my face, searching. Flick down to my throat. "He bruised you."

I touch my throat where William grabbed me. The flesh there is tender. I twist gingerly out of the hold on my shoulders, turn to the mirror on the wall above a small decorative side table. My skin is dark, the color of caramel, maybe even a shade or two darker. I don't bruise easily, but there are fingerprint-sized bruises on my throat. My eyes are reddened. My voice is hoarse, raspy.

Presence behind me, hot and huge and angry. "That little fuck is lucky Len got to him before I did."

That makes me shudder, because I'm pretty sure William will never again be as pretty as he once was. Nor as . . . healthy. "I'm fine."

"He's cost me money. You can't work the rest of today, at least. Maybe longer. You can't see clients with bruises on your throat."

So much for concern, it would seem. I push away a knot of bitterness.

"Did Len check the tapes?" I ask.

"Why do you care?"

"I heard what he said to his friend. He should be stopped."

"A report has been filed. The police are investigating." It is not an answer, but then I know better than to expect a confirmation of the cameras and microphones.

I know they are there, but no one will outright confirm it. It is some kind of secret, as if I am not supposed to know that every move I make, every word I speak is watched and overheard. It is for my own protection, I do realize that. Today's events prove as much. But most days, the utter lack of privacy grates, weighs heavily.

"I will be able to work tomorrow," I say.

"Dr. Horowitz will be by later today to check on you. Take it easy for the rest of today." A nose in my hair, near my ear. Inhalation, exhalation, slow, deliberate, with ever so slight a waver in the exhalation. "I'm glad you're okay, X. No one will ever put their hands on you ever again. Clients will be even more thoroughly vetted from now on. That should not have happened. If you'd been seriously hurt, I don't know what I would have done."

"Trained a new Madame X, probably," I say, recklessly. Foolishly. Stupidly.

"There will *never* be another Madame X. There is no one else like you. You are special." This voice, these words, low, quavering with potent emotion, I do not know how to absorb them, how to react to them. "You are *mine*, X."

"I know, Caleb." I can barely speak, do not dare glance in the mirror, do not dare witness such vulnerability, such strange and alien passion.

Fingers, just the tips, the pads, brushing down my cheek. Tracing my high cheekbone. I finally must glance in the mirror, see the dark hair head-and-shoulders above me. Nearly black eyes, pinning me in the reflection. Fingertips, trailing down the side of my neck. Hand, twisting, reaching around my throat, fitting fingers one by one to the bruises, but gently, tenderly, barely making contact.

"Never again."

"I know." I whisper it, because it hurts to speak, and because I somehow dare not speak any louder.

I see the tableau, frozen in the mirror glass: Charcoal suit coatsleeve, slim, tailored, molded to a thick arm. Coat unbuttoned, tie knot just barely visible over my right shoulder, a perfect triangle of crimson silk against spotless white. Dark, potent eyes on mine, a hand clutching my throat. Possessive, owning, yet somehow gentle.

A promise, not a threat. Yet . . . still a warning. *Mine*, that hand on my throat says.

A sudden, deep inhalation, and then I am alone at the mirror, watching a broad back and wide set of shoulders recede.

When the door clicks shut, I can finally let the breath I've been holding rush out, can slump, shaking, hands on my knees. Step out of my bright red Jimmy Choo heels, leave them at the mirror, one upright, the other tipped onto its side.

I suck in a breath, let it out. Another. Shake my hand, curl fingers into a fist, a vain attempt to stop them from trembling. A sob rips out of me. I stifle it. Another, louder. I cannot, cannot. If I give in, that door will open again and I'll succumb to the need for comfort. And I, at war with my disparate selves, need that physical comfort, that carnal reassurance . . . and I also loathe it. Hate it. Revile it. Feel a deep, secret need to shower and scrub the memory of it off my skin as soon as the door closes behind that broad and muscular back.

Yet I need it. Cannot fight my body's reaction to such raw, masculine, sexual, sensual primacy.

I grab a throw pillow from the couch, cross my arms over it, bury my face in the scratchy fabric, and let myself cry. The camera is behind me; it will only see me sitting on the couch, finally processing the events of the morning. It will only see me engaging in a normal, natural reaction to trauma.

I shake all over, shaking so hard my joints hurt, sobbing into the pillow. Alone, I can strip off the armor.

It isn't until I've nearly cried myself out that it hits me: That was the first time in recent memory that a visit came and went, and I remained fully clothed the entire time. An anomaly.

I let my tears dry, find my breath, find my equilibrium. Set aside the pillow. Stand up, shake my hands and toss my hair. No more weakness. Not even alone.

I glance at the clock; it is 7:48 A.M. What am I going to do with the rest of the day? I've never had a whole day to myself. It should be a luxury, a precious gift.

It isn't.

A whole day, alone with my thoughts?

I am terrified.

Silence breathes truth; solitude breeds introspection.

FOUR

You are a woman. I was not expecting this. The dossier listed your name as George E. Tompkins. Twenty-one, five-seven, only child and heir to a Texas oil baron's rather significant fortune. George Tompkins. No photograph. I was expecting a Texas kid, all twang and "y'all" and a big shiny belt buckle and scuffed Tony Lamas.

Nine A.M., because Caleb canceled my first few appointments of the day so I could sleep a bit later . . . and apply extra concealer over the angry black-green-yellow bruises on my throat.

Eight-fifty-eight A.M.: *ding . . . knock-knock*. "Madame X?"

A lady is never caught speechless. So I blinked, summoned my smile, and ushered the tall, lanky Texas kid into my condo. Speechlessly, but with the expected grace.

You are tall, lanky . . . with prominent breasts that can't quite be hidden, even behind a baggy white button-down shirt. An actual bolo tie. Yes, scuffed Tony Lamas. And yes, a shiny belt buckle larger than both my fists together. Stunning green eyes, hair somewhere between dark blond and light brown, expensively cut and styled . . . short, swept off to one side, parted neatly. A male haircut, not a pixie cut, but a true male style. No earrings, no bracelets, no rings, no necklace. No hint of femininity whatsoever, except those breasts, which I imagine are simply too large to hide, so you don't bother.

You stride past me, back ramrod straight and stiff, a swagger to your walk, a sway/sashay that's a strange mix of masculine and feminine. You peer around at my home, the Van Gogh *Starry Night* print on the wall, the Sargent portrait that is my namesake on another. The white leather couch, dark hardwood floors, high ceilings, exposed support beams crossing the ceilings made out of the same imported African teak as the floor. The built-in floor-to-ceiling bookshelf—more African teak—filled to bursting, stacked three deep in places, with books. Fiction of all kinds, biographies, translations of ancient classics, current literary novels, thrillers, horror, true crime, indie-published romances, nonfiction on subjects as far-ranging as biology, physics, psychology, history, anthropology . . . I read just about everything. It is my only pastime, my only form of entertainment. You spend several long moments in silence, perusing my collection of books.

"Must read a lot," you say. Your voice could be masculine or feminine. High enough to be a woman's, low enough to pass as a high-voiced male.

"I do."

You eye me. Not just look, not just see, but *examine*. Intelligence shines in your vivid green eyes. Curiosity, nerves, confidence, defiance. Complex eyes.

I know what you see when you look at me: five-eight in my bare feet; long, thick, black hair, straight, raven black, glossy, hanging to midbicep when it is loose, which is rarely; I am built with curves, bell-shaped hips and buxom, but I am fit, toned, athletic, lithe—my diet is rigorous, my exercise regimen strenuous and unforgiving; black eyes that I am told seem to see too much and give too little away; high cheekbones, full lips, delicate chin, classic heart-shaped face. I am exotic. I could be Spanish, or Middle Eastern. Even Islander, or Hawaiian, Filipino.

I am beautiful. Uncommonly beautiful, my features possessing the kind of symmetry and perfection that only comes along once in a generation. Exquisite. Breathtaking.

I know what I look like.

I endure your scrutiny without flinching, without looking away.

Another lesson learned early: to establish authority in any situation, wait out the silence, force the other person to speak first.

You concede. "I'm George."

"Good morning, George. Welcome. Would you care for some tea?"

"Got any coffee?"

I shake my head. "No, I'm sorry. I don't drink coffee."

"I'm fine, then. Don't really care much for tea." You amble about the living room, peer out the window from a far enough distance that I suspect you're afraid of heights. Yes, you shudder subtly and turn away, shrugging uncomfortably. Move to the Van Gogh. "This an original?"

I laugh, but kindly. "No, unfortunately. The original is at the MOMA. That is a reproduction, but a rather excellent one."

You move to the *Portrait of Madame X*. This one captures your interest for a few moments. "This is interesting."

I do not comment. I do not talk about that portrait, or its relevance to my name. I do not talk about myself at all.

Finally, you turn away and take a seat on the couch, extend your long legs and cross them at the ankle, fling an arm across the back of the couch. I perch on the armchair catercorner to the couch, a mate to the one in my bedroom. Knees together, legs angled to one

side, ankles crossed beneath, red Jimmy Choos on display. That's a
ploy, that display of my shoes. See if you look at them, notice them.
You do not.

Time to take this appointment by the scruff. "You are not what
I was expecting . . . Miss Tompkins."

A scowl, then. Curl of the upper lip, corners of your mouth
downturned. Disgusted, derisive. "Name's George."

"Explain."

"Explain my name?" You seem truly baffled, then angry. "You first."

Ha. Neatly parried. Point, Tompkins. "I am named for that painting." I point at the Sargent.

"And I'm named for the state."

"So your name is Georgia, then?"

You give me a hard stare, eyes gone hard as jade. "Last person
who called me Georgia ended up needing dental implants."

I smile. "Noted."

Another long, awkward silence. "So. How's this little program
of yours work, Madame X?" A pause. "And do I really have to call
you Madame X all the damn time? It's a helluva mouthful."

"Simply 'X' is fine, if you prefer." I let some hardness enter my
gaze. You don't look away, but I can see it requires effort. You have
backbone. "I'll confess, George, that your case may require some . . .
modification of my usual methods."

"Why? 'Cause I got tits and a twat?"

My lips thin at your vulgarity. "Yes, George. Because you are a
woman. My methods are geared for men, and my clientele are,
exclusively—at least until now—men. Or rather, boys hoping to
become men."

"What is it you do, then? Dad was pretty vague. Told me I had
to come to New York and see you, and do what you told me, and I
didn't have to like it, but I couldn't fuck it up."

"That's all you were told?"

"Basically."

I chew on the inside of my mouth and stare out the window, wondering, thinking. "Your father may have been confused about the nature of my services, in that case."

You lean forward, drawing your feet together, elbows on knees. "What are your services?"

"Consider it . . . etiquette training, of a sort. Manners. Comportment. Bearing. Appearance, speech patterns, first impressions."

"So you teach rich little assholes how to be less douchey."

I blink and have to stifle a laugh. You really are funny. "Essentially, yes. But there's more to it than that. Bearing comes in to play a lot. How you present yourself. How the opposite sex perceives you. How you assert yourself, even passively."

"How are you supposed to passively assert yourself?" you ask.

"Body language, strategic silences, posture, eye contact."

You stand up, pace away across the room, stand in front of the couch looking over at me, and then abruptly sit again. "And how exactly are you, a woman, qualified to teach guys how to be more manly?" You tilt your head. "I mean, that's really it, isn't it? Most dudes these days, especially the rich ones born with a silver spoon an' all that shit, they're just pussies, right? Not an alpha among 'em. They're all just cocky, smarmy, arrogant, pushy, conceited, self-absorbed, entitled little douche-guzzlers. Couldn't charm or flirt a girl into bed no matter how hard they try, so they rely on their wads of cash and fancy cars to do the work for them."

"I sense bitterness, George," I say, deadpan.

You laugh, your eyes brightening, head thrown back, a real belly laugh. You loosen. "You might say so. Been forced to pussyfoot around dickheads like that all my life. Dad had this idea that we had to fit in with the elite wealthy, since we have the same kind of money. 'Cept, we ain't like them. He's a rancher, an old-school Texas cowhand from the ass-end of nowhere who just happened to stumble into the oil business. I do mean stumble, too. Gambled the pink slip to his old dually against a hand of Hold 'Em. Got damn lucky, and won the deed to some land that just happened to have oil wells on it. Bing-bang-boom, a few good investments and a whole hell of a lotta luck later, we was rolling in hundos. But he thought he could buy his way out of being blue collar, which meant stuffing his hick ass into tuxedos, and me into frilly bitch dresses, and us going to fancy-dancy soirées. Problem there is, you can take the hick out of the country, but you can't take the country out of the hick. So we stood out. Them high-society boys, they sniffed me out real fuckin' fast. Knew I wasn't the kind of girl they was used to. Knew there was just . . . something wrong with me. And I had long curly hair then, too, and girly-ass dresses. But they still knew."

"Knew what, George?"

You eye me. "Don't play, X."

"You either." I eye you right back.

You lift a shoulder in faux-laconic dismissal. "They knew I'm a dyke."

"Excuse me?"

"You heard me."

"Say what you mean, George, and don't be vulgar about it. That's the first lesson."

"Whatever." You sigh. "They figured out I'm a lesbian. That clear enough for you? They could tell I'm a true-blue rug-muncher from Dykesville, Lesbiana."

I roll my eyes. "You make jokes at your own expense, George. It's unbecoming."

"Who's coming?" You quirk a corner of your lips up at your own joke.

I harden my eyes. "George."

"All right, all right." You hold up your hands palms out. "I know what unbecoming is. And yeah, I do make jokes at my own expense."

"And not just at your own expense, but that of others who also have chosen your lifestyle."

Your eyes blaze, and I realize I have erred. Your lip curls, your chin lifts. "Shows how much you fuckin' know."

"My apologies, George, what I should have said was—"

"It ain't a *choice*, you prissy bitch. You think I'd have *chosen* this? You think I'd have chosen to be gay? A gay girl from Lubbock, Texas? Really? A gay country girl from one of the least tolerant states in the damn country?"

I let out a breath, slowly. I don't smile, exactly, but I let my eyes show my contrition. "I'm sorry, George. It's not a choice, and I know it. I merely misspoke."

"You know what it was like, for me?" you ask. I shake my head. "No, course you don't. You *couldn't*. I never came out, not outright, you know? But they knew, even before I stopped playing dress-up for Dad. They knew, and they talked. I'd go to the parties and the get-togethers at the country club, and all that, and they'd hit on me. Like, what the fuck? Why? They knew I was gay, but still they hit on me? One of 'em, he cornered me in the ladies' room after a party one night, and he—tried to force his self on me. He was gonna fuck me straight, he said. Well, he was a pussy, and I grew up roping steer and breaking horses. Let's just say that it didn't go so well for him."

"You dissuaded him from his efforts to force you into heterosexuality, I take it?"

"I beat his ass into hamburger, is what I did. Knocked his teeth in, and I do mean that literally. I also stomped on his balls so hard I popped one of his nuts. And I also mean *that* literally."

I cringe. "Rather effective, I suppose."

You smirk. "Yeah, they gave me a *real* wide berth after that." The smirk fades. "Dad and me had a talk, after that. Guess he had a feeling something was different about me, but was hoping I'd meet the right guy and forget about it. Like it was a phase or some shit. Still half-hoping that even now, I think. That I'll suddenly go, 'Whoops! Guess I don't like pussy after all! Bring on the dick!'"

I can't help another snicker. "George, be serious."

"I am serious. That's what he thinks, back of his head. Ain't gonna happen, though. I told Dad, after I turned Rapey the Straightener into Toothless the One-Nut Wonder, I told him I wasn't gonna play his games no more. I wasn't a normal girl, and I was done pretending. He couldn't handle me just coming right out and saying I was gay. He'd have had a heart attack. So I just . . . told him I wasn't playing around no more, and he got it. Stopped wearing dresses, cut my hair, started going by George 'stead'a Georgia. But I was happier after that, and he could tell. I started showing an interest in his business, in the company. I'm all he's got, you see, since Momma died years back. And he ain't so young anymore. Wanted me to take over for him, and while I was playing at being good little straight girl, I wasn't havin' any of that. Now that I'm more or less out of the closet, I'm willing to help him with the business."

"So why are you here, George?"

You shrug and shake your head. "Hell if I know. I for real thought it was like corporate sensitivity training, or something like that. Like, how to turn down the butch when I'm around the bigwigs."

I let out a breath, stand up, pace away from you, past you to the window, stare out at the passers-by thirteen floors below. "I'll be forthright with you, George. I don't know what I can do for you. I suppose it depends on what *you* want. Normally, I don't pay a single thought to what my subjects want. They aren't really my clients, at the heart of it, you see. Their parents are. I am paid by the fathers

of these—as you call them, cocky, arrogant little . . . pricks." I never
swear. *Never.* But something about you has me twisted into a shape
I don't recognize. "I am paid by the fathers to train the sons to present themselves in a more palatable package. I am not a miracle
worker. I can't force a tiger to change his stripes, meaning I can't
change the basic nature of my clients' children. But I *can* help them
learn to disguise it, I suppose. A dishonesty, but one I am paid very
well to engage in."

"But I'm not your average client."

"You aren't an . . . asshole." The word tastes strange on my lips. But
not unpleasant. I wonder if I'll hear about my language later. I turn to
face you. "And I'm not sure what I'm meant to teach you. Unlike the
rest of my clientele, I would not have you hide your true nature."

You seem stunned. "You—you wouldn't? Why the hell not?"

I shrug. "There is a refreshing quality to your brand of brutal
honesty, George. And you don't seem . . . entitled."

"'Cause I ain't. Daddy and I came from nothin'. I grew up in a
hundred-and-ten-year-old two-room shack on damn near five hundred acres. I grew up riding on saddles older than me, driving
beat-up old trucks older than me, wearing clothes that didn't fit,
eating beans and rice and nearly turned meat. We had acreage and
a lotta head of horses and cattle, but that don't really translate into
cash income all that well. I remember that life, X. I remember having just about nothing, and I know I didn't do dick-all to earn what
we got. Daddy got lucky, yeah, but he busted his ass to turn that
little piece of luck into what it is today. So no. I ain't entitled."

"And that sets you apart, George. By quite a large margin."

"I got a large margin for you, babe." You smirk, and wink.

I suppose the conversation was turning a little too personal for
you. "We return to the question at hand, then. What am I supposed
to do with you?"

"Hell if I know. All's I know is Daddy won't be best pleased if I go back to Texas without having finished this. I promised him I would, so I'm going to. He lets me be who I am and don't say nothin' about it. He don't ask any questions when I say I've got a date, as long as I keep my shit on the DL. And he don't tolerate anybody in the office or who he does business with to talk shit about me either. He's nixed deals because somebody got a case of loose lips about Mike Tompkins's queer daughter. So I guess I owe him something in return."

"I'm just not sure what—"

"Just pretend I'm a dude, X. Do what you do as if I'm just another client's asshole kid."

"But you're not a straight male, or an asshole. And those are the kind at whom my methods are aimed."

"Just . . . pretend, okay? Do what you do, the way you normally do it."

I take a few steps toward you, pushing down my feelings, and drape my mantle of cold hostility over my features. "What I normally do is cut through falsity and pretense and attitude. If this is going to work, then you cannot question me."

"Falsity? What the hell you talkin' about, X?"

"First things first. Sit up straight. Quit slouching. And enough with the endearing Texas drawl. It's too much."

"What's wrong with the way I talk?"

"It's bourgeois, and makes you appear uneducated. If businessmen and -women are going to take you seriously, you must present yourself as competent, educated, and smooth. A bit of a drawl is acceptable, and perhaps even will give you a slight advantage, but the foul language and the nearly unintelligible manner in which you speak identifies you as nothing but a slouching, slovenly, foulmouthed bumpkin from the backwoods." I ignore the angry gleam in your eyes. You want to play this game? Very well, then. Let us play. "Appearing as more than merely blue collar is about enacting a host of changes to your essential nature, Georgia. It's not about the clothes you wear or the car you drive, or the house you live in. Anyone can find a bag of money and buy nicer things. It's about learning to comport yourself with dignity and sophistication."

"You think I sound like a bumpkin?" You sound almost hurt, George.

"I do." I endeavor to slur, to drawl, to draw out my syllables and twist them, and to drop the ends of my words. "Y'all sound like this." It comes out: *yaaaaawl sownd laahk thyiiiis*.

"Got news for ya, missy." You stand up, pushing off the couch with violence. "I ain't never gonna sound all hoity-toity like you."

"Clearly. But is something approaching correct grammar too much to ask for?"

You pace, run a hand through your hair. "I won't ever sound like you." It comes out flat, unaccented but lifeless.

"Keep the drawl, but eradicate the poor grammar."

"That ain't   that won't be easy."

I nod. "Better. You'll still sound like yourself, but more . . . acceptable in formal situations." I wave a hand at the condo. "Situations such as this, for example. This is supposed to be a formal client/service-provider scenario. We are not friends, Georgia. We are business associates. And I've lost count of how many times you've used the F-word alone."

"I told you, my name is *George*."

"To your friends, perhaps. To your dates. At home, or at the bar. But in the boardroom? Your name is Georgia." My tone leaves no room for argument. "*Be* Georgia. It will simplify things exponentially in professional situations."

"You're asking a lot, X."

"Businessmen are an easily confused lot, Georgia. They understand numbers and money, P-and-L statements, stock assessments.
They do not understand a businesswoman named George. They'll
spend the entire meeting trying to figure out what to think, how
to talk to you. Are you a man? A woman? They won't know. And
that will detract from the point of the meeting."

"So I've gotta go back to pretending to be a prissy bitch woman."

I shake my head. "No, Georgia. Just . . . present them with something even remotely approaching the familiar to them. Wear a business suit. Even a man's suit, if you prefer. But have it tailored to fit
you . . . *properly*. You don't have to accentuate your female anatomy,
but also do not attempt to hide it. Unless you're going for a trans-
gender appearance?"

You frown. "I—no. I'm still a female, but . . . I'm not a girly-girl.
I don't wear dresses. I don't do fussy hair and makeup and heels. I
like men's clothes."

"Do you bind your breasts?" I ask.

"No."

"Will you?"

"Probably not." You hesitate. "Tried it, a few times. I hated it."

I pause, formulate my thoughts. "You have to find a medium,
then. You don't have to mitigate your sense of self. That's not what
I'm asking of you. But if you want the men of the business world to
accept you even slightly, you have to pay a little deference to the
way things are for them. It's unfair, perhaps, but it is reality. There
are women in positions of power. CEOs, CFOs, presidents. But it is
still a man's world, Georgia. And if you wish to play in it, especially
in the upper echelons, then you have to play the game."

"No. I don't. I am who I am, and they can take it or leave it. I ain't gonna change who I am just for a bunch of stiff-necked old dangly ball sacks."

My eyes close slowly. "Georgia. I'm not asking you to—"

"Yes, you are!" You take several stomping steps toward me, stare hard at me. "Change the way I talk, dress different. *Be* different."

"You said you wanted to do this? Well . . . this is what I do, Georgia. I remove the pretense. I cut through the *shit*. Which, in this case, is the confusing way in which you present yourself. Are you trying to be a man? It seems sort of that way, but not entirely. And in the boardroom, business discussions will be forgotten in favor of wondering what they're supposed to think you are. My suggestion is to present yourself as . . . androgynous, I suppose you could say. A male business suit, not a woman's power suit. An expensive bespoke suit, but tailored to accommodate your bust and hips. Sleek, slim shoes. A watch in dark leather with a sleek profile. Let your hair grow a little and sweep it back from your face."

"So you want me to dress like a metrosexual guy, basically."

"If that's the term you wish to use, then sure. It's an appearance that could go either way. The point is, it's *professional*. An appearance befitting the head representative of Tompkins Petroleum. Dress how you wish on your own time. Speak how you wish, do what you wish. Your personal life is your own. But when conducting business—when on the clock, so to speak—portray yourself a businessperson. And I use the gender-neutral construction intentionally."

You perch on the arm of the couch. "Won't they still be wondering whether I'm a man or a woman?"

"Yes. But if you use correct grammar, do not curse and use vulgarity or crude expressions, and dress professionally, and if you prove that you know the business and demand to be respected and taken seriously, those questions of your gender will eventually cease being as important. They'll still whisper behind your back, of course, but if you demand it with your appearance and your behavior, they'll be forced to treat you as an equal when it comes to business."

"What about less formal situations where a suit isn't appropriate?"

I shrug. "Tailored slacks, a tailored button-down, a men's polo shirt in a size that fits snugly."

You seem uncomfortable. "The problem there is when I wear tops that fit, my tits show."

I keep a steady gaze. "So?"

"So, I don't like it. They stare. Makes me feel like that girl in the dresses all over again."

"So let them stare. If it bothers you that much, then bind them, or get a reduction. Wearing baggy clothes in a vain attempt to . . . not even really hide or disguise them, but—I don't even know what the purpose of the baggy shirt is, to be honest." I gesture at your shirt and then pause for a moment before starting over. "Whatever the case, it says you aren't sure about who you are or what you want. Georgia, my point is, you've owned your sexuality, yes? You are a lesbian. Okay, well and good. But you haven't owned your *body*. You have to decide if you're comfortable with your body, with the fact that you are, very obviously, a woman. And a well-endowed one at that. I'm not saying dress like a woman. But don't hide what you look like. That only confuses the issue and makes you seem insecure."

A long silence. And then, "I *am* insecure."

"And it shows."

"So don't hide them, but don't highlight them. Just . . . let them be there?"

"Or do something about the fact that you aren't comfortable with them."

"It's not that simple."

"I'm sure it isn't. I'm distilling a very complicated issue down to the absurdly simplistic."

"Which ain't—which *isn't* exactly fair to me."

"I'm not paid to be fair. I'm paid to get results. It's not me who must do these things, so I have the luxury of stating things that are, clearly, more easily said than done." I move to stand a few inches away from where you are still perched with a hip on the arm of the couch, one foot flat on the floor. "Confidence, Georgia. It's what I tell my clients most frequently. Everyone is attracted to confidence. It's about just enough arrogance and cocksureness to seem aloof, yet approachable. Caring about how you present yourself, caring what you look like, making sure you always look your best, behave above reproach, speak with authority, yet appearing as if you don't care what others think about you. Confidence is sexy. True arrogance is not."

"What about you, X? What are you attracted to?" Suddenly, the air is thick, and tense, and I am caught off guard.

I take a step back. "This isn't about me."

"Isn't it? If I succeed at your little game, then shouldn't you be affected by it?" You follow me, and now you are in my space.

Staring down at me. Eyeing me. Assessing me.

We're of a height—flat-footed you would actually be an inch shorter than I am, but in those boots with the thick heel, we are even. Yet somehow you manage to look down at me. Your presence somehow captures that masculine energy of dominance, of heat, hardness. You are close, too close, nose to nose with me, green eyes blazing, seeing. Your hands go to my waist, clutch me. Pull me flat against you. Breasts smash against breasts. Hips mash against hips. Yet, despite the scent of your arousal in the air, in my nose, there is no thick ridge between us, no physical thickening of desire. It's baffling. Disorienting. You exude masculine need. You hunger. Your hands dig into my hips just so, and your eyes rake down from my eyes to my cleavage, and your lips tip up in an appreciative grin.

I am breathing hard. Gasping for air. Dragging deep lungfuls of oxygen, swelling my chest within my dress, and you notice. Your hips grind. Something in me sparks, flashes. Heats. The strange mix of your softness and hardness is alluring and disorienting. Your hip bones are hard against mine, yet there is softness, too, and when you grind again, I feel the spark once more, when your front rubs against mine.

I am still, tensed, rigid. Frozen. I do not know what to do. What is happening? What am I feeling? What are you doing?

What am *I* doing, letting this happen?

I shove away, stumble backward. "This . . . that isn't appropriate, George—Georgia."

You smirk. Swagger as you follow my retreat. "Ain't so absurdly simplistic anymore, is it, X?"

"You signed a contract, Georgia." I am reminding both of us, and you somehow know it.

"Ain't none of us that simple, babe. You felt it. You felt *me*."

"The contract, Georgia."

You sneer. "Fuck the contract, X. You and your haughty pussy want me, X. You smell me, and you don't like it. I *complicate* shit for you, don't I?" You stand chest to chest with me again. My nipples betray me, go hard. I know you feel it. "You wet, X? All slippery for me? You know how good a dyke can make you feel? I know what you like, 'cause *I* like it, too. Just the same way. No guy can ever lick your pussy as good as I can. I know *just* how to make you squirm, make you want it and want it and want it, and not give it to you till it's too fuckin' much to take. I know, X. I *know*. You want a taste? Get a little dirty? Be a little bad?"

How did this happen? Where did this come from? One moment

we were discussing you, your appearance, everything was proper and in control and at least somewhat familiar. And then, suddenly, apropos of nothing, *this*. You, in my space, in my head, under my skin.

There is a gleam in your eye. Something . . . clever, and malicious. You know exactly what you are doing.

You're fucking with me.

And I do not like it. Not one bit.

"Enough." I stand my ground, steel my spine, razors in my gaze. "Our hour is done."

You smile, a slow, knowing curve of your lips. "All right, then. If you say so."

I have no idea how much time has passed. I do not care. You disrupt my worldview, George. You make it seem narrow, somehow.

My worldview *is* narrow. My worldview is made up of 3,565 square feet. Three bedrooms, one bathroom, and an expansive open-plan kitchen and living room. Floor-to-ceiling windows that look out onto the heart of Manhattan. That's my worldview.

That's my whole world.

And you in it, this sudden seduction . . . it disrupts everything I know.

I, fighting for equilibrium and composure and breath, push past you. Wrench the door open with far too much force. Wait, eyes staring at you but not seeing you.

You swagger to the doorway, boot heels clicking, and stop face-to-face with me yet again. Too close, yet again. "Confident enough for you now, X?"

You've taken control of this, somehow, stolen my grip on what I do and who I am and what I want. I look at you, feigning calm. You smirk, knowing the lie. You push closer, until our bodies are flush, lean in, in, and I think you're going to kiss me. Instead, you lick the tip of my nose. My upper lip. Smirk.

"See ya next week, X. Think about what I said. What I offered. I wasn't kidding, you know. I'll get you out of here, show you a good time you won't ever forget, I can guaran-damn-tee you that, sweetheart."

"Good-bye, Georgia."

"Call me George. We ain't in the boardroom, are we? We're past formalities, I'd say. I've felt your nips get hard, smelled your pussy get wet. Makes us friends, I'd say."

I step back, shaking, and close the door in your face.

FIVE

Evening. Clients are done for the day. It took every ounce of my abilities to compose myself enough that I could deal with the rest of the day's clients. Yet after they are all gone and I am alone, I am still shaken by what happened. No one gets in my space. No one affects me. No one touches me.

No one but—

Ding.

"X. Where are you?" Voice a low, angry rumble.

"I'm in here," I say. "In my library."

I call it a library. Really, it's just a bedroom lined floor-to-ceiling and wall-to-wall with stuffed bookshelves. One corner is left open, a Louis XIV armchair, a lamp, and a little table clustered in the triangle of open space. In the center of the room is a glass case with my prized books, signed copies and first editions of books by Hemingway, Faulkner, Joyce, and Woolf, a copy of *A Streetcar Named Desire* signed by Tennessee Williams, and even a fourth-century illuminated translation of *The Odyssey*.

Prized possessions; gifts.

Reminders.

The doorway to my library is filled, darkened. Dark eyes so filled with fury as to be feral. Hands clenching into fists and releasing in a heartbeat rhythm. I set *Smilla's Sense of Snow* facedown on my thigh. Pretend to a calm I do not feel; such anger is unusual and dangerous. I do not know what to expect.

Five long steps, powerful legs eating the space in a predatory prowl, a quick hand snatches my book and tosses it across the room, spine cracking loudly against a shelf, pages fluttering, a gentle thump as it hits the carpet. I have no time to react, no time to even breathe. A brutally powerful hand seizes my wrist and jerks me upright. Seizes my throat. Fingers at my windpipe, gentle as a lover's kiss, yet shaking with restrained fury.

Breath on my lips and nose, clean of alcoholic taint. Sobriety makes this fury all the more terrifying.

"Georgia Tompkins has been recalled to Texas. You will not be seeing *her* again."

"All right." It comes out of me as a whisper, penitent. Careful.

Lips move against mine, voice buzzing in a rumble like an earthquake felt from a hundred miles away. "What the *fuck* was that, X?"

I swallow hard. "I don't know."

"*Answer* me, goddammit." Fingers squeeze in warning.

"I did. I don't *know* what happened, Caleb. It took me by surprise. I—I didn't know how to react."

"It was unacceptable. I had to force Michael Tompkins and his queer slut of a daughter to sign further nondisclosure agreements, so your *impropriety* won't be leaked to the rest of *my* clientele." I flinch at your cruel and vulgar insult, so casually hurled. I feel offended for Georgia, somehow, though I shouldn't, and do not dare to let it show. "You work for *me*, X. Remember that. These are *my* clients. *My* business associates. You represent *me*. And when you act that way, when you allow yourself to be *touched* . . . it reflects on me."

"I'm sorry, Caleb."

"You're sorry? You let a *lesbian* touch you? Almost kiss you? You let her speak to you that way? And you"—a tremble in that avalanche-rumble voice—"you looked like—like it *affected* you. As if you *liked* it."

"No, Caleb. I was just—"

"Did you, X? Did you like the way she touched you? Did you like the way she felt? Is it better than the way I feel? The way I touch you?" Hands on my waist, where hers were. Lips, brushing mine. A tongue, touching nose, upper lip. Mirroring. Mocking.

"No . . ."

"No, *what?*"

"No, Caleb." This is the correct, expected response. I know this. But I am afraid, and shaken, and unable to breathe, so I forgot.

"No. She doesn't feel better than me, does she?"

"No, Caleb."

I am turned, given a violent shove. I stumble and catch up against the glass of the display case. A foot smacks against the inside of my ankle, tapping my feet apart. Another, to the other side. Now my feet are more than shoulder width apart. Hips against my backside. Reflection in the glass: my face, dark skin flushed, frightened, yet my mouth is opened in a moue, eyes heavy-lidded, lips moist, nostrils flaring, and behind my face a larger one, pale skin, dark hair, dark eyes. Chiseled, sculpted features so beautiful it hurts.

Lips at the shell of my ear: "Were you wet for her, X?"

I shake my head. "No, Caleb," I lie.

"Were your nipples hard for her, X?"

"No, Caleb," I lie.

I am wearing a dove-gray A-line dress, one of a kind, designed and crafted to my measurements by a prominent fashion student studying here in New York City. It is priceless, unique, and one of my favorite garments.

Hands clutch fabric at my shoulders on either side of the zipper at my spine. One sharp tug, and the dress is ripped apart, fluttering to the floor at my feet. I do not breathe, do not speak, do not move. I do not dare.

Bra unhooked, straps brushed aside. Hands cup my breasts, lift them to rest on the cold glass. Push at my spine to bend me forward until my breasts are now crushed against the glass, smashed flat. Panties are yanked down, roughly.

"Caleb—"

"'Please fuck me, Caleb.'" This in a rough rasp. "Say it, X."

I whimper. "P-please—"

"I can't hear you."

I hear a zipper being lowered, feel flesh against my flesh, a hot, rigid erection nestled between the globes of my backside. Hands in the creases of my hips. Hands scour my spine, my back, caressing in gentle circles. Hands delve around my waist, dive between my thighs. Touch me.

"'I've felt your nips get hard, smelled your pussy get wet. Makes us friends, I'd say.'" The words are whispered in my ear, matched with a rhythmic touch, creating a wet sucking sound from between my thighs. "You're wet for *me*, aren't you, X?"

"Yes," I whimper.

"Your nipples are hard for *me*, aren't they, X?"

"Yes," I whisper.

The erection slides, teases. "She can't give you this, can she?"

"No." I swallow hard, hating that my body wants this despite the terror in my gut, despite the pounding knot of confusion in my throat.

"So say it." A moment of silence as fingers move, bringing me to the edge. "Say it, X."

"Please—please fuck me, Caleb." I whisper it, and I am rewarded with a sudden and slow penetration.

I feel misused. Mistreated. Manipulated. I feel dirty.

Yet I want this.

Why?

WHY?

What is wrong with me? My nipples *were* hard for George, I *was* wet for her. Yet I am even harder and wetter now.

And I was not afraid of George.

A thrust, another, a slow and methodical *fucking*. Fist in my hair, pressing my face to the glass.

I see no reflection now, only my books: *For Whom the Bell Tolls*, *As I Lay Dying*, *The Dead*, *A Room of One's Own*.

Long, slow thrusts. Wet sounds. Sweat on my back. Slapping flesh. My breath, in pants, whimpers. I know how I sound: I sound erotic. I whimper and groan, moan and sigh. My voice betrays me. I cannot deny that I am affected, that such carnal skill, such sexual ferocity, such consummate primal power and unrelenting vigor has me heating up and writhing and detonating, that I am made into a helpless thing, made slave to this. To the sensation of being owned, to being used so. In such moments I am not my own, and I hate and need this in equal measure.

I come, violently, and I hate myself for it.

Lips at the shell of my ear as I lie bent over the glass, the edge cutting into my belly, gasping for breath, near tears: "To whom do you belong, X?" Each word is enunciated carefully, precisely.

"I belong to you, Caleb." It is the raw truth, however I may feel about it.

"Whose body is this?" A slap to my backside, sharp but not precisely painful.

"Yours," I murmur, just above a whisper.

I am pulled upright, a broad, hard palm cupping the back of my neck. Eyes bore down on me, pierce me, dark and still furious, but now fraught with glints and fractions of other unknowable emotions. Fingers delve between my legs. Swipe, smear, gather still-hot, just-spilled seed. Touch it to my tongue. I taste it, musk, tang, saltiness, my own female essence woven around the masculine. "That's me, inside you. You taste us?"

I nod. I cannot speak.

Fingers pinch my nipple, hard. "Your sexuality belongs to *me*, X. No one else may even so much as fucking *smell* you, do you understand me? You. Are. *Mine*." The pinch does not subside, the pain a sharp ache making me tremble, making some part of me twist and writhe and need. I hate, hate, *hate* my body for reacting thus. "Do you *understand*, X?"

"Yes."

The pinch goes harder yet, hard enough to make me whimper. "Yes, *what?*"

"Yes, Caleb!" I gasp.

Fingers release my nipple, and my knees buckle with relief. I cannot stop myself from falling. Arms catch me, lift me easily. Carry me into my bedroom, settle me with exquisite gentility. Too gently. The tenderness hurts and confuses worse than the pain, worse than the demands of ownership, distress me more than the sexual dominion.

"Sleep." It is a command.

And I . . . ?

I obey.

wake abruptly, disoriented. My blinds are open, letting in the moonlight and the scintillating shine of countless windows from the skyline. I reach to my bedside table for the remote that lowers the blackout shade.

The remote is gone. My noise machine is gone.

My heart sinks.

I rise, still naked, and move to the window. Look up. The black-out shade is still there, installed above the window. But without the remote, there is no way to lower it.

Tears prick my eyes. This is my punishment, then. Without the curtains and the noise, how will I sleep?

I won't, or not well.

I fight the weakness. Lie down, cover myself with the blanket, pull it over my head, attempt to sleep. But after only a few moments I feel like I'm suffocating, choking on my own hot, recycled breaths. I toss the blanket away. Stare at the ceiling.

I am awake now.

Frustrated and angry, I kick the blanket away, roll off the bed, stalk into my en suite bathroom. Turn on the shower, hot as it will go. Step in, hiss at the scalding heat. I do not lower the temperature, though. I scrub. Mercilessly, I scrub. Until my skin is red and almost bloody, I scrub. Every inch of me, as if I could scour away not just the feel of those harsh, brutal, yet sometimes tender hands, but also to scour away whatever sickness inside me causes me to react to it, to need that touch, whatever venom has poisoned me into needing that sexual domination.

If I could bleed it out, I would.

In a moment of insanity, I take the disposable razor I use to shave my legs and elsewhere. Place the blade on my upper forearm. Drag the razor sideways, and feel the sting as it slices my skin apart. Shocked by the sudden pain, I drop the razor and watch as blood wells crimson on my arm, sluices away, washed down the drain by the shower. I am fascinated by the spill of my own blood, watch it run.

But I do not attempt to cut myself again. I do not have the courage to seek that way out. I am too much a coward. I still wish to live.

And then, without warning, I am slumped on the floor of the shower and sobbing, shower water beating warm down on me, and I am racked by sobs, sobs, sobs. My fists beat at my skull. My fingers claw at my eyes, my hair.

"Fuck." It comes out from clenched teeth. *"FUCK!"* I shriek it, finally, but the word emerges as a wordless wail, and even that is muffled by the sound of the shower.

It feels good to curse, though.

I find enough strength to stand, to shut off the shower, dry off, and dress in a T-shirt and panties.

Seeking comfort, I pad to my library on bare feet, pruned toes. Maybe a few hours with Smilla will calm me.

The door is locked.

I try it again. Rattle it. Shake it. Slam my fists against the wood.

Another punishment.

I twist in place and rest my back against the door, fighting yet more tears. And as I lean back against the door, my eye casts across the room at the remaining bookshelf.

Which has been emptied of every book.

Except one, a new title.

Obedience to Authority: An Experimental View by Stanley Milgram.

SIX

A week with no books is an eternity. I have no television, no radio. No visitors or friends, save my clients. No late-night visits, either; a long and conspicuous absence. I am going mad. After my clients are done for the day, I pace. Walk the perimeter of my world, wall to wall to wall, window to window, corner to corner. I do not mutter to myself, but it takes considerable restraint. At night, I do not sleep. I toss and turn, stare at the ceiling. In the end, I always find myself at the window, forehead pressed to the glass, arms crossed beneath my breasts, hands cupping my elbows, watching. Watching.

Observe the foot traffic, as is my wont.

See her, down there? A young woman, not yet thirty. Less than that even, perhaps. It is hard to tell from this distance. This late at night, past midnight, she is dressed in a business power suit. Tight pencil skirt, navy. Matching blazer folded and draped across one forearm. White blouse, no nonsense, plain yet tailored. Three buttons are undone, though, revealing a bit too much cleavage for her to be going anywhere but home or the bar. A tan purse hangs from one shoulder, slim, small, nearly invisible strap. Dark wedge heels, either navy or dark gray. Hair in a neat bun. Yet the way she walks, it tells a story. Quickly, legs pumping swiftly despite the narrow confines of her knee-length skirt. Too quickly. And her face, buried in her cell phone. The set of her shoulders. She's upset about something. She reaches the corner, pauses at the intersection, and stuffs her phone into her purse. Straightens her shoulders. Breathes deeply. Tosses her head, as if summoning indifference, courage.

Even from here, I can see the screen of her phone light up in her open purse. From this distance it is nothing but a tiny white glow. She hesitantly withdraws her phone, reads the message. Turns it off and stuffs it back into her purse without sending a reply. But instead of walking onward when the light turns, she remains at the intersection, waiting for something.

A sleek, expensive black sedan pulls to a halt on her side of the intersection, approaching her. Stops even with her. The rear passenger door is shoved open from within. She shakes her head. Steps backward. My heart pounds. She's gesticulating angrily, finger stabbing, stabbing. She is shouting, clearly. Backs up another step. Another. The driver's-side rear door is thrown open, and a tall man unfolds from within. My heart skips several beats. That hair, dark, artfully messy. That confident, arrogant, predator stride. Those shoulders.

It isn't possible.

Yet my eyes tell me it is.

The woman backs up, almost out of my field of view. She is shaking her head. Speaking, head shaking. She holds up her hands palms out as if to ward off an attack, but I could tell her, should I be close enough to speak to her, she does so in vain. Those massive, powerful hands lash out with the swiftness of a striking serpent.

Grab her shoulders. Tug her close, body to body. I see those thin, expressive lips moving, saying something. She shakes her head, but she doesn't pull away. Why isn't she pulling away?

Because she's being kissed, full and furious, a demanding kiss. Even from here, I can see her knees go weak. All that's keeping her upright is those brutal hands, clutching her backside and keeping her pressed hard against that firm, taut chest. Her hands clutch, grab, feather through hair, possess.

She is allowed to touch?

A kiss?

Those lips do not kiss me.

My hands do not reach up to touch.

What is this fury within me? This disgust? This fear? This confusion? I am nothing but a possession. I know this. I do not *want* to be kissed. Not by *those* lips. I do not *want* to touch, not that body.

I will this to be the truth, despite seeds of doubt.

She, clearly, is held to different rules than I.

Yet just as clear is the domination, the masterful knowledge of female anatomy and arousal, and how to manipulate until ownership is complete. I know that all too well. She is subsumed, there on the sidewalk. She is walked backward until her backside bumps up against the front passenger door of the car. She melts. Surrenders. The sidewalk is not empty; this is New York, and it never sleeps. No one is ever alone on the street. Yet the scene up against the door of the car is a private one, an erotic one. Over a wide shoulder I can see her mouth, hanging open. Hands dig beneath her skirt waistband. I know that touch. The arousal, the inevitability of climax.

Right there on the street.

I watch her come. She goes limp, held up yet again—or still. A moment passes. And then she is left alone, leaning back against the car door, skirt twisted out of place, hair coming free of the bun, blouse rucked and rumpled. Purse forgotten, hanging from an elbow. The rear driver's-side door is closed behind that tall, powerful form. She hesitates. Straightens her skirt. Adjusts her blouse. Replaces the strap of her purse on her shoulder. Fixes her hair.

Takes a deep breath.

Walks away.

Good!

Run!

Keep going, girl. Do not be seduced, do not be ensorcelled.

Three steps, she makes it. And then, like Lot's wife, she turns to look back. Unlike Lot's wife, however, she does not turn to salt. But she is equally doomed, for all that. Her gaze locks on the still-open rear passenger door. She cannot resist. I can almost hear it, the siren song of a carnal god beckoning her closer, drawing her in, closer and closer to a dark, hungry, and merciless maw.

Closer, closer.

And then, the fool, she ducks, bends, and slides into the car. I see a hand reach, tug her off-balance so she falls forward, legs akimbo, skirt wide and showing too much leg, hiking up, baring a skimpy black thong. She kicks, fighting to sit up, and the hand whips down to crack against her backside. She stills, and the hand remains, cupping her buttock. Another hand, and the long suit-sheathed arm attached to it, reaches, grasps the door handle.

I watch, mesmerized, as a face I know all too well appears from out of the shadows of the interior, dark eyes lifting, rising, meeting mine. Lips do not quite smile, because gods do not grin or smirk. But there is a ghost of something like amusement or satisfaction on those beautiful and fiercely masculine features.

A moment, then, when I cannot look away, seeing and being seen.

Was all that for my benefit?

Orchestrated to prove a point?

I turn away, stomach lurching. I could vomit, but I do not.

M adame X. How are you today?" Your voice is smooth and polite
as you enter, take a seat on the couch.

"I am well, Jonathan," I lie, "and yourself?"

"All right, I suppose." You shrug, but your voice betrays an infin-itesimal hesitation.

"You suppose?" I query.

You've come a long way since our first meeting. Some of my best work, you are.

"It's nothing." You wave a hand, glance at my bookshelf, still empty but for that one title, which I dare not remove. Nor do I read it, though; my little act of rebellion. "Where'd all your books go?"

I hunt for a suitable lie. I can think of nothing. I did not expect you to notice or care. I shrug. Say the first thing that comes to mind. "I am having them replaced."

You rise. Stride to the shelf, pick up the book, examine the title. Silence, then, as you read a few pages from the middle. "That's fucked up, X."

"Having my books replaced?"

You shake your head, lift the book in gesture. "No. This."

I have not read it, know nothing about it. I cannot betray my ignorance, however. "Why do you say that, Jonathan?"

You shrug. "This book. It's a social experiment. There's a teacher, and a student. The teacher asks questions, and if there's a wrong answer the teacher shocks the student with an electric shock machine. Or something like that."

"You gathered that from the little bit you just read?"

You grin at me. "Oh, no. I took a psychology class in college, and we studied this book. It was a while ago, so I don't really remember a lot about it, but I remember even then thinking how fucked up the experiment was. The results though, that stuck with me. Obedience is a social construct. So is authority of one person over another. It's . . . something we agree on, allow ourselves to go along with, even if it's detrimental to our well-being. We agree to give someone else authority over us. Or, vice versa, we take power, authority, or whatever, and use it, even if it goes against our morals in some other way. It's messed up. Shows how dependent we are on social constructs, even though by and large we don't even realize what's happening, what we're doing."

"Aren't social constructs like that what compose the very fabric of society, though?"

You nod. "Yeah, for sure. But when you become aware of them, even briefly, it can mess with your head. I went around questioning everything after we studied that book. Every interaction, I looked at like it was something new. Like when you say a word so many times it loses its meaning, you know?"

"Semantic satiation," I say.

"Yeah, that. Eventually I went back to normal, stopped thinking about things quite so objectively. But for weeks, it was fucking weird. You realize the little tacit agreements we make without realizing it, you know?"

I shake my head. I follow intellectually, but in practice? No. My experience is more . . . limited. "Let's pretend I don't know, Jonathan. What do you mean?"

"Well, in terms of obedience and authority . . . we give people authority over us. Why do I let you boss me around? Why do I come back here week after week, let you say the things you say to me, let you tell me what to say and how to act and how to dress, when I know nothing about you? We aren't friends, we aren't involved like in a relationship, I personally am not even paying you. Yet here I am. Why?"

"Your father."

"Exactly. But I hate my father. I really do, X. So why am I here?"

"Because he holds control over something you want."

"Right. Exactly. Money. The future of the company. I sacrificed my childhood for his company. My father sacrificed my childhood for the company. He was never home, and when he was, he was in his office, working. I was always expected to excel, to be the best. To get the grades so I could go to the Ivy League school, so I could get the degree that would tell *him* I've earned the right to inherit the company. So I did all that, and yet I don't get to just . . . take over. Or even start near the top. No, I've got to start at the bottom, as an apprentice. Sure, I get it. Work for it, learn the business from the bottom up. Sure. Great. But I went to work with him every weekend, X. Every fucking weekend. I didn't play with my friends, I didn't play sports or video games or go the park or ride my bike. I went to the office with him and watched him work. 'It'll all be yours someday, Jonathan,' he'd say. 'So pay attention.' I paid attention. I know every contact, every account. I know it *all*. I'm ready. But he still holds out. Makes it impossible for me to move up. Promotes other guys over me when by all objective standards *I'm* the more qualified, son of the company president or not. He makes me come here and do this with you, because apparently I'm not *man* enough, either. Which, *obviously*, means letting some stuck-up bitch boss me around and insult me." You glance at me, cringing. "Sorry. I'm just—"

"It's fine, Jonathan. I'll let it go, this once. And besides, I *am* a bit of a bitch, but then, I'm paid to be, aren't I?"

You totally ignore the fact that I've spoken. "But the point is, I do it because I still keep hoping I'll be good enough. I give him the power over me, because I want what he has. I want what's *mine*."

You duck your head, briefly, and then glance at me, your eyes perhaps a bit too sharp, a bit too knowing. "We all have a motivation for letting others control us, though, don't we?"

"Why, Jonathan . . . I barely recognize you, right now. Such introspection is unlike you." I must keep the conversation focused on you.

In my current circumstances, I dare not allow this line of discussion to become focused on me. That would be . . . very bad.

"I'm a rich asshole, X. I get that. I own it, and I'm not going to apologize for it. I was given everything I ever wanted, and then some. Except now that I've done everything asked of me to take my place at his side in running the company, now . . . I'm still not good enough. I wasn't good enough for him to want to spend time with me as a kid, so I went to work with him, hoping he'd notice me. He never did. I think he never will. But I still give him authority over me."

"Where is all this coming from, Jonathan?" Against all reason, I find myself thinking that just maybe there might be a decent person under the skin of the rich asshole.

You shrug. "He told me if I did this, came here and let you teach me or whatever, he'd make me junior VP of operations. So I'm here. I'm trying."

"Indeed you are. And making good progress, too. We're actually holding a worthwhile conversation, and that's improvement indeed."

"Yeah, well. The nasty, contrary old fuck just gave Eric Benson that position, even though he outright *promised* it to me. We still have, what, three more weeks of this? And he gave it to Eric fucking Benson. Benson is a fucking tool. A goddamn sycophantic suck-up prick. Never has any ideas of his own, he just goes along with everyone else and kisses ass and flashes that stupid grin of his with those stupid cheap-ass veneers. Fucking asshole."

I do not know what to say to you. It is not my job to be your

confidant, your confessor, your shoulder to cry on, or your friend
with whom to commiserate. It is my job to make you less of an
asshole.

"When is enough enough, Jonathan?"

You glance at me with miserable eyes. "What?"

"How much is enough? How long will you tilt at the windmill?"

You groan in frustration, lean back, and run your hands through
your hair. "Gah. Enough with the fucking riddles, X."

"It's not a riddle, it's an allusion. It's from *Don Quixote*."

"I *know* who fucking Don Quixote is, X. I did go to fucking Yale,
you know."

I did know that, and I didn't go to Yale, or anywhere else. I don't
say that, though. You don't need my superiority right now. You need
a nudge in the right direction.

"If you know who Don Quixote is, then what is it I'm trying to
tell you, do you think?"

You frown at me, and I can see you thinking. "Stop tilting at
windmills."

"What did Don Quixote think the windmills were?" I ask.

"Giants."

"Correct. But what do you think his greatest failing was?"

"Thinking the windmills were giants."

"Wrong. Thinking he could slay them even if those windmills
had been real giants. He'd have been squashed like a mosquito."

"And you think I'm not only tilting at windmills, but at a giant
I can't slay in the first place."

I remain silent. You must work some things out for yourself.

"What am I not doing right, though? What's wrong with me
that he can't just—just—"

"Jonathan," I scold.

"What?"

"Stop whining and *think*."

You glare at me, but, to your credit, you don't lash out at me. Instead, you rise and pace to the window. My window, the one at which I stand and watch the passersby so far beneath and imagine stories for them.

"When I was three," you say, cutting a regal figure at the window, one hand in your pocket, the other propped on the glass, head ducked, voice quiet, "I drew a picture. I don't remember of what. I was three, so it was probably a bunch of scribbles, right? But I was *three*, and I wanted to draw a picture and give it to my dad. So I gave it to him, and I remember being excited that he'd looked at me, that he'd looked at my drawing. And you know what he did? He took it, looked at it, at me, and he didn't smile or tell me how good it was. He said, 'Not bad, Jonathan, but you can do better. Try again.'" You let out a long breath. "I was fucking *three*. And that was . . . that was the first time. I went back to my little desk with my little crayons, and I remember drawing another picture. Being proud of it. Wanting to give it to him and have him tell me it was great, that he loved it. Only he'd left, gone back to work. And the first picture I'd drawn was in the garbage. Not wadded up or anything, I just . . . I remember seeing it shoved down in the trash can with ripped-up envelopes and a Kleenex and other trash. That was the first time I remember feeling not good enough. And I've spent every single fucking day since then trying to get him to look at my goddamned pictures and tell me how nice they are. Twenty-three years."

I sit sideways on the chair, one leg crossed over the other, watching you at the window. I wait for you to speak again, and it is a long silent time before you do.

"He's the giant. Not a windmill, but a real giant. And I have no hope of slaying him, do I? So why am I trying? That's what you're asking, isn't it? Why bother?"

"No, not why bother. That's the wrong question."

I stand up, step carefully over to you, my nude Gucci Ursula high-heel sandals going *click-click-click-click* on the floor. I am within touching distance, close enough to smell your cologne, which is subdued, faint, and alluring. Close enough to realize how tall you really are, and that I may have done my job a little *too* well with you.

"Then what's the right question, X?" You turn, a half pivot. I do not back away, and pretend not to notice your gaze flowing over me.

"What *should* you tilt at? That's the question. We are all of us facing something, charging at something. Aren't we? But we have to choose which giants we attempt to slay."

Hypocrite, I. There is no choice for me. It has been made on my behalf, and that in itself is a giant I cannot slay. But this isn't about me. And I must appear wise.

You nod, understanding. Your eyes are on me. I hold your gaze and wait. A glance at the clock would tell me the hour is up, but then I know that already, I can feel it. I can feel the passage of time. My life is measured in one-hour increments, and thus I am finely attuned to the sensation of an hour's passage, used to the slow caress of each minute, the slippery tread of each quarter hour sliding over me. An hour has passed, yet you are still here. Staring down at me as if seeing me for the first time.

"X—"

I back up. "Choose your giant, Jonathan."

You follow me step for step. "I think maybe I'll start going by Jon." Your eyes, brown and richly textured in arcs of light and darker shades, fix on mine. You are not leering, or staring; worse, you are *seeing*.

"Jon, then." I meet your gaze, and I must focus intently on keeping erect the wall of neutrality between us. "Choose your giant, Jon. Tilt wisely."

A step. Not even a step, more of a slide of one Italian-leather pointy-toed loafer, and a single sheet of loose-leaf paper could not fit between my body and yours, and though we are not touching, this is illicit, a stolen moment. You do not—cannot—fathom the risk you take. The risk *I* take.

"What if I choose to tilt at this windmill, X?" You ask this with your intention telegraphed in the whisper of your voice, in the way your hands twitch at your sides as if itching to take me by the waist or by the face.

I keep my gaze and my voice calm, neutral; the direst threats are best delivered sotto voce. "There are giants, Jonathan, and then there are titans."

Click . . . ding.

I breathe a sigh of relief . . .

or is it thinly veiled disappointment?

SEVEN

do not expect the knock at the door. It comes at 7:30 P.M., Saturday. I have imagined dozens of fictional stories by now. It is all I have to do. When the knock comes—*rap-rap-rap-rap*, four firm but polite taps—I jump, blink, and stare at the door as if expecting it to burst into flames, or come to life. Regaining my composure, I smooth my skirt over my hips, school my features into a blank mask, and open the door.

"Len. Good evening. Is anything the matter?"

Len's broad, weather-worn face seems hewn from granite and expresses the same measure of emotion. "Good evening, Madame X." A black garment bag hangs over one arm. "This is for you."

I take the bag. "Why? I mean, what is it for?"

"You are to join Mr. Indigo for dinner this evening."

I blink. Swallow. "Join him for dinner? Where?"

"Upstairs. Rhapsody."

"Rhapsody?"

A shrug. "Restaurant, near the top of the building."

"And I'm to join him there? For dinner?"

"Yes, ma'am."

"In public?"

Another shrug. "Dunno, ma'am." Flick of a wrist, revealing a thick black rubber tactical chronograph. "Mr. Indigo expects you in one hour." Len steps through, closes the door, and puts his back to it. "I'll wait here, Madame X. Best go get ready."

I shake all over. I do not know what this is, what is happening. I never join "Mr. Indigo" for dinner. I have dinner here. Alone. Always. This is not how things go. It is out of the norm, not part of the pattern. The warp and weft of my life is a careful dance, choreographed with precision. Aberrations leave me breathless, chest tight, eyes blinking too swiftly. Aberrations are unwelcome.

Dinner at Rhapsody with Mr. Indigo. I don't know what this means; it is semantically null.

I shower, even though I am already clean. I depilate, apply lotion. Lingerie, black lace, French bikini and demi-cups, Agent Provocateur. The dress is magnificent. Deep red, high neckline around my throat, both arms bare, slit up the left side nearly to my hip, open back, Vauthier's signature asymmetry. A runway haute couture piece, probably. Elegant, sexy, dramatic. The dress is enough of a statement on its own, so I opt for simple black high-heeled sandals. Light makeup, a touch around the eyes, stain on the lips, color on my cheeks.

Heart hammering, I step out into the living room, ready in forty minutes. It would not do to keep Mr. Indigo waiting, something tells me.

"Very lovely, Madame X," Len says, but it feels like a formality, part of the charade.

"Thank you."

A nod, an elbow proffered. My lungs are frozen and my heart is in my throat as I take Len's arm, follow him out into the foyer beyond my door: thick ivory carpet, slate walls, abstract paintings, a table with a vase of flowers. A short hallway leading to an emergency stairwell: *Caution, emergency exit only, alarm will sound.* The elevator doors are polished chrome, mirror-bright. A window near the emergency exit, showing the Manhattan skyline, summer evening sunlight coating gold on glass.

The foyer beyond my condo is smaller than I thought it would be.

A keyhole where the call button would be, a key on a ring from Len's pocket inserted and twisted, withdrawn, and the doors slide open immediately. There are no buttons, only another keyhole with four degrees one could turn it to: *G, 13, Rhap., PH*—Len inserts the key and twists it to the Rhapsody marker, and then we are in motion. Only there is no sensation of motion, no lift or dip of my stomach. A brief silence, no wait music, and then the doors slide open with a muted *ding*.

My expectations are dashed. Shattered.

No hushed chatter of a fine dining establishment in full evening swing. No clink of silverware on plates. No laughter.

Not one person in sight.

Not a server, not a patron, not a single chef.

The entire restaurant is empty.

I take a step forward, and immediately the doors slide closed between Len and me, leaving me alone. I feel my heart twist, hammer even faster. My heart rate is surely a medical risk, at this point. Table after table, empty. Two-tops, four-tops, six-tops, all round white-cloth-covered tables with chairs tucked in, napkins folded in elaborate origami shapes, silverware placed just so on either side of the flatware, wineglasses in the upper right corner. Not one light in the restaurant is lit, bathing me in golden shadows of falling dusk streaming in from the thirty-foot-tall panes of glass ringing the entire perimeter of the restaurant, which occupies the entire floor of the building. The kitchen sits at the center, open-plan, so the diners on three sides are able to see the chefs preparing the food, and the tables on the other side, a glimpse of the windows and the skyline. The elevator in front of which I am still standing is one of four forming the back wall of the kitchen, and there is a plaque above "my" elevator that proclaims it to be a private lift, with no public access—in place of a call button, there is a keyhole.

A thousand questions are bubbling in my brain. Clearly, my condo is only one of many in this building. Yet the foyer beyond my condo provides access only to the elevator and the emergency stairwell. The square footage of the condo, however, is not sufficient to take up the entire thirteenth floor. Why a private elevator that only goes to four places, and requires a key to access? Does each of my clients get a key? Or is there an elevator attendant?

Why is the restaurant empty?

What am I supposed to do?

A violin plays, soft high strains wavering quietly from off to my left. A cello joins it. Then a viola, and another violin.

I follow the music around the kitchen and discover a breathtaking vision: a single two-person table draped in white, set for two, a bottle of white wine on ice in a marble bucket on a stand beside the table, and a half dozen or so tables have been removed to clear a wide space around it, with thick white candles on five-foot-tall black wrought-iron stands forming a perimeter. The string quartet is off in the shadows a few feet away, two young men and two young women, black tuxedos and modest black dresses.

In the shadows just beyond the ring of candles stands a darker shadow. Tall, elegant, powerful. Hands stuffed casually in charcoal-gray trouser pockets. No tie, topmost button undone to reveal a sliver of flesh. Suit coat, middle button fastened. Crimson kerchief folded in a perfect triangle in the pocket of the coat. Thick black hair swept back and to one side, a single strand loose to drape across a temple. That ghost of amusement on thin lips.

I watch the Adam's apple bob. "X. Thank you for joining me." That voice, like boulders crashing down a canyon wall.

I didn't have a choice, did I? But of course, these words remain lodged in my throat, alongside my heart and my breath. Careful steps in high heels across the wide room. Come to a halt beside the table. I watch long legs take a few short strides, and I'm staring up at a strong, clean-shaven jawline, glittering dark eyes.

"Caleb," I breathe.

"Welcome to Rhapsody."

"You rented out the entire restaurant?" I questioned.

"Not rented so much as ordered them to close it down for the evening."

"You own it, then?"

A rare full smile. "I own the building, and everything in it."

"Oh."

A twitch of a finger, gesturing at my chair. "Sit, please."

I sit, fold my hands on my lap. "Caleb, if I may ask—"

"You may not." Strong fingers lift a butter knife, tap on the wine-glass gently, the crystal ringing loudly in the silence. "Let's have the food brought out and then we'll discuss things."

"Very well." I duck my head. Focus on breathing, on slowing my heart rate.

I feel rather than see or hear the presence of someone else. Look up, a man of indeterminate age stands beside the table. He could be thirty-five, he could be fifty. Wrinkles at the corners of his eyes and mouth, young and intelligent eyes, light brown hair, receding hairline.

"Sir, madam. Would you care to see a menu?"

"No, Gerald, that's fine. We'll start with the soup du jour, followed by the house salad. No onions on mine. The filet mignon for me, medium rare. Tell Jean-Luc *just* this side of rare. Not quite bloody. For the lady, she'll have the salmon. Vegetables and mashed potatoes for the both of us."

Apparently I'm having salmon. I'd have rather had the filet mignon as well, but I hadn't been given a preference and I didn't dare protest. This was abnormal in the extreme, and I wasn't about to have anything else taken away.

"Very good, sir." Gerald lifts the bottle of white wine. "Shall I present this, sir?"

"No, I did choose it myself, after all. Marcos should have set out a bottle of red for us as well. Have that opened to breathe, and serve it with the entrées."

"Very good, sir. Will there be anything else I can do for you at this moment?"

"Yes. Have the quartet play the suite in G major instead of the B minor."

"Of course, sir. Thank you." Gerald bows at the waist, deeply.

He then scurries and weaves between the tables, whispers to the viola player, who holds up a hand, and the other three players let their instruments quaver into silence. A brief meeting of heads, and then they strike up again, a different melody this time. Returning, Gerald uncorks the wine with elaborate ceremony and pours a measure in each of our glasses, hands me mine first.

I shouldn't be nervous to take a drink, but I am. I drink tea and water, exclusively. I have no memory of drinking anything but tea and water.

What will wine be like, I wonder?

It's the little things; focus on the minor to keep one's self from hyperventilating about the major.

I watch, mimic: forefinger, middle finger, and thumb on the middle of the stem, lift carefully. Take the tiniest of sips. Wet my lips with the cool liquid. Lick my lips. Shock ripples over me. The taste is . . . like nothing I've ever experienced. Not quite sweet, not quite sour, but a little of both of those things. An explosive flavor bursting on my tongue.

Dark eyes watch me carefully, following every move, following my tongue as I run it along my lips once more. Watch me as I take another sip, an actual sip, this time. A small mouthful. Roll it around my mouth, coolness on my tongue, a starburst of flavor, tingling, sparkling. Light, fruity.

It's so good I could cry. The best thing I've ever tasted.

"Like it?" That deep, rumbling voice, following a long casual sip, the glass replaced on the table, adjusted precisely so.

"Yes," I say, keeping eagerness from my voice. "It's very good."

"I thought you might. It's a Pinot Grigio. Nothing overly fancy, but it will pair very well with the soup and salad."

Obviously, I know nothing of this. Wine pairings, Pinot Grigio, string quartets . . . this is a foreign world into which I am being suddenly and inexplicably immersed.

"Pinot Grigio." I nod. "It's delicious."

A crinkle around the eyes, a lift of one lip corner. "Don't get too used to it, X; don't want you developing any expensive or unhealthy habits. This is a special occasion, after all."

"It is?" I have no clue what occasion it could be.

Gerald appears, then, bearing a round black tray. Two low, shallow, broad white china bowls, containing a red soup of some kind. "The soup du jour is a creamy gazpacho Andaluz, made using the traditional elements of cucumber, bell peppers, and onions. Fresh, house-baked bread was used to thicken the soup, and it is garnished with a diced medley of the aforementioned vegetables. Chef Jean-Luc is confident there is no gazpacho Andaluz so good this side of the Atlantic Ocean." Gerald rotates my bowl a quarter turn, presents my soup spoon with a grandiose flourish and a bow—not so deep a bow as the one offered to my companion . . . host . . . lover . . . warden. . . .

"Very good, Gerald. Thank you." Some indefinable note in that chasmic voice contains a warning: *Get lost, if you know what's good for you.*

Gerald is gone in a blink, vanishing into the shadows.

I dip the spoon into the red liquid, lift it delicately to my mouth prepared for heat, unsure of the flavor about to meet my tongue.

"Oh! It's cold," I say, surprised.

"It's a gazpacho." This, amused, not quite condescending. "It's a cold soup. The Andaluz was originally served after the meal, but here in the States it is most frequently served prior, in the English and American tradition."

"Cold soup. It seems . . . antithetical," I say, and then ladle another spoonful into my mouth.

"Perhaps so, in theory," comes the response, between mouthfuls. "In practice, however, it is quite good. Prepared properly, at least, and Jean-Luc is one of the best chefs in the world."

Despite the surprise of the soup being served cold, it is delicious, creamy and bursting with the ripe flavor of fresh vegetables. I wash it down with a sip of wine, and although I have a vague notion that white wine is supposed to be paired with similarly colored foods, the light, fruity flavor of the wine does indeed offset the cold vegetable soup in a delightful contrast. Neither of us speaks as we finish the soup, and Gerald appears as I am scraping the last smear of red from the bowl. He takes the bowl from me and replaces it with a salad, does the same on the other side of the table.

"Continuing with the Spanish theme, this evening's salad is a simple affair of cucumbers, onions, and tomatoes, lightly flavored with red wine vinegar and olive oil." Once again, Gerald rotates the plate in front of me, bowing, presenting the brightly colorful salad, artfully arranged in geometric shapes.

The wine goes even better with the salad, each bite feeling spritely on my tongue, the wine tingling and coruscating.

More long moments of silence as we eat the salad. My wine goblet is empty for perhaps fifteen seconds in total when Gerald appears yet again from the shadows and refills it.

"Dispense with the formality, Gerald, and pour the rest of the bottle." The command comes quietly and cannot be gainsaid, so firm and confident is the voice.

Total authority. Absolute expectation of obedience, even in so simple a matter as pouring a larger glass of wine than is, apparently, formally acceptable.

"As you wish, sir." Gerald pours the wine into my glass first, twisting the bottle to prevent glugging.

Alternating between the two goblets, Gerald makes sure each of us has exactly the same amount, down to the last drops. Remarkable precision, performed with ritual familiarity.

The salad is finished. The quartet lets a moment of silence pervade, and then they strike up again, in practiced unison. I sip at my wine, savoring each droplet. At last, however, I can contain myself no longer.

"Caleb, you said this was a special occasion, but I must confess, I have no idea—"

"Hush and enjoy the experience. I am aware of your ignorance, and I will enlighten you in my own time. For now, drink your wine. Listen to the music. I handpicked this quartet from among the most promising students at Juilliard. Each of the musicians is among the best in the world at his or her respective instrument."

I am not expected to reply. I lean back, pivot slightly, rest an arm across the back of my chair. Attempt to appear at ease, comfortable. How long passes, I cannot say. Minutes, perhaps. Ten or fifteen. I fight restlessness. Cross my legs, uncross them. Glance at the windows, wishing I could stand and stare down, watch the people, examine the city from each new angle, see new portions of the skyline. I know the view from each of my windows as well as I know the sight of my own hands. A new perspective would be something to enjoy.

Eventually Gerald appears with an already-uncorked bottle of wine. The bottle is darkest red, nearly opaque, and has no label. He pours a thimbleful into a clean glass, too little to really drink. I watch with fascination a ritual clearly familiar to both men, the swirl of the tiny amount of liquid around the bottom of the goblet; inhale through the nose, goblet tipped at an angle, just so. A sip, then. A wetting of the lips, swish around the mouth. A nod. Yet instead of filling that glass, Gerald fills mine first. A strange ceremony, that. Present it to the man for testing and approval, but pour it for the woman first. Inexplicable to me.

"This is from the estate at Mallorca, yes, Gerald?"

Gerald nods, setting the bottle down with great care. "Correct, sir. Bottled and shipped here for your exclusive reserves. One of a thousand bottles available, I believe, although Marcos would be the better man to ask for precise numbers." A gesture at the shadows. "Shall I summon him, sir?"

A minute shake of the head. "No, it's all right. It just has a slightly more pungent bouquet than the last bottle, is all."

"I think, sir, that this bottle is the first of a new batch only recently arrived."

"Ah. That explains it."

Gerald nods, bows. "I believe the main course is ready, sir."

A wave of the hand, a dismissal.

I am puzzled. Overwhelmed. Estate in Mallorca? Exclusive

reserves of a thousand, unlabeled bottles of wine? An entire building in the heart of Manhattan?

"Where is Mallorca, Caleb?"

"It's an island in the Mediterranean Sea owned by Spain. I—or rather my family—own a vineyard there, among other places."

Family? It's hard to think of this man as having a family. Sisters, brothers? Parents?

Gerald appears with a large plate in each hand. Salmon, pinkish-orange, surrounded by grilled vegetables—cauliflower, broccoli, carrots, green bean sprouts—and thick, lumpy mashed potatoes topped by a melting pat of butter.

I have yet to taste the wine, which is ruby in color, the shade of freshly spilled blood. I put the glass to my nose and inhale; the scent is earthy, ripe, pungent, powerful. I try a sip. I have to suppress the urge to cough, to spit it out. I swallow, school my features into the blank mask. I do not like this, not at all. Dry, rolling over my tongue with a dozen shades of decadent flavor.

"Don't like that wine as much, I take it?"

I shake my head. "It's . . . so different."

"Different good, or different bad?"

I am in dangerous and unfamiliar territory. I shrug. "Not like the Pinot Grigio."

A noise in the back of the throat. A laugh, perhaps. If I didn't know better. "You don't like it. You can say so, if that is the case."

I demurely slide the goblet away from me an inch or two. "I would prefer some ice water, I think."

"More of the Pinot, perhaps?" My goblet is tugged closer to the other side of the table.

I shrug, trying not to appear too eager. "That would be wonderful, Caleb. Thank you."

A single finger lifted off the tabletop, a turn of the head. Subtle gestures, made with the knowledge that they will be noticed. Gerald appears, bending close. "Sir?"

"The lady does not find the red suitable to her palate, I'm afraid. She'll have more of the Pinot Grigio. I'll finish this myself, I suppose. No sense wasting it."

"Immediately, sir." Gerald hustles into the shadows and is gone for only a few moments before returning with a single glass of the white wine.

I was expecting more of the uncorking ritual and find myself slightly disappointed that I wouldn't get to see it again. So strange, so lovely, like the waltz of a gourmand. No matter. I drink the wine and enjoy it. Feel it in my blood, buzzing warmly in my skull.

The salmon, of course, is very good. Light, flavorful, pleasurable.

Nothing is said during the course of the meal. The only sound is the quartet playing softly from the shadows, the clink of forks. At long last, both plates are pushed away, and I follow example by covering what I didn't finish with my napkin. Gerald removes the plates, vanishes, and reappears with two plates, each of which contains a single small bowl, in which is . . . I do not know what it is.

"Chef Jean-Luc offers Flan Almendra, a traditional Spanish dessert for sir and madam, to finish the evening."

"Thank you, Gerald. That will be all."

"Of course, sir. And may I just say what an extraordinary pleasure it was to serve you this evening." Gerald bows deeply and then departs.

Flan turns out to be somewhere between pudding and pie, with a crunchy almond crust. I eat it slowly, savoring it, forcing myself to be demure, a lady, and not devour it as I would wish to, were such barbaric behavior allowed.

Through it all, my brain is whirring. A single question, burning: Why? Why? Why?

I dare not ask.

At long, long last, there is nothing left to eat, and only the last inch of wine remains in my glass. My red was claimed long ago, and the bottle finished. I truly do not know how so much thick, pungent wine can be drunk so swiftly.

"X." The voice, buzzing in my head. In my bones. It's a little loose sounding. "You've been very patient this evening."

I can only shrug. "It has been an enjoyable evening, Caleb. Thank you."

"I've decided today is to be your birthday."

I have no thought in my head, no capacity for rational thought. The pronouncement has left me utterly unhinged. "Wh—what?"

"Since we know nothing of you prior to our . . . meeting, I decided—rather belatedly, I do admit—that you require a birthday." An easy shrug. "Today is July the second. The exact midpoint of the calendar year."

I try to breathe. Summon words. Thoughts. Emotions. "I—um. Today is my birthday?"

"It is now. Happy Birthday, X."

"How many years would it be?" I can't help asking.

"The doctors, on that day, presumed you—with a high degree of accuracy, they told me—to be nineteen or twenty. That was six years ago, so I'm going to say that today is your twenty-sixth birthday."

Six years. Twenty-six.

Puzzle pieces flit and float and flitter. Gazpacho Andaluz. Spanish red wine. Spanish cucumber salad. Spanish flan.

"Andaluz . . . Caleb, is that a place in Spain?"

An expression of curiosity. "Andalusia, yes."

"Did you find something out about me? Is that what this about?" I cannot stop the question.

Cannot phrase it any more respectfully or politely. Curiosity flares in me. Hope, too, but just a spark, a fragile, easily extinguished, guttering pinpoint of light.

A pause, a hesitation. Tongue sliding over lips, roll of a shoulder, shifting in the chair. "Yes. A little something, at least. I had your DNA analyzed."

"You did?" I blink, breathe in, wonder if it is normal to feel as if I have been somehow opened, pried apart, what little privacy I have invaded.

"Yes. When you were sleeping, the last time I visited you, I took a piece of your hair from your hairbrush, and swabbed the inside of your cheek. You sleep like the dead to begin with, and you were . . . *very* tired. You barely stirred." A self-satisfied glint of the eye, not quite a smirk. "My scientists were able to trace certain markers in your DNA and determine with a surprising degree of accuracy where your ethnic heritage originates."

I am breathless with anticipation—that phrase, it occurs in fiction quite frequently. But in reality, it is not an entirely pleasant sensation. "What—*ahem.*" I have to start over. "What did your scientists discover?"

A hand, manicured fingernails, trimmed cuticles, large and powerful and graceful, waving at the table. "Can't you guess?"

"Spain?" I suggest.

"Precisely. They are clever fellows, those geneticists. They're still working, comparing markers and whatever else it is they do, trying to narrow it down, get more specific results. They tell me with time they might be able to tell me a specific region of Spain, things like that. But for now, all we know is . . . you, Madame X, are Spanish." Those eyes, dark, expressive, hard, hungry, raking over me. "You look it, too. I've long thought that might be it. My Spanish beauty."

Clever fellows. Geneticists on the payroll. *My scientists.* Who has scientists on retainer?

"I would have had Jean-Luc prepare a traditional Spanish main course for us, but I thought that might be laying it on a bit too thick. Spanish food is also very rich, and you are not accustomed to such fare. I wouldn't want to overburden your digestive system as well as your emotions all in one night, you know."

"Yes, I see." My brain supplied relevant-sounding words at the expected moment, but in truth I was numb, dizzy, spinning, and fending off what felt like an anxiety attack.

"Do you need a moment, X?"

I nod.

"Take a moment, then."

I stood up and moved with great relief away from the table, away from the ring of candles, away from the huge and overwhelming presence. Away from the music. Deep into the shadows, to the window. Night had long ago fallen over the city, so now light came from countless yellow and white squares in neat horizontal and vertical rows across the horizon, from streetlamps far below, from red departing taillights and white approaching headlights.

I am Spanish.

I had your DNA analyzed. Such an easy phrase, so easily spoken. What does it mean to me, to know I am of Spanish origin? Nothing; everything.

My eyes prick, sting. My lungs ache and I am dizzy, and I realize I have been holding my breath. I blink and breathe. Such wrenching emotion over what? Knowing where in the world my unnamed and unknown ancestors came from? Weakness.

I've decided today is to be your birthday.

Another fact that feels both weighted with meaning and utterly devoid of it as well. A birthday?

A girl with dark hair walks by, dozens of stories below, on the opposite side of the street, holding her mother's hand. It is much too far to see much else. They know their origins. Their family. Their past. A mother's hand to cling to. A daughter to sing sweet songs to. Perhaps a daddy, a husband waiting for them.

"X?" A single letter, spoken in a murmur that would be a whisper for anyone with a smaller voice.

"Caleb." An acknowledgment is all I can manage.

"Are you all right?"

I shrug. "I suppose."

"Which means no, I think." Warm palm on my waist, just above the swell of my hip. "What's wrong?"

"Why?"

"Why what?" True confusion.

"Why have my DNA analyzed? Why tell me? Why give me an arbitrary birthday? Why bring me here for dinner? Why now?"

"It was meant to be—"

"Are you going to give me a Spanish name now, too?"

A fraught silence. I interrupted, spoke out of turn. In dark and gritty noir novels, someone would say, *Men have died for less*, and with the man behind me, it might just be true. It seems possible; I look down at the hand on my waist. It looks capable of violence, of delivering death.

"Your name is Madame X." A harsh rumble in my ear. "Don't you remember?"

"Of course I do." When one possesses only six years' worth of memories, each one is crystalline.

"I brought you to the MOMA, the day they released you from the hospital. All of the museum at your disposal, and you spent the whole time in front of two paintings."

"Van Gogh, *Starry Night*," I say.

"And John Singer Sargent's *Portrait of Madame X*." Another hand on me, this one lower, below my hip bone, where it becomes thigh.

Pulling me backward, taut against a hard chest. "I didn't know what to call you. I tried every name I could think of, and you'd just shake your head. You wouldn't speak. Couldn't really, I guess. Had to roll you around in that wheelchair, remember? Hadn't relearned to walk yet. But you pointed at that painting, the Sargent. So I stopped, and you just stared at it and stared at it."

"It was the expression on her face. It looks blank, at first. She's in profile, so you'd think it might be hard to tell what she's thinking. But if you look closely, you can see something there. Beneath the surface, maybe. And the curve of her arm. It looked strong. She's so delicate, but . . . that arm, the one touching the table, it's . . . it looks strong. And I felt weak, so helpless. So to see such a delicate-looking woman with something like strength? It just . . . spoke to me, some-how. Reassured me. Told me that maybe I could be strong, too."

"And you are."

"Sometimes."

"When you need to be."

"Not now."

"Why?" Breath, wine-laced, from lips at my ear.

"It's all so much to process. I don't know what to think, Caleb."

"You'll figure it out." Teeth on my earlobe. I shiver, tilt head away, close my eyes and hate my weakness, my involuntary chem-ical reaction. "Come. One more surprise for you, back down in your room."

I was not at all sure I had room within me for more surprises, but I allowed myself to be led away from the window with its mes-merizing view of the city. To the elevator. A key, from a trouser pocket, inserted, twisted to the *13*. Descent, moments of utter silence in which my heartbeat is surely audible.

As I am led into my living room, the first thing I notice is that my books have been replaced on my shelf. Heart leaping with hope,

I turn and see that my library is open once more. I am allowed to leave the strong-armed embrace, wander into my library. Sweep my hands over the spines of my dear friends, these many books. My gaze falls on this title, that: *The Forge of God*; *Wool*; *I Know Why the Caged Bird Sings*; *Lolita*; *Breath, Eyes, Memory*; *A Brief History of Time*; *Influence: Science and Practice*; *American Gods* . . . everywhere my eyes look, a book that has taught me something invaluable. I could cry from joy at having my library back.

I turn, let a tear show: gratitude emoted. "Thank you, Caleb."

Somehow the distance between doorway and room center has been traversed invisibly, silently, and a thumb trails through the wetness on my cheek. "I think you've learned your lesson now, haven't you?"

"Yes, Caleb."

Deep, long, gusting breaths, swelling that great, powerful chest, eyes raking down my form, eager and hungry and admiring. "My Spanish beauty. My X." There is a note in those words, in the delivery of them . . . it must be the wine, the alcohol pushing aside some of the granite wall veiling whatever emotions roil behind those eyes, which have always seemed to me the ocular equivalent of Homer's "wine-dark seas."

"Caleb." What else do I say? There is nothing.

"Look in the display case." The words hold a thread of satisfaction. There is a new tome in the case: *Tender Is the Night*. F. Scott Fitzgerald. "It's a signed first edition, the original 1934 version with the flashbacks."

There are white gloves in the case, of course. I open the case, don the gloves, withdraw the book with shaky breath and steady hands. The inscription, in Fitzgerald's own hand: *From one who wishes he could be at 1917s 20th*, in that crabbed, looping script, the name below, the curlicue *F*, the double-bar downstrokes of the twin

*T*s in *Scott*, the crossbar looping and swooping to merge with the second *F* that begins *Fitzgerald*.

"Caleb, it's . . . it's incredible. Thank you, so much."

"It's your birthday, after all, and birthdays require gifts."

"It's a marvelous gift, Caleb. I shall treasure it." I look up and see that the time for admiring my gift is over with, for now.

Time to show my appreciation.

Some things cannot be rushed.

This night, insatiability comes in the form of my body being slowly unwrapped, inch by inch. The dress unzipped, lowered to bare my lingerie—nostrils flare and eyes go heavy-lidded and hands reach; evidence of my "Spanish beauty"—and then the lingerie is peeled off, tossed aside.

Naked, I wait.

"Undress me, X."

To reveal that body is like unveiling a sculpture by Michelangelo. A study of masculine perfection done in unforgiving marble. Each angle carved with a deeply piercing chisel. My hands work and my eyes devour. My heart resists, twists, beats like a hammer on an anvil. My body, though. God, my body. It knows something my metaphysical heart and cerebral understanding do not: Caleb Indigo was created by an artist for the express purpose of ravishing women.

Specifically, in this moment, this woman.

And I hate my body for it. I tell it to remember the way of things. That this is expected of me. Required. Demanded. I *must*; my will does not enter this equation.

And my body? It has a response: *I do not care about requirements . . . all I know is a singular desire: TOUCH ME.*

Touch me.

Touch me.

My body says that, as does the body I have now laid bare.

So I obey. I obey my body and the tacit command within the two words so recently spoken: "Undress me."

Touch me, that order implies.

So I touch.

Stroke into life the erection as large and perfect as the rest. Well, it was already fully alive and ready; I merely gave it the attention it was begging for by standing so tall and thick and straight.

Hands go to my shoulders, gently and implacably push me to my knees. I cast my eyes upward and obey. Mouth wide, taste flesh. Lips curled in to sheathe my teeth, hands plunging in a slow rhythm. Watch now. Quick breaths go ragged, hands clutch my hair, voice box utters guttural moans. Taste smokiness, essence leaking.

"Enough. Jesus, X." A curse, more rare still than a smile.

Suddenly, I'm airborne, carried into my room and tossed unceremoniously onto my bed. I scramble backward, knock aside pillows, but I'm too slow. Lip curled in a snarl, eyes feral, hands reaching and gripping my hips. Tugging me roughly, and my heart leaps a mile from chest to throat as hips wedge my thighs apart. Face-to-face?

I dare not think, dare not even hope. Breathe, cling to broad hard shoulders . . . exhale sharply as I am pierced.

Movement, face-to-face.

I can't breathe.

This is a night for firsts, it seems.

I dare to flutter my hips to the rhythm of our sex, dare to keep my eyes open and see. There is turmoil. Desire. Conflict. Heated need. Demand. Fire. Urgency.

And also in me?

I shy away from parsing and enumerating my own emotions. To do so would be to open Pandora's box, and I dare not.

Desperate movement now. Eyes on mine. Unwavering, piercing

directness. There is a world in those dark orbs, a whole galaxy a mere mortal such as I cannot fathom.

Close.

So close.

Breath leaves me. Neither of us looks away.

Oh God.

Hands claw and clutch, grip and tug and bruise.

"Fuck. Fuck!" And then total absence. Everything ripped away, heat, presence, breath, body.

The moment is gutted.

"Caleb? Did I do something wrong?"

That huge body stands at the window, silhouetted, erotic male sexuality in shadow, shoulders bowed, head bent, hands wide and high on the frame, hips narrow and trim, buttocks firm and clenched and bubble-round and taut looking, legs like Grecian pillars. Shoulders heaving.

"Over here, X." A command, uttered so low as to be nearly inaudible.

I hear it, though, for I am painfully attuned to every whisper, every breath.

I rise, move tentatively to the window. Touch a shoulder with trembling fingers. "Are you okay? Was it me?"

"Shut up. Stand at the window." So unexpectedly harsh. Almost angry.

At me?

I dare not question again. That tone brooks no argument.

I stand at the window, shaking all over. Turn my head, look over my shoulder. Oh. That face, cast into shadow now, but not the shadows of absent light, rather the shadows of veiled emotion, features smoothed into unfeeling stone. Only the lips slightly pursed and tightened betray the tumult within.

I shake with cold, goose bumps pebbling on my skin.

A foot nudges mine apart, and then arms like boa constrictors snake around my chest, clutch my breast, another around my waist to clutch my hip. Behind me, bent at the knee, a moment to fit that hot thick erection to my opening, and then a hard upward, inward thrust. I gasp, a shrieking exhale of surprise and pain. So hard, so sudden, so rough.

No gentility here, no tenderness. None of the eroticism of only moments ago. This is what I've always known. Roughly thrusting, roughly using. Grunts in my ear.

I stand straight upright and cling to the arms gripping me, slippery with sweat and corded with muscle. Mad, wild thrusts from behind, straight up and down, legs bent wide and far apart.

Finally, when I think surely the moment of climax must be close, I find myself shoved forward so I'm bent double at the waist, hair fisted and jerked so my head snaps backward, a hand gripping my hip crease with bruising force.

Pound, pound, pound.

I whimper, shriek, and then— "Caleb!"

Slow now. Still just as rough and harsh and wild, but slowly.

Uttering that name, it was a plea. A protestation. All I could manage.

I feel the release, the hot gush.

The hands release me, suddenly, and I fall forward, bump up against the window. Opening my eyes, I look out the window and see across the street, an office tower black in the night, all the windows darkened save one, the window opposite my own. A figure in the light, watching.

What a show.

Hands, gentle now, lift me, cradle me, set me on my bed. I fight tears. I ache. My heart aches, my soul. What did I do to deserve so rough and thoughtless a fucking? There was no mutuality in that. No thought for my pleasure.

I let myself drowse, escape into sleep.

But a sound buzzes in my ear, slips through the curtain of unconsciousness. A voice. "I'm sorry, X. You're mine, and only mine. You can't know. I wish you could, but you can't know. You can't know, or you'd—no. You're *mine*. And I don't share."

Nonsensical words. I know who owns me; that is one mistake I shall not make again.

An apology?

Gods do not offer apologies.

EIGHT

need a date for an event, X." You glance at me sideways.

"Ask a friend." I pretend to be busy stirring milk into my tea so I don't have to look at you.

"None of my friends are suitable."

"Ask one of your many girlfriends, then."

You laugh. "I don't have *any* girlfriends, X."

My turn to laugh. "Ha. I can smell them on you, Jonathan."

"There are girls, but they aren't girlfriends."

"So you really are a quintessential playboy." It is said with a hint of humor, and an edge of truth.

"Guilty as charged. But again, none of them are suitable. They aren't classy enough for this event."

"What is the event?" I shouldn't ask, because I know where you are going with this, and it isn't possible.

"It's a fund-raiser, a charity thing. But it's super upper-crust. Invitation only, ten grand entrance fee, and that's just to get in. There's a guest list that's going to read like the Academy Awards. I can't bring any old skank in some slutty dress, like I usually do for these things. I need someone with presence, and class."

"Jonathan, I know what you're—"

"I need *you*, X."

"I am not available."

You frown. "You don't even know when it is."

"It doesn't matter when it is." My tea is very well stirred at this point, but still I clink my spoon against the china.

"I'll pay you normal rates for your time, of course."

I look up sharply, eyes blazing. "I am *not* an escort, Jonathan Cartwright."

"That's not what I meant! I swear, I just . . . I know you're not— I meant, it wouldn't be, like, a *date*-date. It'd be part of my training. See how I do. A test."

Nicely recovered. I hide a smile. "I see. Very clever. But still not a possibility, I'm afraid."

You are suddenly on the couch beside me rather than standing casually at the window as has become your habit. Too close. Cologne tickles my nose. I glance sideways, see your Cartier watch, a square chunky thing of silver with a black leather strap, masculine and elegant.

"Why not, X?"

I cross my legs knee over knee, sip my tea. Do not look at you. "It's . . . not done. Not possible. Not for me. Not with you. Not with anyone."

"*Why*, X?" Your hand ventures along the couch back.

I freeze, silently begging you not to do that, not to put your arm around me. *Don't do it, Jonathan. For me, and for you, don't do it. I've come to like you, against all odds, and I don't want to see anything happen to you.*

"Jesus, X. You are the prickliest woman I've ever known. I'm not even touching you and you're all tensed up."

"I am *not* prickly."

You snort. "All right, babe. Whatever you say." Sarcasm is rife in your tone.

I fix you with a glare. "Babe?"

You hold up your hands in mock surrender. "Sorry, sorry. But you *are* a little . . . standoffish."

I stand up, empty teacup in hand. I am not even cognizant of having finished my tea, yet the cup is empty. I move into the kitchen, rinse the cup, set it upside down in the drying rack. I feel you, a foot away.

"If I am prickly or standoffish, perhaps it is for a reason." I compress myself into the smallest area possible up against the sink as you invade my space. "It's a warning, Jonathan. One you would do well to heed."

"Hands off, huh?"

I let out a breath as you back away. "Yes. Hands off."

"Property of Indigo Services?" Your voice is sharp.

I catch my breath and look up. Suddenly you seem to see more deeply into the truth of matters than I had assumed you were capable. "*Don't*, Jonathan. Just . . . don't."

Yet you do. "Are you a hermit, X? I mean, I've never seen you even step over the threshold of this condo."

"Jonathan. Stop."

You pace away, out of the kitchen. Glance around. "I mean, damn, X. I don't see a TV, or a radio, or a computer. I don't even see a fucking pencil sharpener. Like, I don't see one single electric appliance, except for the fucking refrigerator and toaster. And the thing with the elevator? The whole scary-as-fuck elevator operator-slash-bodyguard? Or is he a prison warden? Do you have a cell phone? Shit, even a landline? Do you have any contact with the outside world in anyway what-so-fucking-ever?" You come to a stop behind the couch.

I cross the room and step up close to you, razors in my gaze, ice radiating off me. "I believe it is time for you to leave, Mr. Cartwright."

"Why? Because I'm asking questions you aren't allowed to answer?"

Yes, exactly. I do not say that, though. God, no. That would be disastrous. I just stare you down, and, to your credit, you do not look away. You just return the stare, possibly seeing more than I am meant to allow.

You reach into your hip pocket and withdraw a slim silver case, depress a button, and the case flips open, revealing business cards. You slide one card free, close the case, stuff it back into the pocket of your slacks. A shuffled step, and you're crowding me, staring down at me. The card pinched between thumb and forefinger, you slide it into the V of my cleavage without touching my skin.

The card stock pokes at my flesh. Your eyes are too knowing. Too perceptive. When did you stop being a spoiled boy and become this confident man? You do not rile my flesh, you do not incite panic or breathless fervor in me, but that is no fault of yours.

There are giants—which I can see you becoming, in time—and then there are titans. And even though you have found your footing, discovered the fire in your belly and how to harness it, you are no titan.

But your proximity unnerves me, nonetheless.

"'Bye, Madame X. I can honestly say that without you, I'd never have had the courage to live up to my potential. So . . . thanks."

Your hand lifts, hovers a hairbreadth away from my jawline. Your face is an inch from mine. I think for a terrifying moment that you are about to kiss me. I cannot breathe; my heart does not beat. I do not blink. You have me trapped against the back of the couch, and I do not dare put my hands on you to move you. To do so would be tantamount to striking a match in a room full of dynamite; there is little chance an errant spark will find a fuse, but the risk is simply too great.

You back away, one step. Two. A breath, a single lift of your chest, your chin rises. And then there it is, that insouciant smirk, knowing, a little mocking, ripe with boyish, roguish humor. You whirl, twist the knob, jerk open my door, and you're gone.

When the door has clicked closed, I withdraw your business card from my cleavage and examine it.

Jon Cartwright

Owner, Cartwright Business Services, LLC

Tel: (212) 555-4321

E-mail: jecartwright@cbs.com

You started your own business. I am inordinately proud of you.

When my door opens rather suddenly, I don't look up, assuming perhaps you forgot something.

It isn't you.

"Well, well, well," a deep, leonine voice says. "Looks like our little Jonathan has grown up."

"Caleb." I glance up sharply and take a step back, surprised. "Yes. It seems he has." I extend the business card, feigning casual disinterest. I don't think it is a believable farce, however.

Dark eyes flick over the card. "Good for him. He has the poten-tial to do well, I think. Perhaps Indigo Services will offer him a contract."

I remain silent. Business endeavors are not within my sphere of knowledge or influence.

Smooth, panther-silent strides across the room, sit, recline with

kingly elegance in the Louis XIV armchair. Examining Jonathan's
card. Speculating. "You parried his questions and advances very
adroitly, by the way. Well done."

"He's harmless."

"No, he isn't. You're wrong there, I'm afraid. He's not harmless
at all." The card flips, flips, flips, twirled between index, middle, and
ring finger.

I dare. "What do you mean? What harm is there in him?"

"His questions. His curiosity." Eyes, burning like balefire, scorching me. "He wouldn't understand the truth, X." The card flies through
the air like a knife, then flutters to the floor.

The truth. Which truth?

I remain silent, knowing my input isn't required as yet.

"You will accompany Jonathan to his event."

I manage an admirable pretense of casual surprise, when inside
I am utterly stunned, faint enough that I could have been knocked
over with a feather. "I will? Really?" I sound more eager than I
should.

I am not eager; I am terrified. Or rather, I am eager *and* terrified
in equal measure.

"You will. You will be well guarded, however. Len and Thomas
will be at your side at all times."

"Why?"

"Why Len and Thomas? Or why am I sending you with Jonathan?"

"Both, I suppose."

"Well, Len and Thomas because they're the most suited to watching over you. Len is as vicious as he is vigilant, and Thomas, well . . .
let's just say he has a rather specific skill set." A pause. "As for why
I'm sending you? It will allay suspicion. The event itself is very private, so there will be no cameras, no press. Everyone else attending

will have their own security, as well, so it's as safe an event for you to attend as anything."

I still don't quite understand, but I say nothing. I don't need to understand.

I'm going *out*.

"Say something, X."

"I'm not sure what to say, honestly."

"Are you excited? Scared?"

I shrug. "Both."

"Understandable. After what you've been through, I can see how you might have mixed feelings about it."

I nod. "Mixed feelings. Yes." I sound faint, slightly incoherent. It's too much to take in. To process. Too many thoughts, too many feelings, too many questions. Too many doubts.

I find myself waiting, expectant. A distraction would be welcome. Yet when long legs unfold and eyes stare down at me from such great height, they are distant, a little cold. Calculating.

"I have much to do today, X. I'm afraid I have to get going."

"You aren't . . . staying?" I know how I sound, and why, and I hate it. I hate that I sound disappointed, needy.

"No. I can't, but you know how much I wish I could." Cold and calculating becomes hot and amused. "You know how much I wish I could stay, don't you, X?"

"Yes, Caleb."

"But you understand why I have to go."

"Yes, Caleb."

Yet despite claims of pressing matters, I feel an erection crushed against my belly, hands feathering up my thighs, lifting my dress hem. Slipping under the elastic of my underwear, slipping into me. Curling, circling, dipping, swiping. Swiftly, no play or pretense.

I come in moments.

"Your mouth, X." I sink to my knees.

Unzip. Free the slide-and-hook clasp of custom-tailored trousers. Taste flesh. Smoky essence. My hands and mouth on firm, clean, masculine flesh, and then it's over, faster than I would have thought possible, considering how long it can last under other circumstances.

"Thank you, X." A sigh, now-slack manhood tucked away. A few strides, and the door is silently swinging open. "I'll send someone with a suitable gown for the event."

I remain where I am, kneeling in the middle of the living room, dress rumpled, lipstick smeared, hair mussed by gripping fingers. "All right."

"Don't look so sad, X. I'll be back, and we'll have some proper time together."

"All right."

"X." This is a scold. "What is it?"

"I don't understand you, is all."

A long, long silence, the door half open, expression hidden in the doorway. "You don't need to."

"I'd like to, though. I try to."

"Why?" Curiously inquisitive, strangely sharp, subtly tender. All in one word.

"I . . . you're what I know. What I have. *All* I have. Yet I don't *know* you. And I don't get much of you. Of your time, of *you*. And when I do, it's . . ." I shrug, unable to articulate any further.

"In your own words, X . . . it's for a reason. It's a warning." A step out the door. The conversation is over.

But I hear five words sling out of my mouth like reckless bullets: "I saw you. With *her*."

"X." This is growled. Snarled.

"That girl. She was upset. She was angry with you. I saw you *fuck* her, right there in the limo. The door open, for all the world to see. *I* saw. And I—I know you saw me. You looked right at me, and you—you fucking *smiled*." Why on earth do I sound so angry, so jealous, so crazed?

"Goddammit, X."

"I know I mean nothing to you, Caleb, but must you flaunt it in my face?" I am reckless. This is insanity.

The door slams closed. *BANG!* "You need to think very carefully about your next words, X." This is spoken in a voice that resembles the edge of a scalpel.

My chin, on its own, lifts. Dares rebelliously upward. "So do you."

Three lunging steps, a brief sensation of weightlessness, and then I'm pinned against the wall as if I weigh nothing, hard hips crushing mine to the wall, a hand on my throat, cutting off my oxygen in a way that somehow does not hurt.

"Let's get one thing straight. *You* belong to *me*. Not the other way around. Do *not* presume to speak to me as if I owe you *shit* for explanations regarding *anything* I do or with whom I do it."

I blink. See stars. Darkness encroaches my vision.

"Do you understand me, X?" This is whispered so low as to be nearly inaudible.

I dip my chin ever so slightly, lift it. I am released. I drop to the floor, gasping, oxygen rushing into my brain in a sweet, cool flood.

I barely notice as my favorite window is darkened, the frame filled. Shoulders hunched, head hanging. "Fuck. X, I'm sorry. I overreacted." Pivot, a glance at me. "Are you okay?"

I am sprawled, very unladylike, against the wall, knees indecently apart, dress hem hiked up around my thighs. I gasp. Merely breathe. I do not answer. I do not have the strength.

Or the courage. That has been choked out of me.

I very intensely dislike being strangled, I am discovering.

Soft footfalls, huge, hard, heavy body crouching beside me. A hand extended to touch. Hesitant, gentle.

I flinch away.

The hand withdraws. "Fuck. *FUCK!*" The last word is shouted, sudden and frightening.

I jerk away, unable to bridle my instinctively fearful reaction.

"I'm sorry, X." The hand, on my shoulder.

I go very, very still. Tense. Frozen. Eyes shut, jaw clenched, fingers fisted on my thighs. I do not even breathe until the hand and its accompanying presence is withdrawn. And even then, I take a slow, careful breath. Watch out of the corner of my eye. Harsh, angry steps. The door, jerked open. Slammed closed with such violent force that the door splinters and the frame cracks.

I hear the elevator door, and then silence.

I sit where I am for I don't know how long. Eventually I hear the elevator again, male voices.

Len.

"Ma'am?" Beside me. Lifting me to my feet. "Come on. I got a guy that's gonna fix your door for you. Why don't you go lay down, huh? You want some tea or something?"

I shake my head, wrench free of Len's grip, as gently solicitous and careful as it is. "Nothing." I whisper it, my voice hoarse. "Thank you."

I move into my bedroom, lie down on my bed, still wearing my dress. Len tints my window black, turns on my noise machine.

"You shouldn't make him angry, ma'am. It's not smart. You got a tiger by the tail, you best not rile him. Know what I'm saying?"

"Classic apologetics for domestic abuse, Len." My voice is raspy again. I don't think I'll have bruises, though.

"I'm not apologizing, just saying."

"Apologetics is—you know what, never mind. Thank you, Len. That will be all."

"Okay, then." A pause. "I'll be by tomorrow, with the designer."

"Designer?"

"The outfit, for that rich bastard kid's event."

"Jonathan, you mean."

"Yeah, whatever. They're all the fucking same."

I don't answer. I feel my eyes grow heavy. Ignore the turmoil in my heart, in my head, ignore the burn in my throat and the sting in my eyes.

I hear the noise of my front door being replaced, and then silence.

I sleep.

Darkness. It is thick and raw and ravenous. A rumbling beast, with gnashing teeth. Red eyes, luminous orbs.

I stumble through the hungry blackness on bare feet. Stub my toe, feel a new stab of pain pierce the all-over agony as a toenail is ripped away.

Another beast, with glowing white eyes. Loud, roaring.

Howls, wailing, rising and ululating and deafening, all around me. So many monsters, iron-fleshed and fast, smashing heedless through the blackness, bright eyes and glowing red tails.

Stumble, my path in the darkness lit by lightning, my bones shaken by thunder, my trail erased by a deluge of cold rain. I am not weeping or screaming, because I hurt too badly to do so, because to weep requires breath, and I have no oxygen, no breath, lungs scorched from the hungry flames.

Flames.

They are somewhere behind me, still flickering and smelling of roasted flesh.

The beasts circle around me, roaring, flashing their too-bright eyes, claws reaching, trailing bandages and needles.

Squares, endless squares above me. Squares pierced with a

million, million dots. One hundred and ten thousand four hundred and twenty-four dots, black holes spiked into the white squares.

Voices, buzzing around me like echoes from a thousand years ago.

Words. Sounds that should be comprehensible, but aren't. Words, words, words, that mean nothing. Nothing.

Loss.

Agony.

Grief.

Agony.

A face, over and over and over.

Dreams of flames.

Dreams of darkness.

Darkness.

No more darkness. Keep the darkness at bay! There are beasts in the blackness. They want my blood, desire my flesh.

I cannot breathe.

I am drowning in an ocean of darkness, and I cannot breathe.

"Breathe, X." A command.

I breathe, drag in a long painful breath.

"Breathe."

I breathe.

Hands caress my face; a body cradles mine. I find comfort even as dimly remembered fear pulses through me. "Caleb."

"Just keep breathing, X. You're okay. You were dreaming."

God, the dreams. They ravage me, pillage my soul.

Awareness returns with a jolt like lightning striking a tree. "Let me go." I crawl away. "Don't touch me."

"X—"

I scramble off the bed, hit the floor in a pile of limbs, huddle in the darkness against the window. A shadow rises in the darkness, male shoulders, that face, angular and beautiful, angelic in its perfection, even in shadowed profile. My door is open, letting in a sliver of slight, a lance of brightness spearing the darkness, setting a too-handsome profile into relief.

"I'm sorry. You know that's not easy for me to say, to you or anyone else. I don't ever apologize. Not for anything, no matter what. But I'm apologizing to you, X. I'm sorry. I shouldn't have done that, and I'm sorry." Beside me, crouched, pale arms bare, wearing nothing but boxer-briefs.

"I know." It's all the forgiveness I can muster.

"Are you hurt?"

"No."

A finger, touching my chin, lifting my face so I'm gazing up into shadowed perfection. "Look at me, X."

"I am." Those eyes, so dark, so unknowable, so piercing, they are open and sorrowful and worried.

"Don't be afraid of me."

"I'm not." Oh, I am a skilled liar, when I must be.

Lifted, I am cradled against a hard warm bare chest. I can hear heartbeats, slow and steady. Hands, running up and down my arms, smooth my hair away. I am still in my dress. I don't know what time it is.

My heart crashes in my chest.

"Sara."

"What?" I allow myself to sound as confused as I am.

"Her name is Sara. The girl you saw me with. Sara Abigail Hirschbach. Her parents are Jewish, prominent members of the Orthodox Jewish community here in New York. Her father is a business associate of mine. And Sara . . . well, we have a complicated history. An on-and-off sort of thing. She would like it to be more 'on' than I would, even though I've explained that I do not and will not ever care for her that way. Yet she keeps coming back for more of what I do give her. Which is purely physical."

"Why are you telling me this?" I struggle to keep my voice neutral.

My question is ignored. "I'm going to be truthful with you, X. Never expect anything from me. What you know of me, it's all there is. And the truth is . . . you know the real Caleb Indigo far more thoroughly than any of my other . . . acquaintances, let's call them . . . ever will. They get less than you. Less of my time, and less of me in those brief moments. You . . . you are special, X."

"How many are there?"

"How many what?"

"Acquaintances." I let venom into my tone.

"There are many. I will make no apologies for who I am, X. The beasts in your dreams? I am like those beasts. Always hungry. Never sated, never satisfied. And the many, many girls whom I . . . visit, they are snacks. A bite, here and there. Enough to tide me over until I can *feast*."

Hot, hot breath on my flesh. My dress is ripped open, top to bottom.

"Caleb . . ."

"*You* are the feast, X."

Lips on my skin. Hands devouring flesh. Fingers seeking my wetness, my hidden heat. There is fear within me, but it only serves to excite. I fear, oh . . . *deeply* do I fear. I fear the prowling predator behind me. I fear the claws in the shadows, the ravening beast whose appetite cannot be slaked. I fear, but I shiver with excitement when I catch a glimpse of it, and I wonder if it is coming for me. And when I see the eyes and the gleam of moonlight on talon, I know it is coming for me. It will devour me, for I am but a soft thing, all underbelly and easily parted flesh.

But this night? This night I find I have claws of my own. *"No,* Caleb." I wrest myself free, naked but for panties. Cross my arms over my breasts, my chest heaving with fear and need and anger and myriad tumultuous emotions too turbulent and intermixed to name. "No. You *hurt* me."

Silence, fraught with tension.

Feet stab precisely through pants legs, shirt buttons are fitted through openings swiftly and without fumble. Socks and shoes slipped on, suit coat draped over a thick forearm. A hand slips into a trouser pocket and withdraws a phone, brief white glow of the screen, repocketed. Keys jingle, rotated around and around an index finger. "I'll give you some time, X, if that is what you need. And I will say it one last time: I'm sorry I hurt you."

There is a promise hidden between the lines of those words: *Your time to get over this is limited.*

The question that boils within me as my front door opens and closes and I am left alone is very simple: Can I get over this? What do I do if I cannot?

Can I forgive? Should I? Do I even *want* to?

I fear not.

And I fear what that means for the coming days.

NINE

You stand alone outside my door, hands stuffed in hip pockets, hair slicked back, wearing a sleek, slim tuxedo with a narrow bow tie at your throat. Handsome, young, confident. Debonair.

You could be Jay Gatsby.

"Madame X. Good evening." You lean in, kiss me formally on both cheeks. "You look lovely."

I do, truly. A stylist had arrived early this morning, pulling a rack stuffed to overflowing with garment bags. A short, stout man with artificially silver hair, wearing a woman's pantsuit in pale peach with four-inch heels and offering me a quick, genuine smile, helped me in and out of thirty-six dresses before settling on the one I'm wearing now. The dress is some brand I'd never heard of, a designer whose logo is a single thick Z stroke. A student, maybe, or a new designer. Gem wouldn't specify, saying only that the designer didn't matter, not in this case. That I looked my absolute best was all that mattered. The dress is deep crimson, floating loose from my hips to brush the floor around my feet, the skirt made of some light, gauzy material that feels like it should be sheer but isn't. From the waist up, the dress is somehow sexy to the point of indecency without actually revealing much at all. The back is open, plunging down to the very base of my spine, showing the slightest hint of my tailbone. The open back cuts in deeply around my ribs, too, so that I am in effect bare from just beneath and beside my breasts to just above my backside. A triangular patch of crimson silk covers me from throat to diaphragm, offering not a single glimpse of cleavage, yet is cut to cling and drape to sultry effect, the triangle of fabric somehow supporting my not-insignificant breasts into mounded prominence. A thin, nearly invisible strap wraps around my throat, clasping at the back of my neck with a delicate hook-and-eye. Gem applied double-sided tape to the edges of my breasts where a hint of side cleavage is visible, keeping the dress from coming loose and revealing more than intended. I insisted on my favorite pair of black Jimmy Choo heels. Gem had brought a rather excessive selection of gaudy, diamond-studded shoes he wanted me to try on, but I insisted on my own, because if I was going to spend the evening nervous and worried and out of my element, I would feel better in familiar shoes. Hair, makeup, all done simply and to great effect, hair piled up on my head, a few wisps escaping to frame my face, minimal makeup, just a touch of eye shadow, some stain on my lips, some contouring on my cheekbones.

Your compliment is delivered with deceptive ease. But as we wait for the elevator, I feel your eyes on me, raking up and down, looking away, stealing back to me.

"Is everything all right, Jonathan?" I ask, my tone sharp.

"Just fine, just fine."

"Then stop staring at me."

You quirk an eyebrow and grin. "Can't help it, X. You're just so beautiful it hurts. I can't believe Caleb"—you glance back at

Thomas, and correct yourself—"*Mr. Indigo*, I mean—agreed to let you come."

Thomas. My bodyguard for the evening. A giant of a man, very literally a giant. Seven feet tall and enormously muscled. Skin black as midnight, head shaved to the scalp, eyes always shifting and moving, seeing, assessing, intelligent and cunning eyes that never look at me directly. He has not said a single word, and I do not think he will, unless absolutely necessary.

"It was a surprise to me, too, honestly."

"What changed his mind?"

I let silence linger for a moment before answering. "He keeps his own counsel, Jonathan. I cannot speak to his reasoning, nor will I attempt to."

I can see Thomas's reflection in the elevator door; he looks almost amused, if so rugged and brutal a face could be said to have such a mundane expression. A *ding* announces the arrival of the elevator. The doors slide open and Thomas steps into the opening, gestures for us to enter with a sweep of a huge hand. I take the back corner diagonally opposite to Thomas, and you stand beside me. Too close. Your cologne is faint, distractingly delicious, light and citrusy and exotic. Your body traps me into the corner, and though you do not look at me, you are somehow still aware of me, and I am aware of your awareness. It is disorienting. I breathe out to tamp my nerves, and though I breathe shallowly, your gaze flicks to my breasts behind the crimson silk, you watch my breasts swell and retract. I tilt my head to the side, stare up at you with a scolding eyebrow lifted, lips pursed.

You blush adorably and shrug. I stare at you until you look away first. That wrist motion, though. There it is, extend the arm, flick the wrist, ostentatious, a broad gesture dramatically delivered to reveal a fantastically expensive watch. A Bulgari, pink gold and brown alligator skin.

"Don't do that, Jonathan," I say, without looking at you.

"Do what? I just looked at my watch."

"You made a show of it. No one cares how expensive your watch is. Doing so only serves to draw attention to your shallowness."

"Oh come on, X. It's how I check the time." You sound petulant.

"True wealth does not draw attention to itself. True power does not clamor for notice. Command it without seeming to seek it."

"Got it," you mumble.

"Speak clearly," I snap. "You are not a boy to mumble when scolded."

"Fine, I got it. Okay? I *got* it." You shake your head and sigh. "Jesus."

"This is your test, Jonathan. And I am with you, so your performance had better be flawless."

"Then don't get on my case about every little fucking thing. Makes me self-conscious, and that's when I mess up."

The elevator opens, revealing an expansive underground garage full of shiny and expensive-looking automobiles. You angle toward one, something long and low and sleek and black with only two doors, a trident logo adorning the nose.

There is a harsh rumbling noise from behind us, which takes me a moment to realize is coming from Thomas. It is a grunt, to get our attention. Thomas inclines his head to one side, indicating a different car. This one is long, low, sleek, and white. Len stands outside it in a tuxedo to match Thomas's.

"Come on, kids. Time's a-wasting." Len slides into the driver's seat, and Thomas takes three long steps—which cover something near ten feet—and opens the rear passenger side door, ushering me in and closing the door behind me as I sit.

"A Maybach, huh?" You take the redirection in stride, it seems. You wait until I'm seated and then circle around to the other side "Nice. Landaulet Sixty-two?"

"Sure is. Mr. Indigo's own personal vehicle," Len says.

I couldn't care less what kind of car it is. The seats are luxurious, the air cool and comfortable. There is a sensation of smooth power, an incline, and then a bright, blinding wash of light as we exit the garage.

My heart hammers in my chest; I am outside, out in the world for the first time in a very long time.

I cannot breathe.

Your hand squeezes my thigh. "X? You okay?"

I force air into my lungs. Blink, curl my fingers into fists and force myself to breathe. In . . . and out. In . . . and out. I cannot answer you, and I am not, clearly, so it seems an inane question to me. Release my fists. Flatten my palms on my thighs, nudge your hand away. I cannot bear touch, not from you, not now.

Eyes open. Look out the window. The buildings are dizzying, rocketing hundreds of feet in the air, rising all around like a tribe of clustered titans. I am drowning at the bottom of a thousand glass canyons. Horns blare, loud even within the acoustically hushed interior of the car. The Maybach Landaulet 62, as you named this vehicle. Some sort of luxury automobile, I assume. I know nothing of such things and care even less. You seem impressed, which I suppose is the purpose.

The people. So many, many people. Crowds of them, an endless river of heads, hair, hats, and shoulders, swinging arms, blots of color, a black umbrella despite the clear, warm weather of the evening. A roar of an engine from a long, high truck with oversized wheels and vertical exhaust pipes spouting black smoke. A man in a suit darting between moving vehicles, running across the street, briefcase clutched under one arm. So much. It is too much.

"X. Look at me, babe." You touch me. Fingers to chin, bring my face around.

I jerk my face away from your touch, but I look at you. And I breathe. A little, at least.

You smile. "Hey. There you are. It's okay, X. It's just Manhattan." You frown, a subtle lowering of your brows, mouth corners flattening, lips thinning. "You really don't get out much, do you?"

I shake my head. "No. I don't."

"Well . . . if you're overwhelmed, why don't you focus on me, huh? Look at me. Talk to me." You take my hand, hold it palm to palm, fingers wrapped around the edge, as children hold hands. It is platonic, and strangely soothing. "This event, there's gonna be a lot of famous people there. Except for that, though, it's gonna be boring as fuck. Just so you know. Lots of standing around with fancy champagne and cheap scotch, talking about how rich everyone else is. Yachts and private planes, who owns which island and which estate where." You take on an arch, pretentious tone of voice. "Have you tried the Lafite sixty-six? Positively divine, old boy. I have a bottle, you'll have to come to my estate in the Hamptons." You wave a hand in disgust. "Rich old windbags. The famous people are worse, I think. Just stand around and expect everyone to come to them, pay attention to *them*. Like anyone fucking cares. They *do* care, though, you know? That's what has me in such a pissy mood about it. They all *do* care. Been to one of these, you've been to 'em all. There'll be dancing, though. Proper waltzes and shit like that. Good thing I learned, right?"

"Good thing, yes," I say, faint.

"Can you dance, X?"

I blink. "Dance?"

You laugh. "Yeah. Dance. Like the waltz or the cha-cha or whatever."

I finally crack a smile, and feel a little better. "Cha-cha? I think not. I can waltz, however."

You arch an eyebrow suggestively. "You'd probably cause a few heart attacks if you were to cha-cha, I think. Those old goats and their pacemakers wouldn't be able to handle it."

"Handle what?" I ask.

You glance at me, look me over blatantly. "You, X. Doing the cha-cha in that dress. All their blood would rush south, and they'd all keel over dead." You clutch your shoulder and mime a heart attack, then erupt in laughter.

"Not appropriate, Jonathan."

You wave a hand dismissively. "Oh, lighten up, X. It's a joke."

I see Len glance at you in the rearview mirror, and catch a glimpse of Thomas in the mirror as well. They are both either amused or disapproving. I'm not sure how to interpret the look you are getting from them. You've been successful in distracting me from my nerves, however, and for that I am grateful.

Silence descends for several minutes, and then Len brings the car to a smooth halt outside a building. It is just like all the others, it seems to me, although there is an awning extending from the doorway to the street, and when Len stops the car, Thomas exits and holds open the door for me, and then you. You slide easily across the interior rather than exiting street-side. You've done this before. I have to focus on making each movement graceful as I rise from the low vehicle, adjust my dress, and wait for you. As soon as you're beside me, you button the middle button of your tuxedo coat and offer me your elbow. Two uniformed doormen with long, tailed frock coats and bellman caps haul open two huge wooden doors with steel handles running from top to bottom, bowing deeply as Jonathan and I enter the foyer, Thomas striding behind us.

I feel a huge weight on my shoulder and turn to see Thomas staring down at me, broad face impassive, holding up a single finger. *Wait*, the gesture says. Within moments Len is entering as well, moving to stand behind Jonathan while Thomas is behind me.

"All right, gang. Time to go." Len catches my eye. "Once we're in there, I'm going to mingle. Keep an eye on you from out of sight. Thomas will be with you the whole time, though." A glance at you. "And Jonathan? The only thing I'm going to say to you is remember clause three of the contract you signed, yeah?"

Your face tightens. "Yeah, I remember."

"Good. That's all. Let's go have fun." Len rolls his shoulder, fastens the middle button of his suit coat, and nods at the door.

Another pair of uniformed doormen bow as they pull the doors open, and we step through. A short, dark wood-paneled hallway leads to a lectern, behind which is a tall, elderly gentleman in a tuxedo with a red rose at his lapel.

"Sir, madam. Welcome. The name?"

"Jonathan Cartwright the Third, and guest."

"Might I see some identification, sir? For security purposes, of course." The host extends a wrinkled hand, and you hand him a card, take it back. "Very well, Mr. Cartwright, madam. This way, please." A gesture to a third and final set of doors, manned yet again by two uniformed doormen.

As they open the doors, a low hum greets you and me—I do not say *us*, Jonathan, because there is no us. Merely two individuals sharing the same space for a short time.

I must remind myself of this.

A low hum of voices, quiet murmurs, polite laughter. A string quartet and a pianist play classical music in some corner, a microphone stand off to one side against the wall, waiting for a special musical guest, I imagine. The crowd is clustered in groups of four and six, sometimes as many as eight in a circle, all in tuxedos and gowns, expensive watches glittering, diamonds glinting. Eyes shift, heads swivel, subtly scanning for familiar faces.

I know precisely three people here, and they are all making this entrance with me.

No one remarks on our arrival. They notice, see that we are clearly not famous, and their eyes skip over us. Return to conversations and beverages. We are two steps into the room when a young woman in a tasteful but short black dress with an apron at her waist approaches us, tray in hand, bearing flutes of champagne. You take a flute, hand it to me, take another for yourself.

Len has vanished. Thomas looms behind us, close, but not suffocatingly so. A precisely measured distance, I think.

"To you, Madame X. And to being outside that condo."

I blink at your unexpected toast. "Yes. As you say." I clink my flute against yours.

"Don't like my toast, X?" You sip, your eyes twinkling with humor.

"It was . . . not what I was expecting you to toast to."

"What *were* you expecting, then?"

I take a demure sip. It is sweet, bubbly, with a crisp bite. I like it, but not as much as the wine I had with—I shake my head, refusing to let my mind wander from this experience. Refusing to let thoughts of Caleb Indigo sully my enjoyment. If it is enjoyment I'm feeling; it is a foreign emotion, a flutter in my belly, a quickening of the pulse, shortness of breath, anticipation of . . . *something*.

"X?"

I shake my head. "Yes?"

"You with me, babe? I asked you what you were expecting me to make a toast to."

I blink. Breathe. Summon my wits. Smile up at you, feigning easy humor I don't quite feel. "My dress?"

You laugh. "Ah. Your dress. Yes, well . . . that's worth a toast, too, I'd say."

Your eyes are warm, friendly. I sometimes do not recognize you as the arrogant, idle, oafish brat you once were, only a few weeks ago. Even from the last time I saw you, you've gained bearing, confidence. You've found yourself, I think. I set you in motion, but you did the rest.

You lift your flute to mine. "To the sexiest dress in the room."

I smile, toast, drink.

We are still only a few steps into the ballroom.

"Jonathan. Who is your ravishing guest?" An older man, silver hair with a bit of black at the temples. Your eyes, a different nose and chin. "Introduce me, son."

"Dad . . . Jonathan Edward Cartwright the Second, I mean—may I introduce to you Madame X."

In the confines of my home, where I conduct business, with the painting on the wall to lend credence, my name is apropos, a thing of mystery and power. Here . . . it just seems awkward.

I shove down all thoughts, summon my cloak of indifference, my armor of cool dignity. "Mr. Cartwright. Well met."

"A pleasure to meet you, Madame X." Your father's eyes do not communicate pleasure, however. There is hostility. An air of ruthless calculation. "You've done a wonderful job with my son. I must admit, I was skeptical of the program, even though I signed him up for it. But you've done wonders. More than I expected, that's for damn sure. "

You shift from foot to foot, uncomfortable. "Dad, I don't think this is the time or place to—"

"Shut up, Jonathan—your betters are speaking." Your father dismisses you, brusquely, casually, brutally.

You do your best not to flinch, but your expression, which perhaps only I can read so easily, communicates a deep, familiar pain. I see where you learned your mannerisms, and what long-ingrained habits you daily fight to become the man you are becoming.

I feel my claws extend. "I must agree with Jonathan, Mr. Cartwright. This is very much not the time or place to discuss such things. This is a social event, after all, and there are . . . shall I say . . . certain clauses dictating knowledge of who I am and what I do. Clauses that by their nature preclude open discussion in a public setting such as this."

"I see. Well." Eyes narrow in open hostility now. "I suppose I have you to thank for my son's abrupt desire to strike out on his own?"

"You do." I smile and keep my tone friendly, sugar sweet as I pour poison. "He was suffering. His natural talents and skills were being wasted. *You* were wasting your own son's potential. Intentionally, it seems to me. Any chance at real happiness or success for your son was being throttled by your obvious disdain. I did not intentionally guide him away from you or your company, nor did I advise him on any business matters in any way. That's not my job. My job was to show him how to be his own person, and that, now that I've met you, clearly meant helping him overcome the massive handicap of being *your* son. Jonathan will do amazing things, now that he's out from under your thumb, Mr. Cartwright. Much to your loss, as well, I should think."

You choke on champagne. "X, I see some friends of mine over there. Let's go say hi, huh?"

I allow you to pull me away from your father, who is fuming, red in the face, forehead vein throbbing dangerously. Perhaps the senior Cartwright will suffer a heart attack. I find myself not entirely displeased by the prospect.

You haul me across the room toward a small knot of younger men, all about your age, each one with a woman clinging to a tuxedoed arm, glamorous-looking models dripping in diamonds, all shallow smiles and fake breasts. Before we reach the cluster of your friends, however, you pull me to the side, to the bar along one wall. You order two beers, tossing back your champagne as you wait. I sip mine, and wait.

You have something to say, and so I allow you time to formulate your words. That you're thinking before you speak is encouraging.

"No one has ever stood up for me before, X. No one. Not ever, not in anything. And *no one* talks to Dad that way."

"About time, then."

You muster a weak smile, then accept the glass of pilsner, downing half of it before turning back to me. "Yeah, I guess so. The point I'm trying to make here is . . . thanks. I've never mattered to that bastard. I never will."

"You only have to matter to yourself."

"Yeah, I get that. But I think it's just basic human nature to want to matter to your own fucking father."

"I suppose so," I say. "But self-preservation is also an essential factor of human nature."

"Aren't you worried you made an enemy of him?"

I shake my head. "Not at all. There's nothing he can do to harm me. If it made trouble for Caleb, then so be it. Trouble for Caleb is Caleb's business, not mine." I wrap my fingers around your arm. "Let's go say hi to your friends."

You snort. "Those assholes? They aren't my friends. They're just some dickheads I know. Guys like I used to be. Rich, self-centered, conceited, and totally useless. Not one of them has ever done a real day's work in their entire lives. And those bitches on their arms? Just like them. Rich bitches who do nothing but shop on Fifth Avenue and get Botoxed and snort coke and go on never-ending vacations to the Hamptons or fucking Turks and Caicos, all of it on their parents' dime. Not one of them has ever done a single thing for themselves. And I was just like them."

"And now?"

"I always wanted to take over for Dad. I wanted *in*. I wanted to . . . to be a part of what he was doing. He's a horrible person and shitty father, but he's a *hell* of a businessman. So I was never like those guys in that from the time I was a sophomore in high school I was working in the mail room or in the copy room, working my ass off nights and weekends, paying my dues. Dad never gave me a single break for being his son. He ordered everyone to treat me exactly like any other candidate for every position I angled for. And some people, *because* I was a Cartwright, treated me even worse. But I played the game. I sucked it up and did my best. I've worked every single day of my life since tenth grade. I've got my own money. I bought my Maserati with my own cash. I bought my condo with my own cash. I got a business loan on my own and raised start-up capital for my business, all without using a single one of Dad's connections. But none of that matters." You finish one beer and start on the next. I'm on my fourth sip of champagne. "I was supposed to keep working for him, keep being pushed aside and passed over and treated like shit. And now that I'm in business for myself, he hates me even more."

"So it sounds as if you were never actually like them?"

"I acted like them, though. Like an asshole. Entitled. Spoiled. I've never been anything but rich. I do what I want, when I want. Yeah, I earn my own income, but I still ran through women like they were nothing. One after another, just for the hell of it. Treated everyone around me like shit."

"What changed?" I am very curious.

"You." You don't look at me as you say this.

My heart sinks. Twists. "Me? Jonathan, I did nothing but what I was paid to do."

"I *want* you, X. But I can't have you, and I know that. It burns my ass, you know that? We're not even friends. I don't even get that much. But you . . . you're not like anyone I've ever met. You . . . *matter.* You need no one, you need nothing. You don't take shit, not from anyone. I don't know what it was . . . what it is about you that

made me see everything differently. I honestly don't know. I just . . .
since meeting you, I guess I just want to be someone that matters."

"You matter, Jonathan." I dare another sip, a longer one, a
mouthful of tart, crisp bubbles washing over my tongue, rushing
through my brain. "And . . . we *are* friends."

"But only friends." It isn't a question, but there is a faint, vague,
boyish note of hope.

It hurts to crush it.

"Yes, Jonathan. Only friends. It is all that is possible."

"Why?" You turn, pivot to rest a hip against the bar, face me.

I stand with my back to the bar's edge, flute held in both hands,
watching the crowd flux and shift. "I cannot answer that, Jonathan.
It just . . . *is*."

"Can't you change it?"

I let out a breath. "No. I cannot."

"Do you want to?" Your breath is on my ear. You are too close.
Too close. I hate it when you do this. You are my friend, Jonathan.
And that is something monumental to me, but you cannot see it.

I wish I could make you see what your friendship means to me.
But I do not know how.

"It wouldn't matter if I did." I whisper this, because it's something I should not say. But I do, recklessly.

Thomas is far enough away that he cannot overhear our conversation. I don't think. But he still makes me nervous. He's there to
keep me safe, and to keep me close. I cannot help wondering what
he would do if I were to try to leave, here and now. Bring me back,
probably. But . . . where would I go? The world is an expensive place.

A dangerous one, too.

"Why not, X? Why wouldn't it matter?" Your voice is so close I
can feel the vibrations.

Something snaps inside me. "*Damn* it, Jonathan! Stop asking questions I can't answer!" I toss back the rest of the champagne, half a flute's worth, swallow it, feel it rush through me, burn my throat on the way down, hit heavy in my stomach.

I flee. Through the crowd, head ducked, angling for the small discreet doorway hiding the restrooms. Thomas is behind me, following silently at a distance.

I push open the nearest restroom door, lungs seized, eyes burning, chest aching, heart thumping heavily, seeing through a blur. Stall door, slammed open, slammed closed. Lean back against the cold metal door, fight for calmness. Fight for breath.

I do not desire you, not physically. But there is something there, some spark of need. You incite doubt in me. Make me wonder at my own life, at my ordered existence. Make me question who I am.

And those questions bring on panic attacks.

I sniffle. Blink hard.

NO.

I cannot let loose this flood of emotion. I am in control. I am in control—breathe, breathe—I can't do this, not here, not now. Not because of Jonathan Cartwright the Third. You know nothing of me. You want me because you can't have me, and that is all it is. And whatever kinship I may feel for you in return is based on less than that. You represent my most obvious success. That's all it is.

I like my life.

I am content.

I do not need more.

I do not want to know what else may exist, out there, for me.

I am safe under Caleb Indigo's protection.

So why am I fighting tears?

I hear the door open, close. A faucet runs.

Silence, but the knowledge that someone else is out there, fixing her makeup, probably, steels me. I cannot be weak. Will not be. I viciously push down my emotions. Shut them off. Bury them. Hold my head high, and exit the stall.

Freeze.

I am in the men's room.

When I exit the stall, look up, see the man, I am struck dumb. A man stands facing me, a cell phone in his hands.

I am left breathless.

There is beauty, and then there is perfection. I have known many beautiful men. Some rugged, some pretty. Some merely handsome. None of them have ever compared to Caleb Indigo, however, in terms of sheer masculine appeal.

Until now.

This man?

He is the splendor of heaven made flesh.

TEN

"Hey there. Looks like one of us has the wrong bathroom, I think." His voice is low and warm and amused and kind, bathing me in sensation.

I cannot move, cannot breathe. He is looking at me, seeing me with eyes so blue they make my heart stutter in my chest, eyes that defy description.

There are countless shades of blue:

Azure. Periwinkle. Baby blue. Navy blue. Ultramarine. Celestial. Sky. Sapphire. Electric. So many others in variation.

And then there is indigo.

Oh, how ironic.

His eyes, they are indigo.

I try to speak, but my mouth only opens and closes without producing sound. Something in me is broken, off-kilter.

"You okay? You look upset." A quick step, and I am assaulted by the scent of cinnamon gum, laced with hints of alcohol and cigarettes. But the cinnamon, it is in me, in my nose, on my taste buds.

His hand touches my elbow; another brushes past my cheek, not quite touching my skin, sweeping errant hair away from my eyes.

"I'm fine." I manage a cracked whisper.

He laughs. "I wasn't born yesterday, honey. Try again."

My eyes prick. "I'm sorry to disturb you." I force my body into motion, push past him.

He grabs me by the bicep, spins me back around, and I'm pulled up against his hard warm broad chest. "You haven't disturbed me. The opposite, if anything. Take a minute. No need to rush off."

"I have to go."

"All the better reason to stay, then." Holy gods above, that voice.

Warmth, like afternoon sunlight through a window on closed eyelids, warming skin. The warmth of early morning, before true consciousness has taken over, when all of existence is narrowed down to the cocoon of blankets.

I don't understand what he means, but his hands are gently, politely, firmly on my shoulders, my cheek is against his chest—not at all politely, not at all appropriately. And I do not want to move. Not ever. I am at a height that my ear is over his heart, and I hear it . . .

Bumpbump—bumpbump—bumpbump.

Slow and steady and reassuring.

"What's your name?" he asks, a single fingertip tracing an intimate line from my temple around the curve of my ear, down to the base of my jaw.

A simple thing, asking one's name. So easy for everyone else. Something I never considered until today—how impossible a normal interaction such as this could be, away from what I know.

I panic. Push away. Stumble. I am caught, held up. "Hey, hey, it's okay. I'm sorry, it's okay."

I shake my head. "I have to go."

"Just tell me your name."

I won't lie. "I can't."

A snort of amused disbelief. "What, it's a secret?"

"I shouldn't be here." I manage another step away.

"No kidding. It's a men's bathroom, and you are most definitely *not* a man." His hand wraps around my wrist, easily engulfing it and keeping me in place.

A tug, and I'm back up against the tectonic wall of his chest. His fingertip, the one that traced behind my ear, across the delicate drum of my temple, it touches my chin. I must look, though I know I should not—I must look into his eyes, so nearly purple, so arresting in their strange shade of blue. So knowing, so warm, seeing me somehow as if the book of my soul is bare to him, laid open.

"Listen, Cinderella. All I want is your name. Tell me that much, and I can do the rest."

"The rest?" I know— intellectually, cerebrally—that I should pull away, leave, get out of here before anything compromising happens. But I can't. I am a creature in the deep, deep sea, hooked on a line, drawn up to the light. "The rest of what?"

I swallow hard. Everything in me is in a boil, weltering and coruscating and dizzied and mixed up and lost and wild.

"The rest of you and me."

"I don't know what you're talking about."

"Yes you do, Cinderella. You feel it. I know you do." He frowns, and even this expression is dizzyingly gorgeous. "I shouldn't be here either. Not at this party, not in this bathroom, and certainly not with someone like you. I don't belong here. And neither do you. But here I am, and here you are, and there's . . . *something*. Fuck if I have a word for it, but there's something going on between us."

"You're crazy. I have to go." I back away.

My hands shake. Something in the deepest shadows of my being rages against each inch of space I put between us, between him and me. Something in the fabric of my being demands that I stay, that I tell him who I am, that I give him what he demands of me.

But that's impossible.

"Yeah, I am crazy. Not gonna argue with you there. But that has nothing to do with you and me, honey."

"There is no you and me, and stop calling me 'honey.'" I don't dare turn around, don't dare show him my back. I shuffle backward to the door, reach behind me for the handle.

"Then tell me your name, Cinderella."

My hand shakes on the door handle. I push the lever down. Pull the spring-loaded weight of the door toward me, never taking my eyes off his. I need to look away, but I cannot. Cannot. I am trapped by his gaze. Ensnared by his warmth, not just physical heat, but some welcoming, enveloping, cocooning, all-consuming warmth in his soul. It heats the ice in me, spreads through the gaping lonely chasms of my being echoing with cold and absence.

"No." It is a whisper, inaudible over the hammering of my heart. If I give him my name, I will give him all of me.

A name is a thing of power.

"Why not?" Long easy strides carry him to me.

His hands curl around the base of my spine and pull me forward, and the door *clicks* closed, and I'm up against his chest, breathing in cinnamon and cigarettes. "I'll tell you mine, then, how about that? My name is Logan Ryder."

"Logan Ryder . . ." I'm blinking up at him, trying to breathe, my hands flat on his chest, feeling his breath, feeling the thunder of his heartbeat under my right palm. "Hi."

"And your name is . . . ?" He's so close, all I can feel and all I can smell and all I can taste, his scent is all-consuming and his heat is all-enveloping, and I cannot give him my name, because it's all I have to give, currency I dare not spend.

I just shake my head. "I can't. I can't." I back away from him, forcing my legs to obey the prudence of my mind rather than the lust of my heart and body.

"Can I tell you a secret, Cinderella?"

"If you wish." I'm still struggling to make my lungs operate, and it comes out breathy.

"I have no idea what I'm doing right now." His fingers dig into the flesh just above my backside, holding me firmly against him.

As if I could move; I'm paralyzed by this sensation. "Me either," I admit.

He smirks, and one of his hands rises to my face. Cups my cheek. His thumb brushes my cheekbone.

I feel absurdly close to tears, for some inexplicable reason.

"Maybe so, but I'm the one doing this . . ." he breathes,

    and kisses me,

           and kisses me,

                    and kisses me.

Or . . . he would have, but I stumble backward in the fragment of a second before his lips touch mine, put just enough distance between us that the kiss is stopped before it can ruin me.

He sighs, a short, small breath of wonder and frustration and desire.

*B*AM!—*BAM!* A heavy fist pounds twice on the door, and I jump, stumble backward and away until my spine flattens against the door. I stare at Logan, eyes stinging and lungs aching for air, hands trembling.

I jerk the door open and slip out of it, slam hard against Thomas's chest.

"Where did you go?" His heavily accented voice is thick as oil, deeper than canyons.

His hands grip my shoulders, set me several feet backward, away from him, turn me around.

"I went into the wrong bathroom by mistake."

A paw bigger than a bear's wraps around my upper arm, gently but implacably, and compels me away from the bathroom. "Next time, I go in with you."

Away, back to the ballroom. Len is there, arms crossed, eyes unhappy. And you, at the bar a few feet away, drinking.

Something is ended, something else begun.

"Madame X. You should pay more attention to which bathroom you go into." Len's voice is sharp, light faux-friendliness. "You wouldn't want me to worry about where you'd gone, now would you?"

"No, my apologies." I hunt for a suitable explanation. "It was— a female thing. Unexpected. I'm sure you understand."

Thomas's hand still around my upper arm, Len in front of me, I fight for breath, for calmness. Pretend the flavor of an almost-kiss does not still linger on my lips. Hope my frantic pulse cannot be heard over the band. I am dizzy.

The milling and talking has ended, and everyone has paired off into couples to dance, a few people along the edges of the crowd, watching, waiting, drinking.

You sweep me away, onto the dance floor, where couples waltz and spin and sway. Your hands are politely placed on my waist and your hand is in mine, warm and dry and loose. You lead with practiced ease, guiding me through one dance, and then another. We pause when the band takes a break, and we sip at wine that I find too light, too fruity, too sweet. And then the band strikes up again, and you lead me back out, fit your hand to my waist, where your touch cannot be misconstrued as anything but platonic. You make small talk, but I let it wash over me without responding, and you seem to expect this, to understand it, carrying on a one-way conversation about—I don't even know what.

I am not thinking of you.

"Can I cut in?" Oh, his voice. Now sharp and expectant, leaving no room for disobedience.

You do not stand a chance, sweet Jonathan.

Big hard warm strong hands take me, spin me away, and his steps are not as practiced, not as smooth, but powerful and implacable and confident. His hand is not on my waist, not polite, not platonic. His hand is on my hip, cupping me intimately. Not quite inappropriate, but very nearly. Fingers are tangled in mine, rather than clasping like friends.

"Hi," he says, and indigo eyes find mine.

"Hi," I breathe back.

And we dance. We sway and sweep in graceful circles, and time is like water, one song passing, and then two, and I cannot look away. Don't wish to. His eyes search me, and seem to see me. Read me, as if I am a familiar and beloved book, long lost and just now found once again.

"What's your name, Cinderella?" His forehead touches mine, and I fear the intimacy of the scene, his hand on my hip, his fingers twined with mine, our bodies too close.

I must end this dance.

I pull away.

"Wait!" He catches my hand and pulls me back against him.

We are lost in the crowd of dancers, but I know Len is watching and so is Thomas, and so is Jonathan, and this cannot happen, should not be happening. He is too close. He touches me as if we are framed and fitted and formed to belong one to the other, as if he knows me, as if my body is his for the touching.

"Why won't you just tell me your fucking name?" He sounds very nearly desperate.

"I can't." I know not how else to explain it.

"It's just a name, sweetheart."

"It's not. It's more than that. It's who I am." I want to smile, want to throw myself at him, to taste his lips, to feel the hard heat of his chest and the warmth of his arms. I want to say a million traitorous things.

"Exactly." His fingers leave my hand and slip and slide up my forearm, and *God*, his fingertips on the tender underside of my forearm is so intimate and so soft that I can't breathe and I am aroused by that innocent intimacy, my thighs clenching together as I stare up at him, just his fingertips on my forearm, dragging from wrist up and up to elbow, back down, tracing and tickling. "I want to know who you are."

My fingers go to my lips, touch them where his lips nearly touched mine. I shake my head. "You can't."

"Why not?"

"It's impossible."

"Nothing is impossible."

I have no response for that. I can only tug my arm free, and he cannot do anything but allow it. I walk away, and it hurts, it aches, the pull to look back. The pull to return to him and finish the almost-kiss is like a taut wire speared through my heart, plucked to hum like a harp string. Each step away from Logan makes my whole being sing the song of that plucked string.

I find you on the far side of the ballroom, leaning against the wall with a glass of wine in one hand, engaging Len in conversation.

I hear words bandied back and forth that I believe are car terms, the kind of thing I imagine men discuss between themselves in a strange language all their own: horsepower and torque and cylinders.

Thomas, however, is on the edge of the dancing crowd, and those wide black eyes see me, and I wonder how much else they saw.

"Madame X?" You say my name, as if you suspect something.

"I'm fine, Jonathan." I refuse to look anywhere but at the dark red rose in your lapel. I hadn't noticed that before. It matches the shade of my dress exactly.

"They're seating us for dinner." You escort me—guide me—through the crowd, through a set of guarded doors, to an enormous room filled with large round tables with six place settings each.

There is a stage at the front of the room. A lectern, a microphone.

Dinner is a long, quiet, formal affair. Outside fork, inside fork, outside spoon, inside spoon. Ice water. Sip at white wine. Nibble at salad greens, a sliver of bread, then a dinner of shredded quail and spicy brown rice and pea pods cooked in oil. As the dinner ends and a delicate dark chocolate mousse is brought out, a stout, middle-aged man takes the stage, adjusts the mic, taps it. Speaks in slow, precise, measured tones of the items to be auctioned this evening. A priceless original painting. A one-of-a-kind, two-hundred-year-old sapphire necklace. A chair that once belonged to King Louis XVI. An ancient Roman Gladius Hispaniensis.

You bid on the necklace. A hundred thousand. Two hundred thousand. Two hundred fifty thousand. You are reckless with your money, I think. You win the bid.

The sword captures my attention. The scabbard is bronze, the hilt of polished bone, the blade so ancient and pitted and rusted that its shape is nearly lost. This is the crown jewel of the auction, a museum-quality piece of history. Bidding starts at a mind-boggling number. Three men bid: an old man with four wisps of white hair draped across his bald pate, a ridiculously beautiful man whom I assume is a movie star, and—

Him.

The table holds two other couples, one a pair of celebrities, the other an elderly couple ignoring the auction completely. The chair beside Logan is empty, the place setting removed.

He lounges in his chair, a glass of red wine held by the stem in one hand. As the bidding continues, he lifts the glass as his signal, ruby liquid sloshing in the goblet.

The bidding reaches seven figures.

I need to look away, but I cannot.

He is a jaguar, all sleek and perfect features, compact, easy power held in repose, exuding threat simply by his mere existence. Blond hair like a fall of gold, swept back in kinked and wavy strands around his ears, the ends brushing his collar. Indigo eyes sweeping the room.

Finding me.

He does not look away. Even when he lifts his wine in a silent bid, he does not look away.

Neither do I.

You are beside me. Logan is across the room. Caleb Indigo is under my skin.

I have no pulse, no breath, no vital functions. All I am is sight, the war of nerves, the fire of need, the calcification of fear inside my throat.

"Friend of yours?" you ask, your voice low, pitched so only I can hear.

"No." It is the only answer of which I am capable.

"You're a better liar than that, X. I saw you two dancing." You take a long swig of scotch. You have been drinking heavily. I worry. "Logan Ryder. I've heard of him."

"Oh?" I endeavor to sound casual, and almost succeed.

But my eyes are still locked, pulled, hypnotized, drawn to the exotic gaze of the man across the room. I must look away or betray myself yet further. Only . . . I am incapable. Made weak.

My will is gutted by the memory of a near-kiss. I am shredded by the desire to finish it, to consummate the kiss.

"He's kind of a mystery in the business world. Has his fingers in a dozen of the most lucrative pies in the city, but no one knows shit about him. Where he got his money, how much he's worth, where he lives, nothing. Just showed up one day on the scene, investing here and there, in this and that. He's got this uncanny knack for selling off right when the prices are best. He never comes to events like this, though. Total recluse." You sound speculative. "He a client of yours?"

"No."

"But you know him."

"No, I really don't." I sound almost cool, almost even, almost believably casual.

You lean close. "I'll give you your lie, Madame X. I owe you that much."

"I'm not—"

"Just do me a favor, will you?"

"What's that?" I force my gaze away, at long, long last, down to my empty plate. I am unaware of having eaten dessert, but there is nothing left except brown smears and crumbs. I feel his eyes still watching me from afar, even with my own closed, pinched shut.

"Quit pretending I don't know you better than that. Quit pretending I didn't see the way you two danced. You may not know each other, but you *want* to."

"No, I don't."

"Don't you, though?" Your eyes are sharp, too much so.

"No." I swallow hard, force my eyes to yours. "I am loyal to Caleb. But I will agree to drop the subject if you will."

"Fine with me." You stand up. Extend your hand to mine, assist me to my feet. As soon as I'm upright, you let go. "I've had enough of this shit-show. Let's go."

"Very well." I accomplish a miracle: I do not look back. Not once. No Lot's wife, I.

You, Thomas, and Len, you all three escort me out of the building. I am in the lead, escaping the hot confines of that building. Once we are out into the night, sirens howl and horns blare and eight people pass between me and the entrance in a gaggle talking, laughing, trailing clouds of cigarette smoke and gaiety. Fingers tangled in the gauzy crimson at my thighs, I bunch the skirts, lift them clear of the sidewalk. Stare out and up into the night sky, at the window squares, familiar buildings seen from an unfamiliar angle, yellow taxis in serried ranks. Stoplight, cycling from green to amber to red, the lights much larger and brighter from down here.

I ignore Thomas, ignore your questioning stare, ignore Len's puzzled eyebrows raised in an arch. I stride away, skirts held around my ankles, heels clicking on the concrete. Freedom. Ripe, thick air in my lungs, noises in my ear.

The heel of my shoe catches in a crack in the sidewalk and I trip, one foot bare on the cold concrete now. I stumble, nearly hit the ground. But a hard body is there, an arm around my waist.

A door, propped open with a wedge, a suddenly familiar blast of scent: cinnamon, wine, and now cigarette smoke, strongly.

I look up, and there he is. "Cinderella. You all right?"

I cannot be this close to him. Cannot.

I turn away, intending to leave my shoe caught in the sidewalk. I have to get away from him before I kiss him. The need to taste his mouth is overwhelming, the need to feel his arms around me all-consuming.

"Your shoe." He bends, retrieves my shoe, and hands it to me.

I slip it on my foot, and then Thomas is there, a huge hand gripping my upper arm, turning me in place. "It is time to return now, Madame X."

I see a light in Logan's eyes as Thomas gives away my name.

I walk beside Thomas back to the car.

Oh, I turn and look back. I must.

Place a foot in the car, a hand on the roof. Stare out over the long roof and sleek hood, watch the stoplight flash to bright green, the cars in a line accelerating. Another crowd of people passes under the awning, but this is an incidental crowd, none speaking to the others.

He is there, watching me intently, blond hair loose and wavy. A hand in his pants pocket, the other lifting a cigarette to his lips, an orange-glowing circle casting his eyes and forehead and sharp high cheekbones into brief illumination—a pause, and a pall of white smoke curling up and away and dissipating.

This is a vignette, seen in a quick glance, and then Thomas presses me gently but firmly down and into the car, the door closes with a soft *thunk*, and then he is out of sight as the Maybach rounds a corner.

I see him still, though, his eyes on me through the veil of smoke, seeing me, searching me, wanting me as much as I want him.

At my door, accompanied by Thomas, Len, and you, and I wish only for a quiet moment alone, a word with you. Instead, Len and Thomas linger in the elevator doorway, blocking it open, making it clear you will not be going inside with me, but away with them.

"Thank you for going with me this evening, Madame X."

"You are welcome." I offer you a small, tight, sad smile. "Goodbye, Jonathan. And good luck with your business."

"You, too." Your fingers move in your right hip pocket. "Wait."

I pause with my door open. You approach me, take me by the shoulders, turn me around. You stand behind me. I feel you, hear your breathing. Something cold and heavy drapes against my breastbone. I look down, see a huge sapphire. The antique necklace you won in the auction.

"Jonathan—"

"Not up for debate, X." Your hands work at the back of my neck, fixing the clasp. You step back. "There."

I turn, and you smile. Nod.

"Why?" I ask.

You shrug, and there's that smirk, that insouciant grin. "'Cause I can. Because I want to. It looks perfect on you."

"Why did you buy it, Jonathan? Not for me, surely."

That shrug again, less easy this time. "Because Dad was there. To make a point."

"You spent a quarter million dollars to spite your father, to show him that you could, just because?"

"Yeah, basically."

"That's childish." I reach up to unclasp the necklace.

"Maybe, yeah. But it's my childish decision to make. Keep it, X. My gift to you." Something in your voice, something in your eyes convinces me.

I lower my hands. Lift up on my toes, hug you briefly, platonically. "All right, Jonathan. In that case . . . thank you."

"You're welcome." You salute me, index and middle fingers together, touched to your forehead. "See ya."

And you're gone.

I won't see you again. I feel more sadness at this than I'd expected to.

Alone, finally, I stand at my favorite window. Watch the taxis and the delivery trucks pass, watch the nearest stoplight cycle green-amber-red, feeling the memory of free air in my lungs, the sound of horns and sirens and voices, the smell of the city.

Indigo eyes.

Thumb on my cheekbone, lips on mine, some inexplicable knowledge of a secret forever passed in stolen moments in a men's room, the feel of breath on my breath, a warm voice and strong gentle hands, the scent of cinnamon and cigarettes.

I want to cry for what I lost when I left that men's room.

But I cannot, for I do not know what it was I lost, only that it is gone, and that it meant everything to me.

ELEVEN

wake suddenly and completely, sensing a presence. "Caleb."

"X."

It is black, totally. But I smell signature spicy cologne, hear a slight breath inhaled, exhaled. The shuffle of a foot on wood.

"What time is it, Caleb?"

"Three forty-six in the morning."

I don't sit up. I remain on my right side, facing away. I allow myself a touch of venom in my voice. "What do you want, Caleb?"

"I've had enough of your attitude. I said I was sorry. It's over." My bed dips. A hand on my hip, over the blanket.

"Am I not allowed my own anger, Caleb? You hurt me. You frightened me. And over what?"

"You don't speak to me that way. You don't question me."

"Or you'll strangle me? Like William did?"

"Or I will be angry. And that's not a good place for me to be, not for anyone. Least of all for you. I didn't mean to hurt you, X."

"Yet you did, and I'm not okay with it," I say.

I wish desperately to push the hand away, yet it slides up my waist, and fingers hook in the blanket. Draw it away. I'm cold now.

Huge, hard hand, pushing me to my back. I don't resist. Not yet.

"Come on, X. Let it go."

"Don't you think I've tried? I can't. I can't just let it go, Caleb." I finally sit up, wishing I could draw the blankets up around my chest, but they've been tossed aside, and it's dark, and I don't dare risk making physical contact.

"Goddammit. All of this because of that stupid bitch Sara." Anger, raw and rife.

"Sara didn't put her hands on my throat, Caleb. *You* did."

"And am I never to be forgiven for it?"

"I don't know." I remember the taste of come in my mouth, that day.

The way my sexual service was just . . . expected. And given, so easily, without question. I despise myself. I loathe myself for dropping to my knees and putting my mouth on that waiting erection, for doing what I was told without question. Why did I do that? What am I, to offer such ready subservience?

Maybe this is all a refraction, everything distorted by my memory of a so-very-different touch on my skin, the way lips touched mine.

"No." I say this firmly.

"No?" Amused now. "No, you're not going to forgive me?"

"No."

Hands on my arms, groping, seeking, finding the back of my head. Pulling me. Heat and heaviness hovering over me. "I think you will, X."

"Caleb . . ." I squirm, trapped, claustrophobic, feeling his oppressive presence crushing me down and down and down to the bed, until I'm horizontal and hands are feathering over my skin, scraping up the loose cotton of the T-shirt I wear as a nightgown, pushing it up around my throat, baring my breasts to the shadows. All is blackness, and heaviness, and my skin being touched. Palms, gentle but insistent. Fingers finding and tugging away my underwear.

"Caleb." I find strength. "I don't want this, Caleb."

Lips, on my skin, at my belly. Hair tickling my hip. "Yes, you do."

The problem is, my hormones remember what those hands can do. The damp slit between my thighs remembers what those fingers can do, what the erection I know is ready and waiting can do. I remember, and I feel the contradiction. The lies, tangled and mixed. I lie. I do want it. I know what happened was a moment of anger, isolated. And I know, too, that it may perhaps not be so isolated. Perhaps, if I ask the wrong question, say the wrong thing, wish for the impossible, maybe those hands that can offer such pleasure will offer pain once more. Pain as punishment. Another accidental moment of strangulation, even a fist, or an open palm. Who knows?

I remember also a stolen moment in a men's restroom, and the sensation of utter safety.

Who am I, and what do I want?

Does it even matter what I want?

"See? I can smell you, X." A nose, nuzzling my thighs apart, inhalation. "I smell it. You want this. You want me. You've always wanted me, and you always will. You know it, and I know it."

I squirm, heels dig into the mattress, feel my hips lift off the bed at the wet swipe of a tongue. A thrill, lancing through me. Such pleasure, the tongue tip tickling and twirling at the precise spot where I'll feel the most pleasure, zeroing in, flicking.

But stronger than the pleasure is the self-loathing. The hatred of myself for succumbing, for being weak, for giving in, for letting pleasure dictate my actions. For letting pleasure take away what little freedom I have.

I reach down, tangle my fingers in thick hair . . . and shove. "*No*, Caleb." I twist, roll away.

Slide off the bed. Find the light switch, flick it on. Dark eyes, squinting against the sudden light. Mussed, imperfect black hair. A smear of my essence around the expressive mouth. T-shirt, suit slacks—tented.

Barefoot. Beautiful. Brutal.

How did I never see the brutality, before?

"X . . . what's going on with you?"

I'm breaking. The status quo is crumbling. "I can't help wanting you, Caleb. But I *can* help giving in to it."

"Giving in to it? Like it's forbidden, or something? Like there's something wrong with you and I having sex?" A step around the bed, closer to me. Crowding me into a corner.

"What are we, Caleb? Who am I? What am I, to you? Where is all this going? Why am I . . ." I swallow, let out a breath. "Sometimes, Caleb . . . sometimes I feel like a prisoner here. I feel like your captive."

A breath, harsh and long and shuddering. A hand passing down from forehead to chin. "X . . . come on, don't be like this. This isn't you. Why are you asking me these questions?" I'm up against a wall, and big hands land on either side of my face, framing me, hemming me in, trapping me. "You *died*, X. You have no one. You knew nothing of yourself. I taught you to walk again. Taught you to speak again. I taught you how to be a fucking *person* again. I gave you a home. Gave you a skill set. Gave you a job. Gave you a life."

"And in return, all I have to do is have sex with you? Suck you off whenever you feel like it? Never ask questions? Never want more?"

"That's not how it is, X."

"It certainly feels like it, sometimes."

"You're wrong. We have something." A breath on my cheekbone.

Dark eyes fraught with indecipherable emotion. I cannot read this face, cannot read those espresso-brown eyes. This, the proximity, the honesty, it's new and disorienting. It's as if a vein in the mountain has been opened, revealing a fissure, letting out long-pent pressure.

"What do we have, Caleb? Explain it to me." Silence. "You saved me, yes. You've provided for me, yes. I remember all that. I have not forgotten. But this?" I put my hands out, touch hard pectoral muscles, move my hands between my body and the one opposite me. "I don't know what we are. What this is. What you really want from me. I saw you with another woman. You've got a lot of women, you said as much. You visit women all over the city and you fuck them? And then you return here, to me, whenever you feel like you want something different, and you fuck me, too? But I'm not allowed to question that? I'm not allowed to even take a walk outside?"

"You have a panic attack just going outside. You wouldn't know what to do out there, X. We tried, remember? You get overwhelmed. You stop breathing. I'm not keeping you prisoner, I'm keeping you safe."

I do remember. The early days, there would be walks outside, in the city, on the sidewalks, afternoon crowds rushing past us. I'd make it a block, and then the noise and the heat and the countless faces and the babel of voices, the sirens, the cars . . . it all crashed down on me, slammed me to the ground, made my lungs seize and my eyes go dizzy, made the world spin and my head throb and I would have to be carried back inside until I could breathe again, safe in my room, in the darkness, with the mantra whispered in my ear:

You are Madame X. I am Caleb Indigo. I saved you from a bad man. You're safe here. I'll keep you safe. You are Madame X. I'm Caleb Indigo. You're safe with me. I won't ever let anyone hurt you again. It's all just a bad dream now. You're safe. You're Madame X. I'm Caleb.

Suddenly it's there, those words, that mantra, whispered in my ear, now, here and now, in my bedroom, in this moment. Reminding me, bringing me back to when the world was new, when I was being birthed into personhood. When I was relearning what language was, what it meant to speak and listen and walk and think and be alive.

"I am Madame X. You are Caleb." I cannot help whispering it back. "You saved me. You taught me everything I am."

"That's right, X. You're safe here."

And, for the first time in six years, for the first time since the night of dreams and red-eyed monsters and blood, I feel a kiss pressed to my lips, soft and slow and hesitant, as if to kiss thus is as new both for the one kissing and for me.

I dare not even breathe until the lips pull away. Dare not. To breathe would be to inhale the poison of truth, mixed with confusion, laced with seduction.

I press palms to chest. Push.

"I have grown, Caleb. I have changed. I have learned new things. I am not at all sure of anything anymore. Least of all you and I."

"Damn it, X." This is hissed. "Don't do this to me."

A long, long silence. I do not move, for I cannot. The heavy, perfect body still hems me in, traps me against the wall of my bedroom, arms beside my ears, lips not quite touching mine.

"Don't *do* this to me." This is, very nearly, a plea.

I feel something sharp within me. I push again. Harder. Until the wall of chest and arms and thighs swivels away. I dart past heat and anger, slide into my bed, naked but for a thin cotton T-shirt whose hem just barely covers my backside. I turn away from the scrutinizing gaze. Breathe deeply, evenly.

"X?"

I do not answer.

A sigh. It sounds . . . sad. Forlorn. Lonely. Sharpness in me, something hard and callused. Something that remembers a moment in a men's room, when I felt safe.

When a kiss made me feel . . .

Treasured.

I was changed in that stolen moment with a stranger.

And I cannot go back.

TWELVE

A full month passes.

I do my job, pretend to be aloof and untouchable, snap at and insult rich young boys and correct their grammar and their posture, push them to the edge of their tolerance. And then, just when they start to think ill of me, I allow them to guide the conversation, pretend to care when they speak, encourage them, let them test out their charm on me. Pretend to be charmed. Pretend to be *almost* seduced. Pretend to be flustered when they get too close. It's all a game. It's always been a game. But now, it seems even more a game. I am numb within, and the burden of playing pretend is heavy.

Alone, I wait. But my bedroom door is not darkened again. No deep-of-night visits.

What is this thick, curling, yet somehow weightless feeling within? Is it hope? Relief? Should I feel relieved that the visits seem to have ended? I owe my life. My self. My past and my future.

It is a heavy debt.

Something changed, and I cannot pinpoint the precise moment when, or how, or why. Or even what. Something to do with Jonathan, oddly. Seeing his transformation, perhaps the only true success I've ever had, watching him unfold and be reborn out of his cocoon, become a man worth knowing. It made a lie of what I do, for the alteration was all of his own doing. I provided the impetus of seeing the need for change, perhaps, but that at most only. I did no changing.

Now I wonder what service I provide. I once thought I did something worthwhile. But now I wonder. These young men who pass through my life, what do I do for them? And what payment do I receive for doing so?

How have I existed—somehow the term *lived* seems too strong, suddenly—for this long, having asked no questions?

I've been floating along, doing as I'm told, blinded willingly.

Now I see more clearly, but all I am able to make out is outlines of absence, the shape of all that is missing. I see how much I do not know.

And then, one day six weeks after the charity auction event, my door opens, and my heart ceases to beat.

I sit on my couch, sipping tea, waiting for my last client of the day. Oddly, I have received no dossier, no contract. Only a notice stating that the final time slot of the day—six forty-five in the evening—has been filled at the last minute. The client will provide all necessary materials at the time of service.

I sit, leg hooked demurely over knee, and wait. Smooth my dress over my thighs; it's a white dress with a square neckline, the hem falling to an inch above my knees. Blue peep-toe wedge heels. Hair in a deceptively complicated knot at the nape of my neck, the sapphire pendant at my breastbone.

Ding.

Watch my door handle twist, watch the door swing inward.

Shrug my shoulders, square them, let out a breath, force my posture to appear relaxed, my expression blank, indifferent. Tug the hem of my dress closer to my knees, so as to not bare too much flesh.

Saucer in my left hand, cup in my right. Plain white china, gold lining the edge of the saucer and the rim of the cup. Harney & Sons Earl Grey Imperial, a touch of milk.

These details are seared onto my brain.

Watch over the rim of my teacup as the door swings open, a male frame fills the opening. Steps through. Closes the door.

My heart freezes. Lungs halt midbreath. Teacup at my lips, paused. Eyes wide open, unblinking.

It is him.

Logan.

Dark blue denim, tight around thick thighs, a rip at the left knee, right thigh. Rectangular outline of a cell phone in the right hip pocket. Black T-shirt, V-neck, hugging ribs and his powerful chest, sleeves taut around golden biceps. Mirrored silver-frame aviator sunglasses hanging at the apex of the V. Wavy blond hair swept back, hanging around his jawline, a strand across his too-blue, almost purple eyes. Jawline so hard, so strong it could be hewn from seaside cliffs. High, sharp cheekbones. Lips curved in a knowing smile as he meets my gaze. Lips that kissed me, lips that stole my breath and with it my life.

"Found you." I shiver at the intimacy of his warm rumbling voice.

It seems a voice I've always known, a voice heard in unremembered dreams, the dreams you forget upon waking, dreams you wish you could return to as you surface to wakefulness.

I gently set my teacup and saucer on the coffee table, so as not to betray my shaking hands. I cannot take my eyes off Logan. I also cannot speak, cannot offer so much as a polite hello.

He moves toward me, eyes on me the whole while, and sits on

the coffee table, a sturdy thing of thick black wood and polished glass, an antique map of the world under the glass. So close. Knees brushing mine.

He leans forward, into my space. Smiles. "What's the matter . . . Madame X? Cat got your tongue?"

I breathe in, and my eyelids flutter and I am shaken out of my paralysis. Cinnamon and cigarettes. His jaw moves, rolling, lifting, compressing; gum, the source of the cinnamon.

"Logan. I—what are you doing here?" I sound suspicious, worried, upset even. "How did you find me?"

"Once I had your name, it wasn't that hard. Getting an appointment this soon was, though. You are in high demand, it seems."

"Why are you here?" I have to remember to breathe, force each breath in, each breath out.

"I'm your six forty-five." He moves nearer. "I'm here to learn, Madame X."

Every lungful is full of his scent, spicy cinnamon, faint acrid cigarette smoke clinging to cotton. Other scents, too faint to identify. The smells of a man who's gone through the day after a shower, life smell, city smell.

"So. How's this work, Cinderella?" He pinches the handle of my teacup in a big thumb and forefinger, lifts the cup, and examines the contents. "Tea, huh? Got any more? I could use a cup of tea. Or something stronger, if you've got it."

I take the welcome excuse to move away, to find somewhere I might find my breath, my equilibrium. "I have tea, or scotch."

"What kind of scotch?"

"Laphroaig. Single malt, eighteenth year."

"Ah. The good shit." He moves to take my spot on the couch, my teacup still in hand. "I wouldn't mind a tipple, then," he says with a lilting fake accent, eyes twinkling.

"How would you like it?" I ask this faced away now, decanter in hand, tumbler turned upright.

"Neat, please."

I pour a single finger, and then some instinct has me add a second. Replace the crystal stopper. Turn, and watch as Logan puts his lips to my teacup, his lips matched to the pale red imprints of my lips left by my lipstick. Tips back the teacup, drinks my tea, replaces the cup in the saucer. Why does that cause me to shiver, from bones to flesh, scalp to toes?

I hand him his scotch, and his fingers brush mine. My skin burns where his touched me. Tingles. I withdraw my hand, curl it into a fist. Still it shakes, scorched by a momentary glancing touch.

I cannot turn away, cannot look away as he now lifts the tumbler to his lips, and I cannot help but watch as he tilts the glass, the thick amber liquid slipping between his lips, and I watch his Adam's apple bob as he swallows.

I feel a jealousy for the scotch, touching those lips.

And then I feel stupid for thinking such a ridiculous thing.

I blush.

Me. *Blushing.*

I duck my head to cover my embarrassment, but then he's laughing as he swallows and sets the tumbler down. "What?"

"Nothing."

I'm standing in front of the couch, to the side of the coffee table. Close, but a polite, appropriate distance away. Yet he is able to reach up, brush my cheek with his thumb. "You're blushing."

"No."

He laughs again. Stands up, crowds me. "You are. I can tell. Why are you blushing, Cinderella?"

"I'm not blushing. And my name isn't Cinderella."

"You are, and I've decided it fits. I like it."

"You've decided." There's a sharpness to my tone.

So close. Too close. A foot remains between our bodies, but it's too close. The air fairly crackles between us.

He grins, a cocky tilt of his lips. "I'm just teasing, X."

"Why Cinderella?" I hear myself ask.

"Well . . . you showed up, all belle of the ball, mysterious and sexy as hell. Everyone wanted to know who you were. You left in such a rush, you all but left a glass slipper behind. You wouldn't tell me your name. And that dress?" He lets out a deep breath and shakes his head, as if overcome. "That dress. Jesus." He shrugs. "Seemed like a fairy tale to me."

"I see." I move away, stride to the window, and I feel his gaze on me as I walk.

Do my hips always sway so much when I walk? Do my thighs always brush so deliciously against each other with each step?

I watch a man and his wife walk hand in hand together, thirteen stories down. I cannot think to invent a story for them. I can almost see myself down there, walking hand in hand with a blond man. Neither of us talks. We just walk, fingers twined, moving in sync. I don't know where we go, the blond man and I. It doesn't matter; we're just going, and we're going together.

I shake my head, turn around—freeze, gasp. He's there, somehow behind me and I didn't hear him move or sense his presence. Scotch left on the table, hands loose at his sides. Indigo eyes knowing. Seeing. Piercing.

"Who are you, X?" Voice like a bow drawn across a cello string, the lowest, deepest, most soulful note. Caressing me, shivering my bones, making my skin pebble, just his voice. It's like a touch, somehow intimate.

How do I answer? I feel tightness in my throat. "I don't know."

My capacity to lie is snared and discarded by the openness in his eyes.

"You don't know who you are?" Disbelief.

I find myself defensive. "And who are you, Logan Ryder? How would you answer such a question?"

He blinks slowly, stuffs both hands in his hip pockets, gazes at me for a long moment. "I am Logan Ryder. I'm an entrepreneur, an angel investor, and a philanthropist. Unmarried and unattached. A semireformed troublemaker."

"That's *what* you are, Logan. Not *who* you are." I press my back to the window, needing space.

When he's close, I can't breathe, but not from panic. From something else. A chest-tightening anticipation. Memory. Fear of what I might do if he presses in again, the way he did in the bathroom. I have no control when he's near. He short-circuits me, and I am unnerved.

"I was born in San Diego. Grew up poor. Surfer kid. Spent my days on the beach, on the waves. Skipped more school than I attended." His eyes are distant, seeing the past. "Got into trouble. Fell in with the wrong crowd. Did some bad shit . . . saw friends die, and I realized I had to get out of that life or I'd end up either dead or in jail. Seemed to me at the time that the only way out for someone like me was to join the army. So I spent the next four years wearing army green. Never saw combat, but I did get plenty of training in how to work hard and party hard. Got my GED, so at least some good came of it."

"That's your past, not who you are." My palms are flat against the cool glass.

"It's more than anyone else knows about me."

"Oh."

"Yeah . . . oh." He smirks. "I'm getting to the part that starts to define who I am. After I phased out of the army, I was bored shitless. Had some money saved and nothing to do. Bummed around a bit, started getting into trouble again. I've got a knack for trouble, you see. It follows me, and I follow it. We're very closely intertwined, trouble and me. I met this guy at a bar in St. Louis. He was a private security contractor. Talked a good game, got me to sign up for a tour in the desert. One tour as a defense contractor turned to two, turned to three. Good money, bad shit." He shrugs. "Got out after the third, took my money and ran. I'd seen enough. Done enough. So I took what I had, bought a bar in Chicago, redesigned it, rebranded and restaffed it. Sold it. Did it again. Made good money, discovered I had a good head for that kind of thing. And I liked getting my hands dirty, ripping the places apart and rebuilding them. Then I had this investment opportunity . . . over here, in Manhattan. A big money investment, big risk, big return. It . . . didn't pan out. Let's just say that and leave it there."

I sense a major plot hole. "You're skipping something, Logan."

He nods. "Yes, I am. That's a story I'm not interested in telling just yet. It's a big part of who I am, but it's still hard to talk about. Still sort of learning how to move past it, you could say."

"But you ask me who I am. Not so easy to answer, is it?"

He merely shrugs, a Gallic lift of one shoulder. "Is it fair to ask a question I find difficult to answer myself? No. Of course not. But how you answer that question, it tells me something. You, for instance, didn't answer at all. You merely turned the question back around on me. You're defensive. Private. Impossible to know. Who are you, X?" His eyes are deep, and sharp. "Make me an answer. Something. Anything."

I'm not supposed to talk about me. It's never been said outright, out loud. It's an unspoken rule. Don't talk about myself.

But how can I not? He's looking at me, looking *into* me, eyes like the deepest seas, turbulent and roiling and fraught with chasms of such impenetrable depths I could get lost and crushed and devoured.

"I am Madame X." It's an answer, isn't it?

"More." A quiet demand. A command.

"I . . . I don't know." I turn away, desperate, rest my forehead against the glass and fog it with my breath. "You should go."

"I have fifty minutes left, X."

Ten minutes? That's all that's passed? An eternity, stretched thin and twisted into a loop, all within the space of six hundred seconds.

"Tell me one fact about yourself. It doesn't have to be embarrassing, or a secret. Just . . . anything."

"Why?" I whisper it.

This should be a simple conversation, but it isn't, and even the why of that is beyond me. He confounds me, sets all I know of how my life works upon its head.

"Because I'm curious. I want to know."

"I'm Spanish."

He's too close. Leaning in. Breath on my ear. "That wasn't so hard, was it?"

"What happened? With the investment?" Why the hell am I asking him this?

He laughs. "Right for the jugular. It was . . . complicated. Certain elements of the deal weren't exactly legal. I knew it, but I thought I'd gone through enough layers to keep myself clean, you might say. But . . . I got betrayed."

"So you're a criminal."

"Once upon a time, yes. Semireformed, remember. All of my current business endeavors are entirely legal."

"You don't seem the type."

"Which type?"

"To be a criminal."

"I came to a point where I had to reinvent myself." He's still so close I can hear him swallow, hear his breath.

He still smells faintly of cinnamon gum, but that scent is over-powered by scotch. I don't know what he did with his gum; a strange detail to notice. He's not touching me, though. Just standing in my space.

Why am I not pushing him away?

"Reinvention of one's self is difficult," I say.

"Yes. It is." His finger now, index finger, on my chin. Just touching. Not turning me to him, just touching. "Why did *you* have to reinvent yourself, X?"

"Because I . . . got lost." It is the shape of the truth, if lacking in substance.

"You're leaving something out, X."

"Yes, I am."

"How about your real name?"

"I told you already. My name is Madame X."

"That's not even Spanish." There's a smile in his words, though I don't look at him to see it. I can hear it, and it is blinding enough in its beauty, even heard but unseen.

I let out a long, slow breath. "It's the only name I have."

I sense the smile fade. My eyes change their focus, and now I can see his reflection in the window glass. His eyes are searching, a strand of golden hair across his eye. The corners of his eyes are crinkled, as if from long hours squinting in the sun. His skin is weathered, leathery. Rugged. He is beautiful, but hard and sharp, threat seeping from his pores. Yet somehow utterly gentle. So powerful, so sure of his capacity to eliminate any threat to himself that he need not posture. A tiger in the jungle that knows he is king.

"X. Why X?"

My eyes go, of their own will, to the painting on the wall. He turns away from me, and I sigh in relief. But I trail after him to stand beside him in front of *Portrait of Madame X*. He examines it. We stare at it in silence for a long, long time. I, remembering. He, perhaps, seeking clues. He will find none in the brushstrokes, nor in the composition, nor in the subject, nor in the use of color, the black and the white and the browns, not in the arch of her neck or the sharpness of her nose, the paleness of her skin or the drape of her hand. The only clues lie within me.

My voice, quiet in the golden evening light. "I lost myself. I lost . . . who I was. Who I could be. I lost . . . everything. And I saw this painting. I don't know why, but it struck me. I had nothing, no name, no past, no future. And I saw this painting, and it . . . it meant something to me. I saw myself in it, somehow. I don't know. I'll never know. But I chose this painting. Madame X. Other portraits of the time, they're given names. But this one? Just . . . Madame X. She has a name, you know: Virginie Amélie Avegno Gautreau. But in this portrait, she is Madame X. The subject of a painting, no more, no less. Something in that meant something to me."

I expect a comment, something deep and meaningful. Instead he turns and moves across the room to the wall opposite, to Van Gogh's *Starry Night*. "And this one?"

I shrug. "I just like it."

"Bullshit."

I frown at the sudden and harsh vulgarity. "Logan—"

"Tell me the truth, or tell me to shut up, but don't lie to me."

"I wasn't lying. I saw it, and I liked it. I felt empty, and . . . blank. Numb. The kind of numb where you have so many feelings you just stop feeling any of them. I couldn't express them, couldn't express anything. And this painting? It expresses so much. Loneliness, but also peace. Distortion, confusion, passion. Insanity, even. There is something to latch on to, though, in the church steeple. You look at it, and you can see so many things. Whatever your past has brought you, there is something of this painting in you. Of course, then . . . I knew none of this. Not even my name. I just . . . knew I could look at the *Starry Night* and it would help me make sense of some of the many things in my mind."

"I have so many questions." His voice is quiet as he says this, as if admitting a secret he fears will gut him.

"Me, too." There is far more truth in those two words than I can even withstand.

I am compelled to turn away, to let myself collapse on the couch. I find my fingers wrapped around the glass tumbler, eyeing the finger's worth of scotch whisky. Touch it to my lips. And yes, my lips touch the faint smear on the rim where his mouth pressed against glass: an intimacy. My lips burn, my throat burns, my eyes water, I cough and swallow, cough. Liquid fire races down my throat, spreads through my stomach and into my veins.

Oh.

This is why they drink such vile stuff.

The afterburn, the heat in my blood, the dizzy warmth in my skull . . . another taste, another cough-swallow-cough-cough, and the buzz expands.

I could float away.

Elbows on knees, knees together, feet wide apart, leaning forward, staring at the map with its strange spelling and bizarre curvature and not-quite accurate geographical relationships, I am dizzy and floating in the clouds, finding a looseness in my skull, something vital disconnecting. A tether, snaking and curling into itself, no longer attached.

His hand, wrapping around mine. Not taking the glass away, but rather his hand on mine, over mine, engulfing, enveloping, covering. He's on the couch beside me. How? When? He isn't massive. He is perhaps six feet, an inch or two more, at most. Compact. His muscles seem . . . harder, somehow. Thicker, though not as hugely bulging and perfectly designed as . . . I shake my head, forgetting where that train of thought was going. He is a predator. Every muscle honed from use. Nothing spare, nothing excess. I'm staring. Helpless.

My stare is drawn up, away from the sculpture of arms and chest and thighs, up, to tumultuous indigo pools, so bright and vivid as to be nearly luminescent.

Oh . . .

I'm drawn in. Falling forward. I see eternity in that shade of blue.

My hand, beneath his, tightens on the glass. His, on mine, lifts. The tumbler with its scotch contents touches his mouth. I tip the glass upward, my hand forming the motion, spilling the liquid onto his tongue. I can see his teeth, a pink splotch of tongue. I watch his Adam's apple bob. He doesn't cough as he swallows. Now the vessel, nearly empty, is moving to me. My hand under Logan's. Our hands moving in sync. He brings the tumbler to my lips, we tilt it, and I swallow.

Fire burns.

In my throat, in my veins,

between my thighs.

Heat and moisture, fiery and potent as the scotch whisky in my belly, pools between my legs.

Logan's nostrils flare, and I wonder if he can smell my essence. How long has passed now? How many minutes have been taken in the exchange of sips, mine and his? They've passed in silence, how-ever many it is. But this silence—it is alive. Not mere absence of word or sound, but communication of something deeper, some language of eyes meeting and hands brushing and breaths counted, a syntax of sensuous gazes, and something deeper yet, something felt in the gut, something shared that cannot be enumerated or encapsulated or communicated in mere thought or language.

As there is something in the beauty of art that stirs the soul, so is there something in a profoundly vital silence that moves the heart.

His eyes move to my lips as I swallow the scotch, and this time I do not cough. I lick my lips, and his eyes follow the path of my tongue from mouth corner to corner, capturing each last drop of the whisky. His tongue moves, too. Between his lips, and I watch it as he watched me. I can almost taste *his* tongue and lips rather than my own.

His lips part, and he sighs, the air passing slightly through his nose as well. His brows are drawn down, the wrinkle at the bridge of his nose furrowed and deep. The sigh . . . it was the sound he made after kissing me.

Huh. That's how it sounds. *Huh,* but a breath, rather than vibrating vocal cords.

I have that sound captured in my soul.

The tip of my nose touches his. The earth has tilted and I am falling into him. My elbows still on my knees, but my arms are crossed in an X, left hand drooping to my right knee and vice versa.

Three mouthfuls of scotch. I am not drunk; I am intoxicated by Logan.

There is a dab of liquid at the corner of Logan's mouth. I am utterly seized by the need to lick it away. To kiss it away. To taste scotch on his skin. I lean forward, breathing slowly, tongue sliding along my lips.

But at the last moment, I catch myself, stop. I could weep from the need to taste his kiss, to taste whisky-honeyed flesh. Instead, I touch my thumb to his mouth. Wipe. Smear. And then . . .

I suck the hint of moisture off my thumb. Logan's chest makes a sound as of mountains colliding. A groan? A murmur?

Sense returns, albeit in dizzy snatches. I lurch to my feet, stumble away, bedroom bound.

He is too much. Too close. Too intense, too embedded in the

meaning of my need and embroiled in the substance of my desire. I cannot fathom moments without him now. Yet I cannot breathe because he is all of the fractal seconds I possess, he is every stuttered fragment of time, and each breath is a drink of him. Intoxicated, I breathe yet more of him. Drowning, I am become nothing but the taste of his presence, the flavor of his eyes on mine and the glance of knuckle past knuckle, the feast of a memory of a kiss.

I close my bedroom door and collapse backward against it. I hear nothing. Only the thunderous pound of my heart, the knowledge of my guilt. The promise of what cameras have seen, and what I will suffer for it.

I hear my front door open. It's a subtle sound, a *click* of the knob twisting, the latch sliding in. The whisper of weather seal on hardwood.

Suddenly, panic seizes me.

If he leaves now, I will collapse inward like a star under its own weight.

Unthinking, I tear open my bedroom door, flee out, across the living room, the tumbler, now empty, alone on the coffee table. My front door is closing. I catch it.

"Logan?"

I don't know what comes next; I haven't thought this far ahead. I just knew I couldn't let him leave like that.

I see him now. Back turned to me, broad shoulders bowed and hunched, hard fists clenched, beautiful head ducked. An imposing, virile, masculine figure, arousing and erotic.

"Cinderella." He hears my door, twists his head to look at me over his shoulder. He is not smiling, and his chest is heaving as if his breath has been leeched by intense physical combat.

"Prince Charming." It is whispered, barely audible, a small, sibilant sound.

I have stepped across my threshold. Out into the hallway. Out of the purview of the cameras.

Another unspoken rule, violated.

What comes next?

I crash against his chest, and his hands are on my back, low, pulling me against him. We twist, a dancing series of steps, his mouth slanting across mine, not just kissing but tasting, feeling, probing, daring, teasing. We spin. I am lifted free of the ground, and my spine is up against the wall beside my door, a full 360-degree rotation. His hands on my back. Oh . . . lower. Fingertips digging into the soft bubble of my backside's upper swell. I feel his heart beating a double-hammer rhythm in his chest, as furious as my own. My arms . . . slipping serpentine around his neck, hands cupping the back of his head and his nape beneath his hair, soft, firm, warm, strong.

I kiss him.

Push up with my mouth and engage his kiss.

All the world ceases to exist. Fades. Flickers and gutters, a candle flame extinguished.

Oh, this kiss.

It is *all*.

The whole of history and the entire potentiality of the future.

The minutiae of the present, compressed into the singularity of his mouth on mine, his hands tender and strong and confident, gently exploring the curve of my bottom and the bell of my hips. Tug, keeping me taut against him.

I feel his erection thickening between us, so flush against his hard body am I.

I am condensed into a mass of need.

The kiss is rapture, his tongue sliding between my lips, tasting me, slipping and seeking. I taste him in return, kiss him back. Demand with my body his kiss, his touch. His hands move down to the backs of my thighs, cup, curl, and suddenly I am airborne, and my legs seem to know what to do. They wrap around his trim wedge of a waist. I writhe. Moan. Is that my throat, making so needy a noise? It is. His hand is at the back of my neck, under the knot of my hair, his other arm beneath my bottom, supporting me, holding me.

Our kiss is one of starvation, as if we've both gone all our lives without this, knowing in our guts we needed it and not having a name for it or a definition of it but now here it is and we cannot live without it another moment. A kiss of utter need.

I writhe, my legs around his waist, my core grinding against his belly. My breasts crushed against his chest.

I could come from the kiss alone, nearly do.

"X . . ." he breathes, and the kiss is broken.

Ding.

I leap down off him, twist away and dart through the doorway, running for my room. Slam my bedroom door behind me. Dive under the covers of my bed.

I tremble.

I weep, so wired with ecstasy I could light a city. Weep, the tears wetting the sheet under my cheek, overwhelmed, overcome. And, as I weep, eyes clenched closed, I see him. Blond hair hanging around his face, and now his hand brushes through it, pushing it back. His eyes are warm, knowing, caressing me with their ultraviolet light. And I feel him, his body around mine, his hands on me, his lips on mine, his tongue inside my mouth. I taste him. Scotch and faint cinnamon.

Tears on my cheeks, chest heaving with a wild disarray of emotions, I am subsumed beneath a wave of need so potent I writhe on my bed, legs scissoring. My dress is hiked up around my hips, and I am covered under my blankets. I am hyperaware of my hand as it steals across my belly and between my legs. Slips under the elastic of my underwear. I lick my lips and taste the salt of tears and the faint impression of scotch and the flavor of Logan's lips. I feel his mouth on mine. His hands on my backside, caressing, squeezing, exploring with such sweet possessive gentility. And his kiss, how it blazed alight within me, fire in my soul, making me feel more alive than I've ever felt.

I touch myself.

I put my fingers to my privates, slip them into my damp heat, and I make myself come, once, hard, immediately upon contact, faster than thought, and I see his eyes, feel his breath, taste his need. I stifle a moan. I writhe against my fingers and pretend they are his, swiping against my clitoris, circling it . . . thus . . . making me come again, harder, and I pretend these are his fingers, two of them, diving deep into my slit, curling up and in, dragging wetness over my clitoris, and they are his fingers, smearing my essence in ever-faster circles until I jackknife under the blankets, huffing wild breaths of hot recycled air, teeth clamped down on my moans of his name.

"Logan . . . Logan . . ." Whispered, desperate.

I have to breathe fresh air. I toss the blankets back to my waist. Wipe at my eyes with my free hand. The one not still caught between my thighs. I'm not crying anymore, but I'm so distraught I don't know how to even feel it all, how to express it. I could scream. Energy boils inside me, my entire body afire with adrenaline and memory and heat.

I *need* Logan.

I need him. God, I need him. He makes me feel alive. I am free in him, *with* him.

I rush to the window. Yes! There he is. Striding across the road, gait loose, easy. Hands in his pockets. He reaches the other side, stops, turns. Looks up. Can he know my window from all the others? It's but a single rectangle of dim light in a city of incandescence. Am I lost in the glow?

I put a hand to the glass, palm flat, fingers spread next to my forehead touching the cool window. He sees me? He raises a hand, waves, once. And then, oh, then he puts his thumb to the corner of his mouth, as if wiping away a droplet of moisture. A gesture, repeated, mirrored. A sign?

Thirteen stories up, yet he sees me? Is it possible?

He turns away then. Descends the stairs down to the subway. Gone.

I quiver with the memory of his kiss, the aftershocks of my fantasy of his touch.

I'd do anything to make that fantasy reality.

Anything.

I know I will never sleep, so I go to my library and pretend to read, pretend I'm not thinking of him. Pretend I'm not machinating, hoping, dreaming—

Fantasizing of impossibilities.

I fall asleep in my chair in the library, lights on, in the silence, dreaming of blond hair and indigo eyes and lips that take me away from here.

THIRTEEN

wake, disoriented, stiff.

And then I remember last night, and my fingertips touch my lips. I smile. I stretch, legs straightening away from the chair, spine stiffening and curling backward, arms tensed and trembling, a full-body stretch, feline and luxuriant.

Ding.

I blink in confusion; have I overslept? I am still in my dress from the previous day, hair messed and tangled and partially knotted, makeup smeared. I can feel makeup caked and flaking at my eyes.

The space of time between the arrival of the elevator and my front door smashing open is infinitesimal. A breath of a moment, less even.

A gargantuan black frame fills the doorway of my library. Thomas. "He sees the video from yesterday." His voice is like the deepest bass note being electronically distorted lower. Impossibly deep, syrupy, and yet somehow smooth as silk.

I am slow, sleepy. "What? Who saw what video?"

Thomas takes three long angry strides toward me, towers over me, and the expression in his eyes is so terrifying I am shocked fully awake. "He *see* you and that man from the auction. With the yellow hair."

"Caleb. He saw the tapes?" I'm starting to fathom the problem.

Thomas grips my arms, twists me, propels me toward the front door. "He is a madman. You must go."

"Go?"

"Or I think you die. He is *mad*." Thomas, with his thick African accent, does not mean *mad* as in angry, I realize. The implication is more frightening than mere anger.

I am barefoot. My shoes from yesterday sit forgotten, between the front door and the library. One, on its side. The other, upside down. I right them with my toes, stuff my feet into them. Shuffle to the door, untangling my hair.

Thomas growls in his chest. "No time for shoes, no time for fixing your pretty hair. *GO!*"

I let go my hair, take a step toward the door, and stumble out into the hallway, into the elevator, which stands open. The key is still in, twisted to the *13*. Thomas, in his tailored Western suit, looks fierce and wild, the whites of his eyes flashing bright, teeth bared. Even in the Western suit, he looks like an ancient Nubian warrior. I can see him with a lion skin, a round shield, and a long spear, dancing in the dust and the baking heat of the African sun.

I blink, and it's just Thomas again, in a black suit with a white shirt, thin black tie, a curly cord trailing down behind his ear and beneath his collar. His eyes go unfocused for a moment, and he touches a finger to the device in his ear, and then looks at me. He reaches in past me, twists the key up to the *PH*—penthouse—and then pulls me out of the elevator.

"Down the stairs." He pushes open what I thought was a fire escape. Locked, equipped with a siren or something.

Just a crash bar and the markings of an emergency exit. No siren wails when I push the door open. A stairwell beyond, grayish-white walls, metal handrails, blue rubber-treaded stairs in a descending square spiral. Shoes in hand now, I run down the stairs. I trip and miss a step, hear Thomas's voice, can't make out the words. Lurch and stumble down the steps so fast my breasts jounce painfully. I miss another step as I reach a landing, trip, crash into the wall opposite. Pause to catch my breath, arm, elbow, and hip aching where I smashed into the drywall. Below, I hear a voice.

"She's coming down the steps." A male voice, nasal and unfamiliar. "Thomas alerted her, I think. Yes, sir . . . I'm on the way up from floor seven. Alan is on the ground floor. We'll find her, sir, I promise. Yeah. I'll update you when we have her. Unharmed, got it. Crystal, sir. Not a scratch."

The voice is echoing from a few levels down and getting closer. Panic chokes me. I push through the door at the landing, marked with a black-painted 10. A clean, modern corridor, pale gray walls, cream carpeting, abstract paintings on the walls. An alcove, men's room, women's room. I duck into the women's restroom, grip the counter and lean, gasping for air, fighting sobs. What is happening? Why did Thomas warn me, help me escape? Does he pity me, worry for me? Where did he think I would escape to? Nothing makes any sense. And the fire escape stairwell not being alarmed puzzles me as well. Perhaps he meant only to give Caleb's anger time to cool off. I don't know. I just know I have to seize the opportunity that is presented. I cannot stay here any longer. Not after what I've experienced with Logan.

What do I do now? I glance up at myself in the mirror. I look awful. I take a deep breath, push down my panic.

Clear thought, rational decisions. Do not act out of panic or fear.

I use my fingers to free my hair from its knot, losing a few long black strands in the process. The black stretchy hair tie has my hair tangled around it, and my hair is a matted disaster. I comb it out with my fingers as best I can and then twist it up into a bun, gathering all the loose strands, wetting it with the sink a little to smooth it all out. Tie it back. Hand soap and water, scrub my face clean. Dab dry with rough brown paper towel from an automatic dispenser—which took me a moment to figure out.

Face clean, hair neat. I straighten my dress, smooth out the worst of the wrinkles as best as possible. Adjust my cleavage. Tug the hem down. Slip on my shoes. Deep breath.

Exit, find the stairwell, glance back, debate trying the elevator. They're looking for me on the stairs now, I assume.

As I'm internally debating, I hear static crackle echoing in the stairwell, a male voice. I move away, follow the corridor around a left turn, slip through a glass doorway into an office. There's a desk, ornate, polished wood. Tall potted plants in the corners, pointillist art on a wall.

A young woman with a headset sits behind the desk, facing a computer screen. "Can I help you?"

"I think I got off on the wrong floor," I say. "Can you point me back to the elevators?"

Her eyes narrow, flick over me. She's looking for something. "May I see your security badge, miss?"

"I—"

She touches a button in front of her. "If you could just wait a moment, I'll have security come up and we'll get you a temporary ID badge."

I turn and duck out.

"Miss? You have to come back!" Her voice is loud, then quieted as the heavy glass door swings closed behind me.

Back to the elevators, touch the call button. Wait, panic rising in my gut. The elevator doors hiss open, and I step into the empty car. This is not the same elevator as stops at my door. There are buttons, dozens of them: G, a numeral one with a star beside it, and then numbers ascending all the way up to fifty-eight. My floor, thirteen, is missing. I look twice: ten, eleven, twelve, fourteen, fifteen . . .

I push the G. Garage? I don't know.

Sensation of descent. Some instinct has me press the two, and the car stops. I get out on the second floor, suppressing panic. I assume there are security cameras everywhere, that the guards are only moments behind me. I have a thousand problems ahead of me, but all I want right now is to get out of this building.

As I step out, peer side to side, a security guard in a black suit, walkie-talkie in hand, strides around a corner, sees me, shouts. "Stop!"

I duck back in, press the DOOR CLOSE icon, jab the first number my finger finds. The uppermost one, fifty-eight. I hear a fist pound on the door outside, but the elevator is in motion. Up, up, up.

I abruptly punch the button for the sixth floor; the elevator stops, the door slides open, and I step out. Peer side to side, see no one. Lean into the elevator, touch fifty-eight again and let the elevator resume its ascent.

I look around: flat white walls, no decorations, bare concrete floor, industrial, raw, unfinished-looking. Exposed beams above, painted black, exposed pipes painted the same. The hallway extends some twenty feet without door or marking of any kind, then turns right. I follow it, and now there are doors on either side of the hall-way, staggered so no door is directly across from another. Door after door. Plain entry doors, no peephole, the door painted the same flat white with large black numerals in industrial stencils. I count: 1, 2, 3, 4, 5 . . . even numbers on the right, odds on the left. I count twelve doors.

I hear the elevator *ding* and the doors open. "Yeah, I'm in pursuit on the sixth floor. Copy that. One second." The same nasally voice from the stairwell.

My heart thunders, my throat closes. I grab the nearest doorknob, twist, push. Oddly, it opens; I was expecting it to be locked.

I have a sense of disorientation, déjà vu. This could be my condo, down to the flooring and the dimensions and the paint. The only difference is the artwork on the walls, and there is no Louis XIV chair here, but the couch is the same, built-in bookshelves are the same, a kitchen connected to the living room via open floor plan, a short hallway leading to the single bedroom with the en suite bathroom, a smaller office opposite the bedroom. Instead of a library, I see exercise equipment: a huge purple exercise ball, free weights, weight machines.

Out of habit, I close the front door behind me. It clicks loudly as it closes. Footsteps, bare feet on hardwood.

"Caleb?" A soft female voice, thin, high, a twang to it.

I have no hope of hiding or ducking back out; I can only hope this girl will be sympathetic to my plight.

Short, petite, with reddish-blond hair, freckles, pale brown eyes. Very beautiful. Heart-shaped face, delicate chin. Expressive, expectant eyes.

"You ain't—*aren't*, I mean—you aren't Caleb."

"No, I am most certainly not."

"Who are you?"

I hesitate, infinitesimally. "I am Madame X."

"That's your name?"

"Yes. And yours?" I endeavor to seem confident.

Shrug, as if it doesn't matter. "I'm Six-nine-seven-one-three. For now. But I'm gonna be Rachel."

My heart twists. "Six-nine . . . what?"

A gesture, pointing at the door opposite. "Across the way, she's Six-nine-seven-one-four." A finger pointing next door. "She's Five. Down the way are Seven and Nine, and across from us are Two, Six, and Eight. That's all of us, for now."

"I'm confused." I have to lean back against the door. Something niggles at me. An idea, a horrible idea.

The girl is dressed in a shift; that's the only word for it. It's not a dress, not a nightgown. It's plain white thin cotton, hangs at mid-shin. She is very clearly nude beneath it. Barefoot. Hair in a simple low ponytail, no makeup, no paint on fingers or toes.

"It's my apprentice number. Who are you, and why are you here?"

"I work for Caleb." It's the truth and hopefully sounds authoritative.

"But why are you here?" The girl steps toward me, suspicion in her eyes. "Ain't nobody ever—" She winces, starts over. "I mean . . . No one ever visits except Caleb. No one, not ever. So who are you, and what do you want?"

I examine the ceiling, the corners where the molding joins. "Are you watched?"

"Watched?" Six-nine-seven-one-three follows my gaze. "You mean cameras?" A snort of derision. "You got to be kidding me. This whole floor is off-monitor. This one, nine, fifty-eight, and obviously Caleb's penthouse up top. Thirteen don't exist, or there's no way to get to it. Rumor is Caleb has a secret lair on the thirteenth floor, like a red room or something. But this floor, nine, and fifty-eight, there's no security cameras or audio. Too much risk, I guess. Can't have people knowing what's going on, right?"

I shake my head. "What happens on these three floors . . . Rachel?"

The girl doesn't answer right away. "I ain't—I'm *not* Rachel yet. Haven't earned my name yet. I'm just Three . . . for now." Side-eyed glance of speculation; a decision reached. "And if you don't know, I probably shouldn't tell you."

I push past the girl, walk to the window, my favorite window, the same one, same place. Slightly lower view, but nearly as comforting. Watch the cars pass, pedestrians. Familiar, soothing. I can almost breathe.

Silence. Padding feet on the wood, I smell shampoo and soap. "You said your name is Madame X?"

"I'm his secret on the thirteenth floor," I whisper.

"What do you do?" She leans against the window frame opposite me, assuming a familiar pose that suggests she spends as much time standing here as I do at my own window.

"If you don't know, I probably shouldn't tell you," I said.

"That ain't fair. I didn't even know you existed. How am I supposed to know?"

"Exactly. I didn't know you existed either, Three." I turn, rest my shoulder against the window. "You said it was your apprentice number. Apprentice what?"

"Apprentice bride." This is whispered. "That's my goal, at least. First I have to make Escort, and then Companion. Then Bride."

"I don't understand."

"Me and all the other girls on this floor, we're the property of Indigo Services. We're part of the apprenticeship program."

"Property?" I can barely get the word out.

A steady, even look. "I signed up for it. So did all the others, so don't you get no look of fuckin' pity in your eyes for me. It's better than being on the streets, and that's where I'd still be if it wasn't for Caleb. I'm drug free. No pimp. No debt. None of that bullshit. It's a way out. I ain't a slave. I know you're thinking that word. You don't know me, so don't you fuckin' judge me, *bitch*."

"I'm not judging you, Three. I just don't understand."

"How can you not? Was you born on fuckin' Mars or something?"

My instincts kick in. "'Were you,' you mean."

Three snarls at me, upper lip curled in a sneer. "I don't get what's so wrong with the way I talk. Caleb's always raggin' on me about it, too."

"Perception is vital. Proper speech creates the impression of class, Three. Proper grammar, lucid, concise syntax. No vulgarity. You wish to be taken seriously? Then you must act like a—" I was going to say *gentleman*, but I have to change tactics. "Like a lady. A woman of class."

"Who the hell *are* you, Madame X?"

"Someone much like you, I fear, only much less self-aware, I'm realizing." I glance at the door. "Can you leave? If you wanted to?"

Three makes a face. "Course I can. I mean, I wouldn't, but I *could*. Door ain't locked, elevator works. Once a week I get to go on a practice date with Caleb up to Rhapsody. I get a new dress, new shoes, get to put on makeup. If I do well, he might take me outside, out there, for the monthly final."

I have to formulate my question carefully. "Three, could you—could you explain for me how the program works?"

A shrug. "Sure. Easy. I was homeless. Workin' the street, right? Got no way to feed myself, so I ended up selling the only thing of any value I had, get it? Myself. Then I met Caleb. He hired me for a whole day. Guess he saw something, I don't know. Potential? Told me he had a program that would give me skills, and eventually a life off the streets. Kind of a training program followed by a matchmaking program, all in one. Right now, I'm in the training program."

"What kind of training?"

Another lazy, indolent shrug. I itch to correct her comportment, but it isn't my job to do so. "Everything. There's a tutor, Mr. Powers. He does the usual school kind of stuff. Helps us get a GED, if we need one, or furthers our education if we have a diploma already. Or he can do guided studies in specific areas. You're interested in science or some shit, he can help you find resources and whatever. Anyway, Mr. Powers is always on me to speak proper, too, but I grew up talkin' like this, everyone I knew talked like this, and some habits are hard to break, you know? And then there's Miss Lisa. She's head of the program. Keeps track of our progress, tells us what we need to do to improve, to get up to the next level. She's the head boss, lead supervisor basically. And then . . . there's Caleb."

"And what does he do?" I ask. I'm not sure I want to know the answer, though.

Three doesn't answer me, won't look at me. Her pale cheeks redden. "I shouldn't be prudish about this, considerin' where he found me. What I was doing." Another pause. For courage, I think. "He teaches us how to please. How to act attractive. How to seduce. How to look, how to dress, how to—how to fuck."

"And he teaches you all of this personally, does he?"

Widening of the eyes. "Oh yes. Of course. He delivers the final exam. Makes sure we're ready for each stage. An Escort has fewer requirements than a Companion, and a Bride has the most of all."

"Requirements?" My voice sounds faint.

Three shrugs. "It's complicated. Learnin' those differences is part of the training, so it ain't like I can just sum it up in one or two sentences, you know?" A glance away, out the window. "I shouldn't be telling you this stuff anyway. Ain't supposed to be talking about it to anyone not in the program. We signed an agreement. But you're the big secret on floor thirteen, so I'm guessing you probably got secrets of your own. You ain't gonna rat me out to Caleb, are you?"

I shake my head. "No, Three. I won't. I promise."

I have a million, million questions, but I don't even know where to start. But Three suddenly bolts upright, away from the window, glances at the plain wall clock.

"Shit! You gotta get out of here. I've got an assessment, like right now!"

"An assessment?"

"Yeah, with Caleb."

"Caleb is coming *here*, now?"

We both hear a voice. One we both recognize. But rather than the usual calm, there is anger, hot and loud. "No, Douglas, it's *not* going to be fucking *fine*. If she didn't leave the building, then she's hiding out somewhere. Fucking *find* her, or there will be hell to pay." Right outside the door.

Three hisses in my ear. "Under the bed. *Go!* Don't even breathe, okay? He won't stay too long. 'Specially not in this mood."

I hustle toward the bedroom, slide under the bed, make myself as small as possible. Arms under my chest, cheek to the dusty hardwood. Barely breathing.

I hear the door open. Hear that deep, gravelly voice. "Three. Good morning."

"Caleb." Three sounds . . . breathy. "I'm fine. How are you?"

"Not well. There's been . . . a problem. It's got me distracted, I'm afraid." Footsteps on the hardwood, and I see shiny expensive tan leather shoes, khaki slacks. "Perhaps we should reschedule your assessment for tomorrow. I'm not sure I can focus at the moment."

"But . . . Miss Lisa told me I've finally got my first Escort gig tomorrow, but only if I pass this assessment." Three sounds genuinely disappointed. "Unless you think there's a chance I might fail . . ."

"I think there's very little risk of that, Three. Your progress has been remarkable."

"You don't think I could . . . help you with your mood?" Three's voice goes low, sultry, rife with suggestion. "I know I can't fix nothin'—"

"Three." It's a warning.

"Sorry, Caleb. I meant, fix *anything*." I see feminine bare feet framed between larger shod ones. Three lifts up on her toes. A silence that speaks of something happening I can't see. A kiss perhaps. Sounds, too quiet to interpret. "I could distract you from your . . . distractions, you know?"

I clench my teeth and breathe shallowly, slowly. They are moving closer, Three walking forward toward the bed, the Italian leather dress shoes walking backward.

It seems Three shall be assessed.

The bed above me dips under weight. Springs squeak. The shoes are inches from my face. Three's feet shuffle, and then one knee touches the floor, the other. A belt buckle jingles, zipper sounds. The khaki slacks droop around ankles, and I get a glimpse of familiar hairy calves. Wet sounds. A male groan. Quiet, faint gagging.

"Very good, Three." This, delivered through clenched teeth. "Mmmm. More tongue, more movement of your whole head. Don't just suck. Alternate using your hands, your lips, and your tongue. Yes, like that." A growl, as Three obviously demonstrates a particular . . . technique, I suppose.

My gut twists. Feelings I don't dare examine rage within me.

Sucking, gagging, male grunts and groans, sighs. It goes on for longer than I would think possible. The sounds taper off for a moment or two, and then resume, silence, a female gag accompanied by a male groan.

"Are you ready, Three?" Low, thickly voiced, teeth clenched, breathless. "I'm going to come. I'll let you decide where you want me to come."

Gagging. Gulping. A long, guttural male groan. Sigh. Three's weight shifts backward as she sits on her heels, one hand planted on the floor. There's come on her hand, white smears across her knuckles. Apparently she didn't elect to swallow it all.

A moment of silence.

"Very, *very* good, Three." An extended sigh, and the weight on the bed shifts backward. "Next time, I would like you to take it all on your face. I don't personally find pleasure in that, but others do, and you need to be prepared for how it will feel."

"Yes, Caleb." Why does she sound so eager?

"Now . . . I want you to tell me the truth, all right? Penalty free for this answer, regardless of what you say. Our last session together, did you fake your orgasm?"

A hesitation. And then Three's voice, pitched low, embarrassed. "Yes—no. Well, sort of. I mean . . . I exaggerated it, some. I *did* come, but not as—as hard as I might have made it seem."

"Why?"

"Because I—I wanted you to think . . . I don't know. I don't know."

"The truth, Three. *Now.*"

"I *wanted* to come. But it's just . . . I can't, very often." Her voice is tiny. So delicate. Mortified. "I've tried. On my own, and with you, and before I became an apprentice. My whole life, it's just . . . it's hard for me to come. And when I do, it's just not very—hard, I guess. I still enjoy things, when you do them to me, I mean. I enjoy them a lot. But I just can't come every time, or not as . . . as intensely as I feel like you expect me to."

"First, a warning. Do not fake it, or exaggerate. Never again, no matter what, do you understand?"

"Yes, Caleb."

"Now stand up and put your hands on the bed."

"But you said penalty free!" A panicked protest.

"I'm not punishing you for your answer, Three, I'm punishing you for faking. I told you at the very start not to ever lie, fake, or pretend. Not about anything. I require absolute truth in all situations." A softening of the voice. "And this punishment won't be going on your program record. This is between us. So you understand that I'm serious."

"But . . . Caleb, I—I understand. Okay? I won't fake again, I swear!"

"Three. Stand up, *now*. Put your hands on the bed, *now*." Slow, deliberate, precise, calm.

Three stands up, twists in place; I can see her knees shaking. The Italian leather shoes slide forward, and I see the pants rise, hear the buckle of the belt. The bed dips very slightly, and Three's feet are spread shoulder width apart. I watch as the hem of Three's shift rises up out of view.

Smack! Hand on flesh.

Smack! Again.

Three cries out. There is pain in that cry, very real pain. But there is also . . . arousal.

Smack!

Smack!

The sounds of spanking increase, punctuated by Three's cries of pain and increasing sexual arousal. My gut is churning. Some part of me is . . . not as horrified by this as I should be. Three is *enjoying* this. Doing this *voluntarily*. Three could leave at will. As the spanking continues, cries of pain gradually become entirely erotic cries of need. Bare feet shuffle on the floor, knees dip, bent body pushing back into the blows, into the touch.

I wonder if there is only the spanking, or if something else is happening. Fingers as well, perhaps, moving inside her privates? From the way Three is moaning and whimpering, I assume so.

I can see how this might be intensely arousing. I feel dirty for eavesdropping on this, and dirtier still for feeling curious, and jealous. But some part of me is finding a dark voyeuristic pleasure in it. I am sick, *this* is sick.

But I cannot get away from it.

I hear Three orgasm. The wail of release is shrill, and loud, and to my ear, genuine.

The white shift is tossed aside, to the floor. Pants drape around ankles. Three cries out. The bed shifts, dips, and is rocked sideways by a forceful thrust. Three is bent over the bed, male feet lined up behind. The sounds of sex are loud, and fast. Three whimpers with each fleshy slap of skin against skin, and then as the tempo increases, the whimpers become cries, and then grunts, and I can tell from the movement of Three's bare feet when accepting the thrusts turns to active participation, pushing back into them.

Male grunt of release, slapping of body on body slows and stops, and Three is breathless, moaning, emitting high-pitched whimpers.

I'm damp between my thighs, aroused, and sick with guilt and shame and confusion.

A moment of silence, then, neither person moving or speaking. And then I see trousers slide up, hear a belt buckle, fabric rustling. I can picture strong hands tucking a pristine white shirt into the slacks, tugging it to blouse just so, stuffing fingers into hip pockets so they don't bulge or fold. A familiar ritual of re-dressing, adjusting; Three will still be naked, of course. Artfully posed, probably, to look sated, glutted, content, drowsy.

I know the pose all too well, having assumed it myself a million times.

"Was that exaggerated, Three?" Arrogant, and assured.

"N-no. No, Caleb." A gasp. "It was real. I came *so* hard, Caleb."

"What do you think made the difference?"

"You . . . spanking me. I—I liked that. It hurt, but I liked it." Three sounds embarrassed. "I liked it a *lot*."

"Don't be upset, Three. You shouldn't feel shame. Know your body, know your sexuality. In time, you will learn to control your sexual encounters. Even when you're being fucked like I just fucked you, from behind, where you have no physical control over what might be happening to you, you will still be able to exert influence over how enjoyable it is for your partner. You will be able to control how fast you both get off, how intensely. I can tell the difference when you fake it, Three. Some men may not be able to, but I can. When you genuinely enjoy and participate rather than just being a passive receptacle, you become a much more exquisitely erotic creature. When you were a whore, it didn't matter. Your johns paid you to let them fuck you, and they didn't give one single shit how you felt about it. But you are not a whore anymore, Three. You will not be paid for sex, implicitly or explicitly. Indigo Services does not provide sex workers; we provide companionship, partnership, and romance. If you have sex with a client, it will be your choice, a mutual decision between you and the client, *after* your service contract has expired. Keep this in mind, for tomorrow. The basic Indigo Services contract expressly forbids any kind of sexual act during the time frame of the services provided. If you choose to engage in sex with the client after the contract expires, that is *your* choice, and you should never feel pressured by the client. If you do experience pressure of any kind, report it to Lisa immediately and that client will be blacklisted. You should not *ever* be pressured into sex by a client. And you should *always* enjoy sex. Do you understand?"

"I understand." Three's voice is small, unsure.

"You enjoy a little pain with sex. I suspected as much, but now we know. Perhaps in the coming weeks, as you begin working as an Escort, we will explore the limits of your enjoyment of pain."

"But you won't . . . *hurt* me, hurt me?" Three sounds breathy, eager, and a little afraid.

"No. Never. You are valuable. To me, and to Indigo Services, and ultimately, you should be valuable to the man who eventually chooses you as his Bride."

"You think someone will choose me, Caleb?" Oh, the doubt, the fear, the vulnerability I hear cuts me to the bone.

"Three, dear Three." I'm not the only one, judging by the tone of voice. "Yes. I do think someone will. How could they not? Your personality shines through in every situation. I realize this program is not the easiest thing to go through. Letting go of your name, your past . . . it's never easy. But through it all, your beauty remains undeniable, and I refer to the beauty of your soul as well as the beauty of your body."

I have never received such kind, genuine, uplifting words. Am I unworthy?

"Th-thank you, Caleb."

"Congratulations, Apprentice Six-nine-seven-one-three, you are now an Escort." This is said with great formality. "Have you chosen a name?"

"Rachel." Three—Rachel, now, I suppose—sounds excited, gleeful.

"Why have you chosen this name?"

A pause. "You'll laugh."

I can almost—*almost*—imagine a subtle quirk of the lips. "I think not."

"I used to watch *Friends* a lot. You know, Ross, Rachel, Joey, Chandler, Phoebe, and Monica?"

"I am familiar. I don't watch television, but it is a common enough part of pop culture that I've heard of it."

"When I was a kid, I'd watch it with my older sister. She'd do her homework and I'd sit with her and—well, and then . . . when I ended up working for Slade, I'd watch it late at night. It was . . . a way to escape, I guess. And I always just loved Rachel the most."

"Do you miss it?"

"What? Watching *Friends*?"

"Yes."

Three is quiet for a moment before answering. "Yeah, some-times. I don't miss none of—I don't miss any of the rest of my past, obviously, but *Friends*? Yeah. They were like *my* friends. Their lives were better than mine. They had easy problems, so I could forget mine for a while. I miss that."

"Perhaps something can be arranged. I do not believe in my girls being distracted by such triviality as television, as you know, but perhaps as a reward for achieving Escort certification I could arrange a viewing for you."

"And the other girls?"

"It is a reward for you, Rachel."

"Which means I can share it, right?"

"Very well, then. Lisa will be in to review and brief you for tomorrow. Once again, congratulations."

Loafers tread quietly away, and I see a hint of white door as it opens, the *thud-click* as it closes. I wait several more long moments.

"Come on out, he's gone." Rachel's hand appears in front of my face, waving me out from under the bed.

I scoot out, sore and stiff, and stand up on wobbly legs. Brush dust away, straighten my clothes. Rachel lounges on her bed, naked. Her breasts are slight, areolae pale pink around her nipples. She is shaved totally bare between her thighs, whereas I am not. I smell sex in the air, musk, seed, pheromones, sweat.

I don't know what to say, what to do. Congratulate her? I don't know. It's hard to look at her. I keep hearing her moans, the sound of her being spanked, how thoroughly she enjoyed it. I can almost see her, bent over the bed, hair in her face, pale skin of her buttocks reddening with each slap. I push away the images.

"Never had an audience before," Rachel says. "Felt a little weird at first, knowing you were listening. But then . . ." A shrug, dismissive.

"What?" I can't help asking. "But then what?"

"But then I forgot. Well, sort of. I was sort of distantly aware that you were there, but that only made it even better." She giggles. "God, I had no idea I'd like being spanked so much. When I was a hooker, things was straightforward. They wanted me on my back, or doggy style. Caleb . . . he's kinda weird about positions, though. Only likes it doggy style or from behind. Bent over, standing up facing a wall, you know? Like that. Never face-to-face. Talked to the other girls about it, and he's the same with them."

The same is true for my own experience. I don't offer this, though. "Hmmm. I wonder what Caleb has against face-to-face sex?"

Another shrug, which is a signature expression, I'm realizing. "Oh, probably commitment issues, you know? Guys like him, it ain't just control, right? Or not control over *us*, the girl he's fucking, but control over himself. Face-to-face, you see the other person's eyes. You see their expression. Makes it more . . . personal, I guess. And with us, for Caleb . . . it ain't personal."

"It's sex, Rachel. How is it not personal?"

An expression of utter befuddlement. "We're just apprentices, you know? Nothin' but girls to be trained. The clients, when they get their match, they expect the girls to be . . . perfect, basically. Educated, well-mannered, and good in bed. Everyone is always like, 'Oh, I wanna bang me a virgin,' but virgins ain't any good in bed. They're clumsy, too quick, no fun in 'em. Boys and girls both. Girls is worst, I hear, because a girl virgin, she's got the pain to deal with. You gotta specially train them, I'd think. A gentleman is coming to Indigo Services for a trophy wife, he wants a woman who knows how to please, who knows what to do with his dick, you know? Who knows how to work it all night long. A virgin cain't do that. Those guys who're shopping the

Bride pool, they don't want to have to train their wife to fuck 'em like they want to be fucked. They want to be fucked by an expert. And you don't get to be an expert at fucking except by fucking."

"So Caleb . . . fucks you until you're an expert." The vulgarity both feels and sounds foreign and awkward on my tongue.

"Right."

"Eight of you at a time?"

"Well, not all at once. Not like, *ménage à* . . . whatever *eight* is in French."

"But you're aware he's having sex with each one of you apprentices?"

"Well, yeah. He's *Caleb*." Like it's something obvious, like, *duh*.

But I understand it. There is something hypnotic about those dark eyes, that commanding presence, utter confidence of primal male sexuality, something entrancing in total dominance.

"Does it bother you?" I ask.

"Not really. I hear it, when it's him and Five, next door. She's a screamer. He's always trying to get her to shut up, but as soon as he's got her going, she starts howling like a damn cat in heat. Annoying as hell, you ask me." Rachel stands up, walks with an air of confidence in her nudity.

I follow her. Some carnal curiosity has me looking at her backside; her buttocks are still pink, and I see a glistening smear on the insides of her thighs, low, a trickle of seed seeping out of her.

I am equally repulsed and aroused. Not at the sight of postcoital drip, but at the memory of my own walk from bed to bathroom, the memory of delicious ache, a sense of . . . satisfaction, almost, at the feel of the wet warm stickiness on my skin.

And then, as fast as the sensations roll through me, they are replaced by disgust, and hatred.

Revulsion.

All of it aimed primarily at myself. At my blindness, my gull-ibility.

At my twisted thoughts. At the fact that *any* part of me found pleasure in what I overheard.

I hear the shower running, splashing, quickly shut off. Rachel emerges with a towel around her torso.

"You're the problem, ain'tcha?" Her voice is sharp.

Her poor grammar and twanging accent and propensity for curs-ing lends a false sense that she is somehow unintelligent; she is not.

"The problem?" I pretend to not understand her meaning.

"Don't play coy with me, *Madame X*. 'Find her,' he said. You're running away from Caleb." The last is an accusation, blatant.

I sigh. "Yes. You're correct."

"He'll find you."

"I know that."

"Ain't nobody else like him, you know. I'm only twenty-two, but I been on the streets since I was thirteen. Met all kinds of men, turnin' tricks. Some of 'em weren't bad, just . . . lonely. Or too busy to bother with even trying to set up casual sex, I guess. Some were curious. A few virgins, here and there. But in all of 'em I ever met, there's never been nobody like him. You must not understand what you're running away from."

"My situation is . . . ." I have to hunt for an appropriate word. "Unique."

"Ain't everybody's?" Rachel eyes me.

"Well, I guess that's true, but I'm different. I don't mean to sound—"

"You're different. You're special. I get it. You're Caleb's big secret on the thirteenth floor. What you don't get is what he's done for me. For all of us here. I know what you think of us. I can feel you judging us."

"I'm not judging—"

"The hell you ain't!" She closes in, her eyes intelligent, proud, and piercing. "I was a meth head. Okay? You don't—you *can't* understand that if you ain't lived it. Alls I cared about was the next fix. I was gonna *die*, and Caleb Indigo saved me. He got me off the street, gave me a place to live, fed me. He's gotten me off drugs. Before, I was turnin' tricks to afford the next high. No one gave a single shit about me, myself least of all. Now, here? I got a reason to live. I got a reason to stay off drugs. I've got *value*, here. Yeah, I know I ain't the only one, but Caleb spends time with me. *Me*, the whore, the drug addict. When he's with me, I'm the only one that matters." This last in a quiet voice that quavers with conviction. "He makes me feel like I could amount to something besides what I used to be. I can get put in the Bride pool, and who knows, maybe I'll even get matched with someone who—who could love me." Such hope, clung to with tenacity. "You run away from all that if you want."

A long silence. I do not know what to say. I have too much in my head, in my heart.

"Garage is your only real shot, I'd say," Rachel says. "Take the elevator down, make a run for it. Good luck to you. I won't say nothing, but if Caleb asks, I'm telling the truth."

"I wouldn't ask you to lie for me." I try a friendly smile. "Thank you, Rachel. And . . . congratulations on your—promotion, I suppose it is?"

She does a part nod, part shrug. "Thanks."

I give her one last smile, one last glance. Then pull open her door, peek, step out. Close the door behind me, a sense of finality in the soft *click*. Stride away from the door marked *3*. Focus on the now, focus on reaching free air, reaching sunlight, reaching the outside.

Step onto the elevator, and my finger hovers over the *G*. But I hesitate. Why am I hesitating?

I need answers. That's why. Who am I? Who am I to Caleb? What does anything mean?

The conviction in Rachel's voice. Feeling like she was the only one that mattered when she was with Caleb . . . that sounds all too familiar.

Instead of *G*, my thumb stabs the *L*, for the lobby.

Descent, my stomach twisting. The doors whoosh open. I step out.

Surprised faces. "Madame X!" Hands reach for me.

I stop them with a glare. "Keep your hands to yourself. Bring me to Caleb." I feign authority.

Pretend I'm not a mess of nerves, shaking, furious, disoriented. Pretend as if everything I thought I knew hasn't just been upended.

Len parts the crowd of onlookers and security guards. A familiar face, at least. "Madame X. Gave us quite a scare. Thought maybe you'd gotten lost." Len's face is impassive, giving away nothing.

"Take me to him, Len."

"Why don't we get you back to your room? Been quite a morning; I'm sure you'd like to rest." A politely phrased command, that is.

"I don't think so, Len. Take me to the penthouse. *Now.*" My eyes are narrowed, my voice hard and cold.

Len blinks twice, lets out a short breath. Lifts his wrist to his mouth. "I've got her, sir. She wants to see you . . . no, she wants me to take her up to the penthouse. . . . Yes, sir. Got it, sir."

Len takes my upper arm, gestures to the elevator on the far right of the bank of doors. *This elevator for authorized personnel only.* A key opens the doors, the same key twisted to the *PH*. Ascent, my nerves ratcheting with each foot the elevator climbs. Len is stoic, silent.

I try to formulate thoughts, try to decipher my feelings.

Everything I thought I was going to say flees when the doors slide open at the penthouse level.

"Madame X. Please, come in." Oh, that voice. Deep as canyons, rough as sandpaper.

FOURTEEN

'm glad to see you've come to your senses." Suppressed fury, teeth clenched.

The doors slide closed behind me, and as soon I hear the elevator whine and fade, I step forward. "You *bastard*."

"Excuse me?" Disbelief, shock.

"Would you like to know where I was just now, Caleb?" I ask this in my sweetest, most innocent voice.

Dark eyes narrow in suspicion. "Where were you, X? Do enlighten me."

I am chest to chest, staring up. I seethe. "I was on the sixth floor."

"I see."

"In room three. I met a very interesting young woman who said her name was, strangely enough, Three. But then, you see, I was privileged to overhear a very . . . illuminating . . . assessment and promotion, in which she *earned* a real name."

"I don't know what you think you heard or saw, X, but it's not what you think."

"It isn't? That's strange, because it seemed very much as if what I heard was *Three* sucking your *cock*." My blood boils at the memory, at the indignity of my own unstoppable arousal. I cannot temper my fury. "I'm pretty sure what I heard was you *fucking* her. Just like you fuck *me*. Which I must say, raises some very interesting questions, Caleb."

"You saw this, did you?" This is said calmly, quietly, in far too even a voice.

"Saw it? No. *Heard* is a more accurate term, I think. I was under the bed, you see. Hiding from you, and your thugs."

Jaw muscles work. "X, there are elements to all this that you don't—that you *can't*—understand."

"Then enlighten me, Caleb!" I shout. "Because it feels like I'm just another one of the girls on the sixth floor. Except, I don't get the future they have. I'm kept in the dark, alone, day after day, serving client after client. But I'm not allowed to form a friendship with any of them. I'm not allowed relationships of any kind. Except you, when you deign to visit me, in the middle of the night. Are you *training* me, too? Like you're training girls Two through Eight? Teaching me to please a man, before you sell me to the highest bidder? Is that it? Or am I just your dirty little secret on the hidden thirteenth floor? The secret you sneak in to, late at night, to have sex in the dark with, after you've finished *training* all the other girls. Or am I—"

"You are *mine*!" comes the venomous hiss, cutting me off. Huge hard hands clutch my face, tilt my head up, brutal fingers holding tight, not allowing me to escape. "You are not like them, X. You're secret because you're special."

"I don't believe you."

"You think I'm selling those girls, X? Is that what you think?" An abrupt change of tactic. "That's not how it is, and if you'd really talked to Rachel, you'd understand that."

"You've got her brainwashed. Like you did me."

"I saved her life, like I did yours! I took her in off the streets and I sat by her as she went through meth withdrawals. I bathed her, and I held her as she shook so hard I thought she'd break a bone, and I fed her with my own hands. That's not something I'd *sell* like a bag of fucking potatoes! I'm giving her a future, and I'm not going to sit here and defend myself to someone who doesn't have the first fucking clue what I'm about!" I am abruptly released, and long legs begin pacing back and forth, impatient, angry. "You know nothing about me, X. Not the first thing."

"That's the point!" I shout. "What do you think I'm trying to—"

"And have you forgotten what I've done for *you*? Who was there for you when you woke up, alone?"

"You were, but—"

"And when you couldn't talk, couldn't walk, who wheeled you around in a wheelchair and carried a notebook everywhere, so we could communicate? Who took you to MOMA? Who showed you the *Madame X* painting? Who held you when you cried at night, *every* night, for weeks? You had no name, no past. I couldn't return your past to you, but what *did* I give you, X?"

"An identity," I whisper.

"And a *future!*" Male scent, heat, fingers gripping my waist. "I built you a life, X. I gave you the best of everything. The best clothes, the best food. An education. Skills. A job, something to keep you from going crazy with boredom! I'm not keeping you prisoner, I'm keeping you *safe!* Have you forgotten all that?"

"No, I haven't forgotten."

"I don't often bring these things up. You know that. I focus on the now, on the immediate future. I move forward. I don't dwell on what was, X. I don't expect repayment or even thanks." Finger and thumb, pinching my chin, lifting my face. Wide, deep, dark eyes penetrate mine. I cannot look away. "What I do expect, X, is *loyalty.*"

"How *dare* you?" I pull away. "Loyalty? When you've got *eight* women just sitting around waiting to *service* you at your every whim? Hoping for a glimpse of you, hoping for the next . . . *assessment*? Yet you expect loyalty from *me*?"

"Do not speak of what you do not understand. And that is something you *don't* understand."

"You show up in my room late at night, and you *fuck* me. That's all it is. Just like them. *All* of them. None of it means anything to you, does it? Not me, not them. We're just . . . receptacles for your . . . *male urges*, prettied up with fancy excuses." I fight a sob. "And you always leave and I just . . . want it to *mean* something. But you never give me anything of yourself. It feels good, sure, but when that's over, what am I left with? You said it yourself . . . I don't know the first thing about you. How *could* I? I don't even know the first thing about *myself*. But why should that matter, right? I'm just there to satisfy you when you feel like picking me."

There is a silence then, and it is a silence more full of tension and volatility than any I've ever felt.

"How can you not see, X?" This, so quiet I have to strain to hear it.

"See what, Caleb?"

"See that you're special to me. I keep you apart. I keep you for—for myself. Those girls, Rachel and the others, I've got to give them away. They're all fucking damaged, and I'm trying to make them whole. I know you don't get it, but that's what I'm trying to do. I don't sell them, I match them. All of them, each one, they'll all get matched with someone who will appreciate them, even love them. It works. I've seen it work. But in order for them to go out and be the wives they need to be, they have to feel beautiful. They need to feel their own self-worth. And when they come to me, when they enter the program, they don't."

A few paced steps brings a body I cannot ignore to stand beside me. A long index finger touches my cheekbone, traces its curve. "But you, X. You're special. I always knew you would be. When I first found you, I just knew I had to help you. And yes, I was eventually going to put you in the program. But I couldn't. I *can't*."

There is a flaw in this logic, somewhere, but I'm dizzy, lost. Heat overwhelms my senses, the sudden and unexpected rush of truth drowns out my logic. Hands span my waist, gripping with fierce need. Lips touch my earlobe. There is tenderness here, and it is so alien and so welcome.

"Why?" I whisper it. "Why can't you?"

"I can't give you away to someone else, because you're *mine*. You belong to me. I can't share you. I *won't*. You're . . ." Adam's apple bobs with a hard swallow. "You *mean* something to me, X." Behind me now.

I've never heard such things from this mouth. Never seen such intensity or openness. I am flooded with doubt.

Lips touch my throat, and sorcery subsumes me, weaves me into the dark thrall of its warp and weft.

"Don't you feel it?" Broad, powerful hands on my belly. "Don't you feel . . . *us*?"

Oh, that word. *Us*. It means belonging. I want it. I want to believe.

"Do you *feel* it, X?"

"I feel it, Caleb." And I do. I do.

I shouldn't, but I do. I am weak. So weak.

I am falling under the spell.

My thighs tremble, my belly quivers and tightens. Need pulses in me. The hard body behind me is huge and powerful and incites something hungry within me. I cannot help but lean my head back, baring my throat. One huge hand slides up my body, cups my breast, and then curls around my throat, gentle, but insistent. The other skates down my body, over my belly, down between my thighs. Cups me, there. Fingers curl and gather the edge of my dress, lift it. Inch by inch, my thighs are bared. Then my hips. Then the black sheer mesh over my privates, the skinny string around my waist.

One hand at my throat, the other at my core. One cupping, the other clutching. One clamped with enough pressure to render me tremulous with a hint of fear, the other digging under silk to find flesh, stealing my breath.

"You're *mine*, X."

I can only moan in response. Fingers curl, slip in, find me sensitive and needy, press just so to set me shaking, knees weak.

I come, quickly and hard.

But I'm not done. Oh no. While I gather my strength to stand up on my own, the fingers slip out of me and unzip trousers. My dress is up around my hips, hot breath on my ear, and now my underwear has vanished, leaving me bare from the waist down, the air cool and my damp core hot. I hear shoes kicked off, pants and belt thud on the floor. Feet nudge mine apart, and a hand pushes me forward. My bottom is bared, exposed. I drip with need. I ache. God, I ache.

The hand on my throat has not slackened its grip, and now, bent forward, that grip is all that keeps me from falling over.

A deep-throated groan, and I am filled. Deep, slow, and hard.

"You feel it, X? You feel us?"

I don't know how to fathom this. Words have never entered this equation, have never been a part of this act. "Yes, Caleb."

"Yes, what?"

"Yes, I feel it."

But it's the same, still. Despite the words, despite the palpable emotion, it's the same. I see only the floor. Feel only what I'm allowed to feel.

But then something changes. A thrust, another. I moan, stumble, shake, only the hand on my throat keeping me upright. I'm dizzy with lack of breath. I'm not being choked, but it is still limiting my oxygen.

Control.

I want more.

"Let me see you, Caleb." I say it, out loud, and I am amazed at my own daring.

The presence within me vanishes, and I am hauled upright by a sharp tug on my hair. Hands turn me. Eyes fiery, blazing, burning, dark and unknowable. "You want to see me?"

God, that body is dizzyingly perfect. All hard angles and huge muscles. Carved, cut, and perfect. I reach, and for a split second I am allowed to touch firm flesh, but only for a moment.

Hands strip the dress off me, make short work of the strapless bra, and then I'm naked.

I am pushed backward, and I trip over something.

So focused on the man in front of me, am I, that I've noticed nothing of the space around me. That does not change now. A couch, I think. I fall backward over the arm of a couch, and male heat and hardness follows me over. On my back, my legs dangle over the edge, hang into space. A broad wedge of male flesh and muscle fills that space, parting my legs. Hands grip my thighs, pull me, and then grip my hips and lift me. I can see the sharp angles and dark stubble, wild, angry eyes, thin slash of a mouth. I have a moment of breath, a moment to look, to see slablike pectorals and grooved abdomen, and then one sharp thrust drives the thick shaft into me.

I let out a gasp of surprise. It scrapes within me, fills me in a strange angle, fullness but different. Hands gripping my hips, I am lifted and pulled backward into the next thrust, which is hard and rough.

"Oh—oh God." It hurts, these hard thrusts, but they feel good as well.

"You're *mine*, X. You fucking *belong* to *me*."

Hips slam in between my thighs, and I am rocked forward, but strong hands keep me hauled taut for the next powerful drive.

Dark eyes do not leave mine. I cannot look away, not even to close my eyes as orgasmic tremors blow through me. Cannot look away, do not.

"Mine." A rocking thrust, sending me over the edge. "Say it, X. Fucking say it! Say you're mine."

I need the next thrust, need it to stay here on the far side of bliss, where everything is nothing, and nothing matters but the heat and fullness and the slight ache and burn and twinge and the grip of hands on my hips and the slam of body against body. Right now, that's all that matters. I am conditioned to need that, this moment, this now. It's all I am.

"I'm yours, Caleb." I say on a whimper, a sob.

As soon as those three words leave my lips, I feel the hot wet rush of release within me, feel that heavy body collapse forward, and I accept the weight, feel hard muscle under my hands. Stubble on my face, cheek against cheek. A moment of mutual breathing, harsh and ragged.

"X." My name, said thus, with such . . . not vulnerability, but something like it—I want to believe everything I've heard over the last few minutes.

I should say something, but what?

Abruptly, the weight is gone, and the cold statue-blank expression is in place. "I have to go."

I lie on the couch, naked and sated, confused, emotionally demolished. I watch the naked body as it is covered inch by inch with expensive clothes. Shoes, last, slipped on, tied quickly.

"Stay." I say it, hoping.

A pause. Hesitation. All I can see is a broad back, trim waist, strong legs. I cannot see the expression on that handsome, too-beautiful face. "I can't. I'll be back, though. You stay here. Don't put on clothes." A rumble, deep-chested, of some deep emotion too thick and male and tumultuous to express in mere words. "Just . . . stay. I'll be back. And X?"

"Yes, Caleb?"

"You are special to me."

I feel something in me twist and expand and bloom with hope.

Silver key, twisted. Elevator doors open, easy strides into the car, turn, and I can see a hint of the storm of emotions. There is much kept hidden, I'm realizing.

Still waters run deep, I believe the saying goes.

The elevator doors close, and I am alone.

Glance away, huge windows letting in the sunlight. Perhaps thirty minutes have passed since I entered this penthouse.

The space is mammoth. Exploring, I realize the entire uppermost floor of the building composes this penthouse, more square feet than I can count. Most of it is open space, divided here and there with half walls and paper panels, or sectioned off with long couches to create informal nooks of space. A kitchen, way off in the distance, all gleaming marble and stainless steel. A balcony, the walls themselves sliding apart and the ceiling sloping back and away out of sight to bare an outdoor area cut out of the structure of the building itself.

There, a set of elaborately painted paper panels inspired by Japanese culture, sectioning off the bedroom. Cleverly layered, three sets form a barrier so that the bedroom cannot be seen from without. A wide, low bed with a white comforter, neatly made. A nightstand on either side, empty of any effects. An actual wall forms the left side of the bedroom, and in it a doorway, leading to the bathroom.

I need a shower, I suddenly realize. I've not had one in a long time.

But when I get into the interior of the bathroom, there is a deep claw-foot tub, and I smile to myself.

I run the water hot, fill the tub. Climb in, skin scorched by the delicious heat, splashing water onto the floor. Sink down, submerged gradually until I'm immersed to my nose.

Immediately, I am assaulted by the chaos in my mind, the furious onslaught of everything I've refused to think about.

I ache between my thighs, and now that the source of that ache is gone, I feel shame, embarrassment, revulsion. Hatred. I fell for the sorcery yet again. Caleb has some way of weaving a spell over me, of making me forget all my objections and all my thoughts and everything that is logical or rational.

Caleb is a god, and gods are meddlesome . . . or so read the ancient myths. As a god, Caleb meddles with my rationality. Manipulates my body and my mind. Drowns my senses with masculine perfection, blinds me with beauty. Now, alone, I can only see the distinct parts that compose the whole, and the effect is not the same. The eyes, the mouth, the jawline; the arms, the hands, the massive musculature . . . these are Caleb. The anger, the coldness, the body heat and skillful touch, the way I can be melted down to nothing. These, too. But all together, it is more.

And I fall for it every time.

I let Caleb spin a web of words and touch, and I let—I allowed myself to be *fucked*, only a few short minutes after Rachel.

I am repulsed . . .

Yet also turned on.

The hatred is for myself.

And for Caleb. For twisting me around, for making me feel like I meant something. How can all my thoughts and protestations and objections be swept away so easily?

Did Caleb even shower after Rachel and before me? I doubt it. I didn't smell evidence of a shower. I lift up and twist, look behind me at the shower stall; it is dry, unused.

Do I have the mixed essences of Rachel and Caleb and me, all smeared together?

Disgust, and deeper than that, shame.

I fell for lies. Believed neat explanations and trite claims that I am special.

And yet, here I am, in this penthouse, in Caleb's tub, bathing, waiting.

The hot water pulls me under, makes me sweat, makes my eyes heavy.

Self-hatred is exhausting.

A noise jerks me awake, upright. I sit, splashing cool water everywhere, the ends of my hair sticking to my back. I wait, tensed, sure I heard something.

Footsteps.

"Caleb?" I sound fearful. Naked, vulnerable, disoriented from accidentally falling asleep in hot water, dizzy from overheating, I am in no shape to fend off Caleb's sorcery.

The footsteps are not Caleb's, however. Shuffled, strange. I look around for a towel, see nothing. Crossing my arms over my breasts, I crouch in the now-cool water, waiting for whoever it is to show themselves.

Shiny black shoes, first. Pants leg, waist, suit coat. It is Len, edging forward while leaning backward, walking strangely.

Ah. An arm around his throat, shiny barrel of a handgun to a temple. I recognize the hand clutching the gun, and the golden forearm wedged under Len's throat.

"X?" I hear his smooth familiar voice, first, and then he and Len are in the bathroom, Logan not quite visible behind Len.

"Logan? What—what are you doing?"

"I came to get you." The gun nudges Len's temple. "He didn't want to let me, and he lost."

I am absolutely speechless, hunched over in the tub, cowering, dripping wet, cold, shivering.

"On your knees, fucker." Logan taps Len on the back of the head with the gun barrel.

Len hesitates.

Logan presses harder, draws back the hammer. "Don't make this messy, man."

My heart stops. Len blinks, squeezes eyes shut, shoulders lift . . . and then Len slowly kneels, a heavy, lumbering motion. Logan is visible now: distressed blue jeans, scuffed black combat boots, a gray V-neck T-shirt tucked behind the buckle of his belt with the rest left untucked, sleeves stretched taut around his arms. Black hat, brim tugged low to hide his face.

"Take off your belt, shoes, and socks," Logan instructs.

Len complies, unbuckling a thin, shiny leather black dress belt, sweeping it off, then sensible black dress shoes and argyle socks.

"Lie down on your side and put your hands by your ankles."

Once again, Len complies, slowly rolling and extending wrists together. Logan, the gun still in one hand pointed at Len, shoves the end of the belt between Len's ankles and the floor, draws the tip of it over Len's ankles and wrists, feeds it deftly through the buckle, all one-handed. Tugs it taut, and then harder, until Len grunts in pain. Only then does Logan stuff the pistol in the back of his jeans. A few quick motions, and the belt is tied in a knot. One sock gets balled up and shoved in Len's mouth, the other stretched around to form what looks to be a painfully tight gag.

The whole process of tying up and gagging Len takes Logan less than thirty seconds.

"You okay?" Logan takes two quick steps to me, kneels in front of me.

His eyes are on mine, and they are the indigo of the deepest ocean blue, calm, concerned.

I nod. "Yes." But then I glance at Len, and I start shaking. "No."

"You hurt?"

"No, I'm not hurt."

He glances around, as I did, looking for a towel. He sees what I didn't, however: a cabinet hidden in the wall. He moves like liquid, retrieves a thick white towel, holds it up for me. "Come on. Easy now."

I stand up, step out. Logan's eyes remain on mine, and though I am naked in front of him, I don't feel as vulnerable as I should. He wraps the towel around my shoulders, cocooning me in it.

"Can you walk?" he asks, his voice soothing and warm in my ear.

"Yes." I take two steps, but then my knees make me a liar. I am still dizzy, disoriented. I feel sapped of strength, and thirsty. Logan's arms are around me, catching me easily. "I'm sorry. I fell asleep in the tub."

"That'll do it. You're overheated." He moves with me, twists sideways out of the door, carries me across the room in easy strides. "I need to set you down. I won't let you fall, though."

I find my feet, lean against him. I feel stronger now, but his proximity is calming, and I'm confused, tired. I never take naps, and I feel as if I've fallen through a hole in the ground into some other place. Like Alice down the rabbit hole. Nothing is right. I shouldn't be in Caleb's penthouse, and Logan shouldn't be here either.

And I certainly shouldn't feel safe in the arms of a man who just bound and gagged someone at gunpoint, using his captive's own belt and socks.

But I do.

Logan produces a key—Len's, I assume—from his pocket. Inserts and twists it to activate the elevator, which takes a moment to arrive, and then the doors open.

Logan nudges me on. "That won't hold him for long. We gotta move, if we want to pull this off."

He brings us to my floor, his arm around my waist, holding me up, helping me walk, swiftly, but carefully.

At my door, he reaches behind himself, withdraws the gun, a black piece of metal that looks small in his hand, held naturally, as if an extension of his arm. He throws my door open, an arm around me, his body in front of mine. The barrel sweeps the opening, quickly and professionally. He sits me on the couch, waves at me in a gesture to stay, and then disappears into my bedroom.

Moments later he's back, a stack of clothing in his hands, shoved at me. "You have literally *no* practical clothes, X. You don't even have practical underwear."

He's chosen a set of black Agent Provocateur lingerie, shelf bra, boy short panties. A pale blue sundress, sleeveless, knee-length, red flowers printed around the hem. Strappy silver sandals, the smallest heel in my closet.

I shrug, take the clothes. "I don't purchase my clothing."

Logan's eyes narrow, but he doesn't remark on that comment. "Get dressed," he says, brusque but with a note of kindness. "We don't have a lot of time." He turns away, shoves his hands in his back pockets, the gun barrel stuffed diagonally in his waistband at his back.

I dress quickly. It's strange how having clothes on can change one's mind-set.

Logan turns, peeks at me to make sure I'm decent, and then turns around completely. He takes my arms in his hands, eyes sincere, warm. "All right, X. I'm only going ask you this one time, and you need to think hard about your answer." His hand goes to my cheek, brushes a lock of damp hair off my cheekbone. "I can take you away from here, if that's what you want. But I'm not going to carry you out of here over my shoulder like some barbarian. You can come with me, or not. It's your choice."

I swallow hard.

This is all I know. Caleb, Len, this condo. I glance to the left: my library, the door open, all my books waiting. My window, my view.

But upstairs, that scene. Bent over, a hard hand on my throat. The sorcery of Caleb's touch, as if my will is somehow subject to such easy manipulation. So easily left alone, no explanation, just an expectation that I'd be there, waiting, ready to do as Caleb instructs.

I don't know what I want.

I don't know Logan. The unknown is scary, and when you have no past, no identity, when you've but rarely ventured out of the small realm of the familiar, everything is unknown and scary.

But Logan is giving me a *choice*.

That, in itself, is enough to sway me.

The unknown is terrifying.

An eternity of the same few things I *do* know . . . that's scarier yet.

"Take me with you, Logan." I strive to sound confident, when I am anything but.

A very small smile crosses his lips. "I hoped you'd say that." His palm lifts, cups my cheek.

That touch, so gentle, so kind, hinting at strength held at bay; I nuzzle my cheek into his palm, and my eyes flutter, close. A moment, only, but it quiets the turmoil in my soul, if only for one fleeting moment.

As my eyes are closed, I feel his breath, his lips touching mine. Sweetly, softly,

He kisses me,

and kisses me,

and kisses me.

All in a moment.

I gasp as his lips leave mine, and then his hand tangles in mine, fingers twined, and he tugs me into motion. "Come on, honey. Time to go."

And he takes me away from everything I know.

FIFTEEN

On the elevator, Logan tugs his cap off his head and fits it onto mine, taps the brim lower over my face. He scrubs a hand through his hair, making a mess of it, the blond locks tangled. But even thus, with his hair in a snarl, he's so sexy my breath comes short at the sight of him.

"We're just gonna walk right out of here, okay? Right out the front door." He slips an arm around my waist, digs his other hand into his pocket, produces his cell phone and hands it to me. "Keep your head down. Pretend like you're engrossed in Facebook or something, yeah? Just act like you can't be bothered to look up."

I take the device in my hands. It's a big glossy black rectangle in a rubber case, with a single round button at the bottom. Logan presses the button with his thumb and the screen turns on, showing Logan with a large chocolate-brown dog, its tongue lolling out. He leaves his thumb on the button for another second, and the screen changes, showing rows of little icons in different colors with various logos. Behind the rows of icons is a stunning photograph of a spiral galaxy.

I have no clue what to do. I don't own a cell phone and have no knowledge of how to use one, so it's likely I've never owned one, either.

I just stare at the screen for a moment, and then glance up at Logan. "I don't know what to do."

He frowns down at me. "What do you mean?"

I lift the phone in gesture. "With this. I've never owned a cell phone."

His eyebrows rise. "You're just full of surprises, aren't you?" He touches the screen with his index finger and swipes left, pulling the screen full of little icons to the right. He finds one icon, taps it, and it expands to reveal a hidden set of icons; he taps one. "Tetris. It's easy. Just fit the little pieces so they make a straight line across. Tap them, and they'll rotate. It's like a moving puzzle."

A couple more taps, and the screen resolves into something like graph paper, lines marking off the screen into tiny squares. A bright yellow square appears, dropping slowly from the top of the screen to the bottom.

By the time the elevator reaches the lobby, I understand the basic object of the game, and I'm engrossed. I intentionally allow myself to become absorbed into forcing the various shapes to fit with others so the line vanishes. Otherwise, I'd be terrified. I *am* terrified; I'm just pretending, even to myself, that I'm not. A video game can't erase my panic at leaving the condo, my fear of being discovered and returned, and punished.

I'm leaving.

With Logan.

I'm leaving *everything* I know, with a man I've met twice.

And I'm playing a video game.

I could laugh from the absurdity of it all.

Logan's arm slides more tightly around my waist, and I lean into him, let him guide me. I keep my focus on the cell phone in my hands, tapping at the squares with both thumbs as I've seen my clients and Caleb do on numerous occasions. Pretending like I'm doing something more important on the device than playing a game.

I am tensed, barely breathing, heart hammering; I expect a hue and cry at every step. I hear voices, faint music, the *ding* of the elevators reaching the lobby and opening. I hear the doors ahead open, letting in a brief slice of the noise from outside, and then they close, returning stifling quiet to the lobby.

I have never seen the lobby of this building before, the few times I've left having entered and exited via the garage, and then always under heavy guard, hustled from the car to the elevator and vice versa as quickly as possible. I want to look around, but I don't. I see the floor underfoot, shiny black squares of marble veined with streaks of gold.

I feel Logan's torso twist and shift as he leads me through the doors, heavy slabs of glass with silver handles. Road noise, blaring horns, engines, squealing brakes. The old panic surfaces, and now my heart rate increases to a dangerous speed, thumping so hard in my chest that it's physically painful. My breath leaves me, my lungs frozen. I can't blink, and my legs won't move.

These panic attacks are why I stayed in Caleb's tower for so long.

Logan drags me, essentially, his cell phone dangling from my fingers.

"You okay, honey?" His voice in my ear, buzzing, warm.

I try to force oxygen in, and sort of succeed, enough to rasp out an answer. "Panic . . . attack."

A man in a suit sweeps past me, accidentally slamming his shoulder against mine, not slowing to even glance at me. I shrink away, my shoulder slamming against the building, and I feel like I'm trying to huddle into the stone, collapsing to my knees. Someone else passes, a woman scantily clad in shorts that barely cover her buttocks and a tank top that leaves little of her cleavage to the imagination; she glares at me, disgust and contempt in her gaze, as if I've personally wronged her somehow. I watch her, stare at her, unable to look away. Has she never witnessed a panic attack before? Why would someone I've never met look at me with such hate?

"X, you gotta pull it together, sweetie. I've got you. No one's gonna hurt you. You're safe with me. You just need to walk two blocks with me, okay?" He's kneeling in front of me, hands on my face. I blink, and his deep, deep blue eyes fix on mine. "That's it. Look at me. You're fine. You're okay. Breathe for me, all right? Deep breath in, ready?"

I nod, grip his forearms with desperate fingers, focus on his blueblueblue eyes, drag in a lungful of hot Manhattan summer air.

He smiles, his face kind and patient, his eyes not wavering from mine. "Good, honey. Good. Another. With me, okay? Deep breath in through the nose, out through the mouth. Keep it going. Good. Just keep your eyes on mine."

I'm breathing, staring up at him, and my heart rate slows a little. Another moment or two of deep breathing, and then he's tugging me to my feet, hand tangling in mine. I've got his cell phone in a death grip in the other hand, squeezing so hard now my fingers hurt. I lean into him, his hard bulk at my side reassuring, his scent on his T-shirt filling my nostrils, fabric softener and the faint whiff of a cigarette. His stride is loose and easy and unhurried, although I notice him glancing in the windows as we pass them, and then when we stop at a red light, he angles to face me, adjusting his hat on my head, but his gaze is down the sidewalk behind us, watching for pursuit.

"I think we're clear," he murmurs to me, feathering fingers through my loose, damp hair, tossing it back over my shoulders. "My truck is close. Half a block, not even that. Feeling any better?"

I'm still terrified beyond all reason, but I'm not in the grip of the panic attack anymore. I jerk my chin in a brief nod. "I'm fine."

He grins at me, squeezes my waist with his arm. "That's my girl. You're doing great."

He's so calm. Doesn't he understand what Caleb is capable of?

His girl? I'm his girl? Or is that just an expression? With Logan, it's hard to tell.

He pulls me around a corner, down a narrow cross street jammed with parked delivery trucks, half the width of the street blocked off by orange and white construction barriers. There's a boxy silver SUV parked between a white produce delivery truck and a tall black van. Logan pulls me to the SUV, helps me up and into the passenger seat. I get a whiff of his scent again, and I inhale, find some strange calm in it as he reaches across me to click the seat belt into place.

We're in motion within seconds, reversing out of the parking spot, accelerating and turning back onto the main road. The car smells like leather and vanilla. He turns at random, I think, left here, right there, three lefts, straight for several blocks, and then another right, his eyes watching his mirrors as much as the traffic ahead.

"I don't see any signs we're being followed," he says to me, a triumphant grin on his face. "We did it, X! You were awesome!"

"Awesome? I had a panic attack as soon as we walked out, Logan. I'm still feeling sick. Nothing feels right. I don't know what I'm doing, I don't know what's happening. Half of me feels like I just made the biggest mistake of my life, and the other half is so relieved I could cry."

"You're allowed to feel however you feel. We'll take everything slow, all right? What do you want to do first?"

I shrug. "I don't know. I don't know anything, Logan."

He nods. "That's fine, too. Just let me take care of everything, then, okay? You think of anything you want, just say it."

He presses a circular knob on the console between us, and loud music fills the air, cacophonous, angry-sounding, a man's voice screaming in rage. I cringe against the door, immediately tensed and confused by the volume and the raw hatred in the singer's voice. Singer . . . a word I'm not sure applies to what I'm hearing, exactly. Logan twists the knob, and the volume lowers to a tolerable level, and then he taps another button, twists, presses the knob, and the music changes, now all drums and keyboard and a more palatable female voice singing.

"Sorry," Logan says. "I suppose Slipknot is probably not your thing."

"Slipknot?"

"Yeah. Heavy metal." He glances at me. "Let me take a wild guess here and say that you don't know what kind of music you like, either?"

"You would be guessing correctly," I admit.

"What *do* you know you like?"

I sigh. "Very little. I like books, I guess I can say that with confidence. Old books, signed first editions, rare versions. Fiction of all kinds."

Logan is quiet for a moment. The song changes, something about uptown funk, although what that is I couldn't say. It's catchy, though, and I find myself bobbing my head to the rhythm.

"If you had to say there was one thing you wanted right now more than anything, what would it be?"

"A shower. A long, hot shower. Comfortable clothes. And then something to eat." I pause for a moment, and then blurt what feels like a secret. "Unhealthy food. Something greasy and satisfying."

Logan smiles at me. "Easy enough. First stop, then, is Macy's."

I didn't realize how wide my eyes could go until Logan led me on a dizzying tour of Macy's department store. I was thoroughly lost within seconds, a few turns down one aisle and then another and I would have been hard-pressed to find my way out. Not that I would have minded, I think. I could have wandered endlessly, flipped through rack after rack of clothes, content to simply look, to simply see all the various things one could buy. Logan was ceaselessly vigilant, seemingly casual as he guided me from area to area, pretending to glance at a shirt or a dress while watching in every direction at the same time.

I choose plain, comfortable clothes: a pair of jeans, a shirt, undergarments, a pair of slip-on ballet flats. I don't try anything on, merely guessing at sizes. Logan seems relieved when we're back in his vehicle, and now he drives a less circuitous route across Manhattan to a quiet, narrow, tree-lined street with low brownstone houses connected to each other in a long row. He parks his truck beside a tree, which is ringed in brick, small lights buried in the mulch at the base of the tree. Three steps up, a key turned in a lock, and then there's a loud beeping noise coming from a white panel on the wall just inside the door. Logan presses a series of numbered buttons, and the beeping stops.

"Disarmed," a disembodied, electronic, vaguely female voice says.

There's a wild, ceaseless barking coming from behind a door somewhere. Logan closes the door behind me, twists the knob to engage the deadbolt. "Come on in," he says. "I've gotta go let Cocoa out of her room. She's friendly, I promise. Exuberant in her welcomes, but friendly."

I don't have time to even panic before Logan vanishes down the hallway, opens a door, and the barking grows louder, louder, and then there's a brown blur and the scrabble of sharp claws on hardwood.

"Cocoa, down, girl!" Logan shouts, but it's too late.

A heavy warm wiggling barking licking mass slams into me, huge bear paws on my shoulders, a tongue slapping wetly on my face, and the dog's weight plows me backward, topples me off balance, and then I'm on the ground, curled into a tight ball, fighting tears, fending off a crazy tongue, a paw on my shoulder, a cold nose shoving under my hands to get at my face.

I don't know whether to laugh or cry.

I hear Logan laughing.

"Get her off me, Logan," I manage to say, past the canine tongue that seems to be trying to see what I ate last via my throat, and how recently I've blown my nose via tongue-examination of my nostrils.

"Cocoa, *sit*." Logan's voice is hard, and sharp.

Immediately, the huge brown animal—which I recognize from Logan's cell phone screen—stops licking me and sits on her haunches, whining in her throat.

"X, say hello to Cocoa." He kneels down beside me as I lever myself to a sitting position on the floor, wiping at my face. "Tell her to shake, X."

I stare at the dog suspiciously. "Will she try to eat me again?"

Logan laughs. "Eat you? She was just saying hi, in crazy puppy language."

I give him side-eye. "Puppy? She's the size of a grizzly bear, Logan."

"She's barely a year old, and not even eighty pounds yet." He cuffs her ear affectionately, rubbing in circles with his thumb. "She's a good girl, aren't you, Cocoa?"

I give my still-damp face one last wipe with my forearm, and then twist on my backside so I'm facing the dog. "Shake, Cocoa."

The dog lifts her paw, a goofy dog grin on her face. I take her paw and shake it as I would a man's hand, and she barks.

"Tell her *good girl*," Logan instructs.

"Good girl, Cocoa," I say, and the dog immediately launches herself at me, tongue first. This time, I try what Logan did, making my voice sharp and hard. "Sit, Cocoa."

"See?" Logan says, grabbing the dog around the neck and hauling her against his chest, letting her lick his chin, laughing. "She's a good girl."

Clearly, the man loves his dog. Something about this makes my heart twist, and melt. I don't know what to do with myself as I watch Logan rub, pet, and kiss his dog as if she were a beloved child. Other than try not to melt, that is.

Finally, Logan stands up, wipes his face. "Gotta go outside, Cocoa?"

Cocoa barks and, with a clicking scrabble of claws, tears across the house to a back door and plants her haunches on the gleaming hardwood, thick tail flailing wildly, her head swiveling between Logan and the door. Logan pulls the sliding glass door aside, and Cocoa lunges through the opening as soon as it's wide enough to fit her bulk. The outdoor space—which I hadn't realized existed in Manhattan—is small but elaborate and beautiful. A small terrace of cobblestone, a round wrought-iron table with four chairs, a gleaming silver grill, and a plot of green grass maybe a dozen steps across, flowering bushes lining the back fence. Logan follows Cocoa out, and I follow him; we stand together, watching the dog prance around happily, circle three times, and then squat to do her business.

It's quiet here. Even in the middle of the day, there is no babel of traffic sounds, no horns or grinding engines or sirens.

"This isn't where I imagined you living," I say, apropos of nothing.

"Expected some downtown high-rise, probably? Big views and lots of black marble?" He shoves a hand in his hip pocket, scraping at the cobblestone with his boot toe.

I nod. "Pretty much."

"I had that, for a while. I hated it." He shrugs. "Found this place, kind of by accident. Bought it, reno'd it myself, and adopted Cocoa. Having somewhere quiet to go, at the end of the day? It's priceless. Having somewhere outside with some green and some privacy? Even more so. And Cocoa to keep me company . . . can't get any better." He glances at me. "Well, it *could*, but that'll happen in time. I hope."

Is he talking about me? He's looking at me as if he might be. But I don't know what to make of that, what to say to it, how to process it. This is unfathomable to me. A dog, a yard, peace and quiet. No view of the city, no endless parade of stories to invent, crossing thirteen stories beneath me. No expectations on my time. Choosing my own clothing. Discovering what I like . . .

It's all too much. I'm choking on possibilities. I turn away, yank the glass door open, dart through, find the hallway and the open door showing me the bathroom. I don't even bother closing the door behind me, I just collapse onto the lid of the toilet, face in my hands. My shoulders heave, and I feel tears sliding down.

I don't know why I'm crying, but I can't stop it.

I jump a mile into the air when I feel a cold nose touch my cheek. She doesn't lick me or bark or jump on me, she just lays her chin on my knee. I laugh through my tears at her expression, wide dark eyes gazing at me, as if she could somehow commiserate, as if she's trying to communicate to me. Comforting me with her presence.

And it works.

I bury my fingers in her soft, silky, short, chocolate-brown fur, scratch her floppy ears, pet her thick neck.

"See what I mean?" Logan's voice, from the doorway. "There's a reason we call dogs 'man's best friend.' This is why."

I sniffle and feel a fresh wave of tears flow over me, hide my face against Cocoa's shoulder and cry on her; her only reaction is to put her chin on my shoulder and very gently lick the lobe of my ear.

Eventually, it passes. I look up, and Logan is sitting on the floor beside me, legs stretched out, back against the wall.

"I'm sorry," I murmur, wiping my face. "I don't know why—"

"Stop," he interrupts. "You don't have to apologize. I know—I get the feeling you've been through a lot. You don't have to tell me anything, I just . . . I'm here to help, okay?"

I struggle for calm, my emotions still running on high, turbulent and mixed up. "Why, Logan? You don't know anything about me. Why do you want to help me?" I wipe at my eyes again. "You just made yourself an enemy of Caleb. And for what?"

He moves to kneel in front of me, nudges the bill of his hat up out of my face. "Don't you worry about him. Okay? Caleb is not your problem anymore. He's mine." His fingers brush over my cheekbones. "As for why I'm doing this? I wish I could say it was pure altruism, rescuing the damsel in distress because I'm just that kind of knight in shining armor. I can't say that, though."

I have to focus on blinking, on breathing, on not letting myself dive forward and inhale his scent and feel his muscles under my hands and taste his tongue and lips and neck. Instead, I just stare at him, and hold myself utterly still. "Why not?"

"Because the truth is, I have far more selfish motivation. I mean, yeah, you didn't belong there, and I just . . . I *had* to get you out. But . . . getting you away from Caleb's cameras and security gorillas . . . getting you alone . . ."

"You wanted me alone?" Why is *that* the only thing I'm seizing on?

"Yeah. I did."

"We're alone now." I've whispered it, my voice dropping to nothing at all, a tiny sound, a breath. His face seems closer, and I can smell him now, and feel his hands on my thighs.

"Yeah," Logan says, his voice not much louder than my own. "That's true."

But then Cocoa barks, a happy *ruff*, as if she too wants to be in on the moment.

Logan stands up. He's breathing heavily, brows lowered, eyes intent. He gestures at the glassed-in shower. "You wanted a shower. I don't have any girly shower stuff, unfortunately, but you can get clean, at least." He pats his thigh, and Cocoa leaves my side to sit at his, tongue lolling out. "I'm going to take Cocoa on a little walk, give you some privacy, okay? I'll lock up and arm the alarm when I leave. Towels and washcloths under the sink. We can go get some lunch whenever you're ready."

He slaps the post of the door, offering me a quick smile. And then he's gone. I hear something jingling, hear claws on the floor, the door open, beeping of the alarm as he enters the code. Then the door closes, and I'm alone.

For the first time that I can remember, I am truly, completely alone.

There are no cameras watching my every move, no hidden microphones recording my every sound. No security waiting somewhere, should I try to leave on my own. No Len, no Thomas . . .

No Caleb.

I have a flash of memory, Caleb's eyes on mine, dark and intense with the fury of orgasm. Hands on me, a moment of something like connection. Face-to-face, for the one and only time.

Had Caleb stayed, what could have been? There is much behind those nearly black eyes, a world of emotion, a world of thoughts indecipherable and deep. Caleb admitted things to me, truths I never thought to hear.

But Caleb walked away.

And now I'm alone.

When showering . . . before . . . I would always disrobe in the bathroom, and dress there as well. If there was any room in that condo that I might have had any privacy, it would have been the bathroom. And I didn't like the feeling of being watched as I did something so private and personal as change.

But now, I can do whatever I want.

I am *alone*.

It feels like the greatest freedom to walk out into the living room, to examine the huge TV and the brown microfiber couch, the stereo, the artwork on the walls ranging from band posters to classic paintings—to do so alone, unobserved. The silence is thick, blissful. The sense of isolation is lovely.

There is a staircase, a landing. On the wall facing the rising stairs is a painting.

Starry Night, by Van Gogh.

I wonder if it means something personal to him, as it does to me, or if it's just another piece of art?

The kitchen is small, clean, inviting. A small dining room, a round table with two chairs, one pulled out as if recently sat in. A pile of magazines and envelopes, a set of keys on a ring. *Logan Ryder*, an envelope says, with an address.

A thought seizes me as I stand in the kitchen; before I can second-guess myself, I reach up behind my back, tug down the zipper of my dress. My heart hammers in my throat. I shrug out of the garment, let it pool to the floor. Bra, and then underwear. I'm naked now, in Logan's kitchen. There's the sliding glass door, the backyard, the high wall. Trees beyond, but no buildings, no one to see unless it's a helicopter flying overhead.

Daring, a little afraid, nervous, I step outside, just for the thrill of it.

I'm outside, totally nude.

I want to dance and scream in joy at the feeling, the freedom. I dare a half dozen steps out into the yard, look around me at the fence rising a dozen feet over my head, blocking my view and that of the neighbors.

And then I hear a voice from behind the fence to my left, and I dart back inside, shaking. I waste no more time getting into the shower, the water just a little too hot. There's a bottle of two-in-one shampoo and conditioner and a bar of soap; I smile to myself as I lather my hair and scrub at my scalp, remembering Logan's claim to not have any "girly shower stuff."

I take a long, long time scrubbing my body. Scrubbing the memory of Caleb off me. Trying to scrub away a lingering thought, a faint, almost guilty wish, a wondering at what could have been, had Caleb stayed.

I scrub that wish away until my skin feels raw. Caleb didn't stay; I was taken, used to sate some kind of need, and then left alone yet again, as always.

But I cannot, no matter how I try, pretend there wasn't a moment, however fleeting, when Caleb's eyes met mine and a moment of intimacy existed. That happened. It was real. I know I didn't imagine it. As quickly as it occurred, however, Caleb squashed it like an offensive bug.

And that, more than anything else, helped prompt my desire to escape. I dared hope for intimacy, for a glimpse of who Caleb is. A glimpse of the man, rather than the figure, the master, the *owner*. But such a hope was—and always will be, I now believe—in vain.

I twist the hot-water knob until my skin tingles with the heat, as if I could scald the hurt away.

Even after all I've endured, my weakness for Caleb remains. I fear him, yet I need him.

And I *hate* myself for it.

I am here, I think, to try to scour away that need. To replace it, perhaps, with need for someone else.

I am drawn to Logan, hypnotized by him, mesmerized, entranced, enthralled.

He is so kind. So thoughtful.

So warm.

But beneath that is a core of ice and steel; behind his indigo eyes lurks the cunning of a predator, I sometimes think, the ferocity of a warrior.

And that, as much as I fear it, also makes me feel safe.

Eventually I know I can linger in the shower no longer, and I turn the water off, find a thick rust-red towel folded into neat thirds under the sink, wrap it around my tingling body. Wrap another around my head to sop up some of the water; my hair is so thick that without a blow dryer, it will be damp for hours. I peek my head out of the bathroom and sense that I'm still alone. I find the bag with my new clothes in it by the front door. I have it in my hand, and at that moment, the deadbolt knob twists, the door swings in toward me, and my heart leaps into my throat.

BEEPBEEPEBEEPBEEP

Cocoa leaps at me, barking, puts wet paws on my bare shoulders. Utter chaos ensues for a wild moment.

Logan is shoving at Cocoa, who is blocking the doorway, which in turn has me stumbling backward. Beyond Logan, rain is sluicing down in hammering bucketfuls, so thick it obscures my view of the street beyond.

The alarm is beeping faster and faster, and Cocoa is on top of me, barking, tail wagging, smearing muddy paw prints on me and on the towel, and her claws catch in the cotton of the towel and loosen it, threatening to tug it away. Logan steps over Cocoa, stabbing at the alarm panel to disarm it, then slamming the door closed.

I shove Cocoa away with one hand, trying to stand up while holding the towel in place with the other.

Logan is soaked to the bone, his gray T-shirt all but see-through now, sticking to abs so grooved and ridged and hard they could be carved from stone, sticking to his lean upper body, hard, chiseled pectorals, broad shoulders. His hair is lank and stringy and sticking to his cheeks and chin.

Rainwater puddles at his feet, and his eyes are hot blue orbs, locked on mine. Neither of us moves. I am not breathing.

The towel covering my torso is hanging loose around me, held up only by one of my hands, the other still fending off Cocoa's muddy and exuberant greetings.

"Cocoa . . . *sit*." His voice is faint, as if he has to remember how to speak. "Stay, Cocoa."

The dog sits . . . on my feet. Wet fur, on my feet. She stinks of wet dog, a pungent smell.

I unwind the towel wrapped in a turban around my hair and hand it to Logan, who, without looking away from me, kneels beside his dog, unclips her leash, and wipes her down carefully and lovingly, each one of her paws, her legs, her long body, her floppy ears, over and over until she's wiggling to get free.

"Go to your room, Cocoa. Go lie down." His voice is still faint, and he's still staring at me, and I can't move, paralyzed somehow by the superheated blue of Logan's gaze.

Cocoa barks once, and then trots into her room.

My back is to the wall, cold against my bare spine. I need to cover myself, but I can't.

Logan is in front of me, standing tall and broad mere inches away, and he's wet, too, but now he's so warm he feels like he could be steaming. I smell him, man-scent as pungent as wet dog.

He lifts his shirt, peels it off, baring a torso that is a sculpted wonder of lean, corded muscle. He isn't a mammoth bear of a man, not like the only other male body I've seen in this state of undress. Clad in those faded blue jeans and nothing else, he is tall, over six feet, but he is a man of razor sharpness, each muscle defined as if cut into his body, each muscle lean and hard. He has no spare flesh or muscle, nothing extra, nothing unneeded. He is all hard lines and deeply etched grooves. There are scars, too. Thin white lines crisscrossing his left pectoral, his right bicep, and left forearm high up near the elbow. Two round puckered scars on his right shoulder, one in the meat of his muscle, the other higher up on the collarbone, and a third lower down, just beneath his ribs. There are tattoos coloring the skin on his shoulder, a nearly indecipherable jumble of images on his left arm from collarbone to just above the elbow, so that they'd be all but hidden if he wore a short-sleeve shirt. I see cartoon pinup girls and flames and a Jolly Roger made of a grinning skull and crossed assault rifles and initials in Old English lettering nearly hidden in a snarl of barbed wire, phrases I can't quite make out in the same lettering. The whole tangle of images begins just above his elbow, designed as if to grow out of a tree whose roots wrap around his bicep, the jumble of images and designs forming the trunk, and the branches extending in skeletal fingers across his collarbone and back toward his shoulder blades.

My fingers itch to trace the images, to sort them and name them and find out their stories.

His shirt plops to the floor, a wet sound. Water streams in rivulets down his face, over his neck and shoulders, and follows the line of his sternum, over his diaphragm, and into the deeply etched grooves of his abdomen.

"You got mud on you," he murmurs, his voice a smooth basso ribbon sliding over me. His fingers trace across the upper slope of my breast, through the muddy paw print.

"Well, I *was* clean," I say, for lack of anything better.

"Now we'll have to fight over the shower."

"You go. This will wipe off."

He reaches down between us, takes the end corner of the towel, lifts it, and wipes at the mud until my skin is clean again. "There. Good as new."

Of course, in lifting the towel, he bared a significant portion of my bare skin, from knee to belly. The air is cold on my skin, and I'm trembling. Or maybe it's Logan making me tremble.

One hand pressed to my chest, keeping me at least nominally covered, I mirror his action, lifting a corner of the towel and using it to wipe at the droplets of water on his chest.

How easy it would be to drop the towel. Some part of me wants to, feels daring enough to risk it. To let him see me. To let him touch me, skin to bare skin.

I wonder if he can read my mind: His hand steals around my back, tugs me to him. I stumble, and willingly fall against him, cheek to chest. Heartbeat, like a drum: *Bumpbump—bumpbump—bumpbump*. His flesh is warm, smooth, firm, damp. My cheek sticks to his chest, but I have no desire to pull away. My hands are on his chest, palms flat against his skin on either side of my head. My left palm is on the right side of his chest, and I can feel the puckered scars there. Bullet wounds, is my guess. My fingertips touch the scars, trace them gently.

Logan murmurs in my ear. "Those weren't as bad as they look. Hit meat and bone, mostly." He takes my hand, moves it down so my fingers touch the wound just beneath his rib cage. "This one nearly got me. Rotated home, took me damn near six months to recover. Nicked the bottom of my lung, narrowly missed a few other important bits."

Who is this crazy woman inhabiting my body? Not me, not the self I'm accustomed to being. This woman, she is wild, daring. She clutches his ribs with both hands, feeling thick slabs of muscle under sensitive, exploring fingertips. This woman, this me, this X? Her lips touch skin. Feather over tattoos, cross the centerline of his sternum, kiss, kiss, kiss, and touch those wicked scars. My lips, his skin; explosive chemistry. Delicate touch, just a breath, motion across flesh, but enough to set me ablaze. I feel him shake under my hands, under my mouth. I kiss each scar. I don't know why. Each long-healed slice on his skin—"Close encounters of the shrapnel kind," he murmurs—a kiss. A burn mark on his forearm, shiny, too smooth, rippled—"Got too close to a hot rifle barrel," he whispers in explanation—kissed.

Every time my lips touch his skin, he inhales sharply, as if my mouth is afire, as if my tongue is white-hot, scorching his flesh.

Bare skin under my hands, hard muscle . . . I'm addicted. Drunk with him. I pause the skein of kisses, lips on his clavicle, and just touch. Fingers on his shoulder blades, tracing the bright ink I can see with eyes closed, even, down low to explore his waist above denim, slipping palms up sides to stutter fingertips over ribs. A poem of touch, a song of kisses.

"X, you gotta stop." His voice is tense, wired, slow with precision.

"Why?" I've never felt such need, felt such pleasure in merely touching. I revel in being allowed to touch as I wish, no guidance, no commands, no instructions. Only touching as I wish, mouth moving of its own volition, my small hands exploring a work of art.

"Because now isn't the time." He grabs my left hand, gathers my right into the same gentle grip, brushes my hair out of my face with his empty hand. "And you keep this up, I'll forget that."

"What isn't it the time or place for?" I look up as I ask this, meet his eyes.

"For what I want to do with you, and how long it's going to take." Oh, the promise in those eyes, those words.

I shiver. "Oh."

"Yeah." He draws a deep breath, as if for courage.

His eyes roam my face, as if memorizing. My hands still pinioned in the gentle circle of his left hand, his right nudges my chin up, tilting my face up to his, the pad of his thumb brushing my cheek and then skating over my forehead, sliding a lock of hair away.

"Damn it," he murmurs,

and kisses me,

and kisses me,

and kisses me.

Breathless, dizzy, heart madly beating, lungs seizing, hands fluttering and clutching, I kiss him in return.

A kiss. Such a simple thing. Two mouths meeting. Lips touching, a little moist, tender yet firm, hungry yet tentative. Hands reach, dare closer to erogenous samples of skin. So simple. Yet so complex, so fraught with meaning. Pulsing with questions, throbbing with possibility.

Does he kiss me to begin something else, something more?

Do I kiss him to beg for more?

Can we kiss to merely kiss, to find each other's fathom, to plumb the depths of desire without the vulnerability of shared nakedness?

I break his hold on my wrists. Reach up, snake both arms around his strong neck, cling to him. Press up against him. We pause for breath, lips touching but not locked, gasping, eyes open and seeing one another from so close that features blur. His eyes are blue like the deepest ocean, the shade of night just past twilight when the sun has sunk and stars do not yet pierce the sky. His hands find my waist, find skin—all there is to find of me is bare flesh, for I am naked, and unashamed, and full of hunger.

The floor falls away, and my legs wrap around the hard wedge of his hips. The taut firmness of his belly is hot against my bare core. He spins, presses my spine to the window. His hands cup my naked bottom, keeping me aloft effortlessly, his tongue delves into my mouth, steals my sense and my breath, steals my will, steals my desire to know anything but this, but his kiss, but this moment.

I clutch his face, palms to faint stubble. I am confident in his hold on me. Given over to him. Lost to this. Anything could happen, and I would want it, as long as it is with Logan Ryder.

I don't know why.

I just know he possesses some secret power over me, and I cannot resist it.

One hand now holds me up, a strong forearm barred beneath me, his other hand sliding up my spine, smoothing over skin, up and up, finding my neck, squeezing, massaging, kneading, and then back down. Soothing, yet arousing. I want to relax into him, and yet I want to devour him. My hands, too, seek more, explore, reach, find. Shoulders, hard and round. Ribs, waist. Broad back, hot skin. Up into his hair, under the damp, wavy locks.

I feel him gather my thick hair into a fist, gripping at the base of my skull, tilt my head back so I'm staring up at him—or I would be were my eyes open—and his kiss plunges me into oblivion. The hold on my hair is delicious. Firm, yet gentle. I cannot break away, should I even want to.

I do not.

I wish only to be kissed, and to eagerly press my lips up to his and taste his tongue in my mouth and clutch and cling to the endless maze of muscle and taut flesh.

How long passes thus? Minutes? Moments? Hours?

I once read in an old text that a moment is one-fortieth of an hour. Perhaps a million moments pass, and I count each one, sear each moment and stamp each moment onto my mind, into my memory. I do not want to ever forget this experience with Logan, should I get nothing else with him.

A myriad of moments.

His hands, both of them once again on my bare bottom, holding, cupping, gently squeezing, then his hand on my cheek, rough, hard, callused, strong, gentle as the sweep of a downy feather across skin. His lips, scouring mine, tilting, nipping, his teeth catching my lip, upper and then lower. The bite of his teeth on my lower lip is a drug, the tug, tug, tug of his teeth an aphrodisiac.

I feel my lower lip pulled away, feel his breath and his tongue, and I am turned into a wildling.

I make a sound in my throat, a noise I cannot describe as anything but a growl.

But then, just when I am contemplating how to reach down between us and free the button on his jeans and grasp his hardness in my hands, Logan sets me down and backs away.

I am utterly naked, the towel dropped and forgotten.

A tableau: me, nude, nipples hardening under his ravenous gaze, desire pooling at my core in dripping slick heat, his zipper bulging, a vein in his neck pulsing, fists clenching and releasing, chest heaving, my breasts rising and falling with my own crazed breath. A moment, where I know he is mere moments away from assaulting me, and I would not stop him, would only encourage him and moan for him and beg him for more.

"Jesus, X." He rubs his jaw with a palm. "You make me fucking crazy." He sounds shaken.

I cannot stand upright, can only lean weak-kneed back against the wall. "I have to know what you want from me, Logan." The words tumble out unbidden.

He tilts his head and frowns. "What I want from you?" He kneels, gathers the towel in his hands, presses it to my chest, covering me.

I am not unaware of a certain reluctance in him as he does so.

I struggle to stay upright, lock my knees, scrape trembling hands through my hair. "I don't trust myself with you. You make me . . . wild. But my situation, it's not . . . I'm not safe. And I need to know what you want. What's happening. I—I—"

He moves like lightning, his hands somehow instantly gripping my upper biceps gently, thumbs tracing circles. "You can trust me, X."

"I want to."

"But?"

"But how do I know? I can't even breathe when I'm with you. It doesn't make any sense. I don't recognize myself, and everything is scary enough as it is without feeling like I'm going to—I don't know. Lose myself. I barely have anything to lose, but even that is . . . at risk."

"I'm not sure I'm following."

I shake my head, pull out of his grip, pace away. "I'm not making any sense. Which is unlike me."

He follows me but doesn't grab hold again. "You know, I've noticed something."

"What's that, Logan?"

"You are very adept at avoiding talking about yourself."

I shrug. "There's not much to say about myself." This, at least, is a truth.

"There's so much to who you are, it's impossible to even know where to start."

I frown. "You make it seem like I'm complicated."

"Complexity, thy name is X." He's close to me again, the damp, cool towel the only barrier between our bodies. I can't help but rest my forehead against his chest.

"That's not true," I protest.

"Then what's your favorite color?"

"I don't know."

"Favorite poet?"

"E. E. Cummings."

"Favorite food?" His voice is in my ear. Rumbling, buzzing, intimate and familiar.

"I don't know."

"Favorite band?"

"I don't know." Instinctively, I turn away from the scrutiny of his gaze, except the towel is only loosely draped against my front, so I now bare my back to him. I feel his eyes on me, on the curve of my spine and the swelling bubble of my backside. "I don't know anything about myself, Logan. I don't know. Okay? I'm not complicated, I'm . . . incomplete."

"Babe. You're complex." His palms skate over my back, both of them moving in soothing circles. "It's not a bad thing. It makes you mysterious. I get the feeling a man could spend a lifetime getting to know you and still not unwrap all your layers."

"You barely know me."

"Exactly." A pause. Fingers in my hair, which is still damp. The intimacy of this moment makes my heart ache. "The only name I've got for you is X. I know you're of Spanish descent. I know you work for Caleb Indigo, and you're hard as hell to find, even for one of Caleb's girls. And *that* is saying something."

Logan has both of his hands on my hips now, holding me pressed back against him, my spine to his chest, my buttocks curved against the rough scratch of denim. I feel the bulge of his erection behind the zipper. I move just so, and were he naked as well—I inhale sharply and push away that need, that desire, that thought.

But we are puzzle pieces, he and I. How else might we fit perfectly together?

I tremble at the possibilities roiling in the dark depths of my basest desires.

"What is your real name?"

Anger, sudden and hot. "I *told* you my real name, damn it!" I try to pull away, but he won't let me. For the first time since I've known him, I get a tiny taste of his real strength.

He holds me in place with his hands on my hips, his grip unbreakable but still gentle and careful.

He is implacable.

"The hell it is!" He's angry, too. "You're trying to tell me your real, *legal* name is Madame X?"

"Yes!"

"Bullshit. I can take a lot on faith, honey, but I won't tolerate being lied to, or having the truth kept from me." His voice is a low growl, colder than I thought he could sound. Here is the man who has killed, the man who was once a criminal.

"I'm not lying." I sound small, and sad, and defeated.

His hands turn me. Tilt my face up to his. "Then what is your name?"

"My name is Madame X. I am named after the painting by John Singer Sargent." I shrug away from him, all of my fire tamped and doused now. Something stings my eyes. Something wet. Why am I crying? I don't know. Or maybe there are just too many reasons to choose one.

I inhale sharply. Square my shoulders. Firm my jaw. Shove down the welter of emotions. Blink until my vision is clear.

And then I walk away.

I make it to the entrance of the hallway, trying to wrap the towel around me, needing to be covered now, and then he's moved past me to stand in front of me, blocking my path to the bathroom and his eyes are conflicted, concerned, confused. A broad thumb sweeps over my cheekbone, smearing a tear across my skin. "I believe you."

"Fortunately for me, my name does not depend on your belief for its existence. Nor do I." There are the claws, out for defense now.

"Are you one of Caleb's girls?" The question is unexpected, throws me off balance.

"I don't know what you mean." My voice is carefully modulated into cool neutrality.

"Of course you don't." He doesn't sound surprised, and he also doesn't sound as if he believes me. He sighs, rubs his face with both hands. "You know what? Let's forget that for the moment. I need food. Will you have lunch with me, Madame X?" He glances at his wrist, at the thick black rubber timepiece there. "Or dinner, I guess it would be, at this point."

"I—" I am hungry. I'm also afraid of Logan's many sharply pointed questions. Hunger wins out over caution. "Yes. I suppose I will."

"Good. You need to get dressed, then, and I need to change." A moment, then, in which neither of us seems willing to turn away first. Finally, Logan sighs. "I'm sorry, X. I didn't mean to question you or make you mad. I just . . . there's a lot I don't know, and I want—I want to know you."

I could weep again at the vulnerable sincerity in his voice. "You're right, you know. I *am* complicated. But I'm also not. It's just . . . hard for me to talk about myself. I am unaccustomed to trying, so you'll have to be forgiving if I'm not always very . . . forthcoming."

"I'll do my best to be patient, but you should understand one thing about me: When I find something I want, I go after it, hard."

I can only swallow hard and wonder how I'm supposed to respond to that. "Okay," is all I can manage.

"Get dressed, X," he says, his voice rougher than it's ever been, "before you discover how much self-control it's taking to not . . . ravish you senseless."

"Ravish?" Once again, I sound faint. I am clearly not myself around this man.

"Ravish. You like old books, right? That's an old-book sort of word. It means—"

"I know what it means." A little sharper, a little more myself.

"Yet you're still standing there, basically naked." He takes a step toward me, and never has a man appeared so primal, so intimidatingly, sexually male as Logan in this moment, his hard, lean, lupine form filling the narrow hallway, naked but for jeans, hands fisted at his sides, head tipped forward so all I can see are sharp cheekbones and fiery eyes. "I had you naked in my arms, X. I could have had you up against the wall. But I didn't."

"Why not?" I breathe the question, frozen in place like a deer that's scented a predator.

"Because you're not ready. Not for what I want."

"And what do you want, Logan?"

Another step. Mere molecules separate us, yet again. A breath, and I'd be in his arms, and I know nothing would stop the inevitable, should our flesh touch again.

"*Everything*, Madame X. I want everything." He towers over me, my head tipped back so I can look up at him, and our lips are nearly touching, but not quite. "Everything, and then some."

He's right.

I'm not ready.

He swivels out of my way, and I let out a shallow breath, one of something very like relief, and push past him. Now I am become Lot's wife: I turn back, press my spine to the door, and my eyes lock on Logan's. I fumble for the doorknob, never taking my eyes off Logan's. Stepping through and shutting the door between us takes every ounce of will I possess, and he does not turn away, does not blink, does not so much as breathe as I put the door between us.

And even then, I sense him there, still, on the other side.

SIXTEEN

He takes me to a tiny Italian place. We walk there, a half hour of walking hand in hand across town.

The streets are wet, the trees dripping scintillating droplets in the golden evening haze. The sun has returned, peeking between clouds and skyscrapers to illuminate everything with a sheen of decadent brilliant light, making everything seem romantic and beautiful and perfect.

I feel no panic at being outside, and it is incredible.

"I love this time of day," Logan says, apropos of nothing. "Photographers call it the golden hour."

"It is beautiful," I say, my heart full of joy at the simple luxury of this moment.

He gestures at the sunlight streaming at us from between the buildings to our left as we cross an intersection. "You know, the Japanese have a word. *Komorebi*. It means the way sunlight filters through the trees in a forest. I've always thought there should be a similar word, something that captures this time of day, in this place. The way the sun is such a perfect gold that you can almost but not quite look directly at it, the way it's framed by the buildings, shines off the glass, turns everything beautiful." He looks at me. "So beautiful."

Is he referring to me? Or to the sunlight, the moment?

We walk on, and I memorize this. His hand in mine, his fingers tangled between my fingers, his thumb rubbing in small circles on the web of skin between my thumb and forefinger. The beauty of the city, the air warm and lush and smelling of fresh rain, the familiar cacophony of New York, freedom, the man beside me.

"There's another word," he says, once again breaking the silence. "This one is Sanskrit. *Muditā*"—he says it *moo-dee-tah*—"and it means . . . how do I put it? To take joy in the happiness of someone else. Vicarious happiness."

I watch him, and wait for him to elaborate.

He glances at me, a smile lighting up his beautiful face. "I'm experiencing *muditā* right now, watching you."

"Really?" I ask.

He nods. "Oh yeah. You're looking at everything like it's just the most beautiful thing you've ever seen."

I wish I could explain it to him. "Everything *is* beautiful, Logan."

"And I just . . . I love that innocence, I guess. I tend to be jaded, a lot of the time. I've seen a lot, you know? A lot of nasty shit, and it's easy to forget the beautiful." He pauses. "I like odd words, because they capture things in ways English doesn't. They capture the beauty of little moments. Words like *komorebi* remind me to put aside my general disillusionment and just enjoy the now."

"What kinds of things have you seen, Logan?" I ask, although I'm not sure why, or if the answer will be something I can stomach.

He doesn't answer, just directs me with a nudge to my elbow through a low doorway into a dark restaurant, accordion music playing, garlic scent strong in the air.

He waves at an old man wiping down a red-and-white checkered tablecloth. "Got a table out back for me, Gino?"

"Yeah, yeah, course I do. Go on, go on. Sit, I'll bring wine and bread for you and your pretty friend." Gino smiles and hustles off into the kitchen, hunched over but moving faster than I'd have thought possible.

Logan leads me through a back door and into a tiny open-air courtyard. I could probably touch both walls if I lay down, but there are four tables crowded into the space, three of them occupied by other couples. White lights on a string are draped around the perimeter of the wall over our heads, hanging on nails driven into old crumbling brick.

We've barely had time to sit, Logan with his back facing the wall, when Gino returns, a wicker basket full of garlic bread in one hand, a bottle of wine and two goblets in the other. He sets the basket of bread between us and then pours the wine, a dark ruby liquid.

"This is a good Malbec," Gino says. "From Argentina, 'cause no good Malbec ever came from anywhere else. It's good, very good. You like it, I think."

"Is there wine I don't like, Gino? Answer me that."

"Shitty wine, that's what," Gino says, setting a glass in front of me. He and Logan both laugh, but if there's a joke, I've missed it.

Both men stare at me, expectant. Apparently I'm supposed to try it first? Another new experience. Tentatively, remembering the last time I tried red wine, I take a sip.

This is different. Smoother, not biting at my taste buds quite as hard. Flavorful, but not overpowering. I nod. "I like it. But I'm not a wine expert."

"Who's a wine expert? Not me," Gino says, "certainly not this joker. No sommeliers here, *mia bella*, just good wine and good food."

"*Mia bella?*" I ask.

"It just means 'my beautiful,'" Logan answers.

"Hey, who's Italian around here, buddy? Not you, that's for damn sure. You wouldn't know *bella* from *bolla*. Leave the language of love to me, heh?"

"I thought French was the language of love?" Logan laughs.

"Nah, nah. Italiano. *Italiano é molto più bella.*" Gino waves a hand. "Bah. French. Sounds like a duck blowing its nose. But to speak Italiano is to sing, my friend. Now. What you have to eat?"

"Surprise us, Gino. But be warned, we're both very hungry."

"Mama's in the back, and you know how she is. You'll need a crane to get you out of here before she finishes with you. You'll be so stuffed you'll beg for mercy. And then she'll make you dessert!" He laughs, an uproarious belly laugh that, although I once again have missed the humor, is nonetheless catching.

I find myself grinning, and sipping the wine, which is, as he said, very, very good.

Alone once more, Logan leans forward, his forearms on the table. "Gino's an old friend. And he wasn't kidding about Maria. She'll keep sending food out until we can't eat any more."

I take a sip of wine. "This is perfect, Logan. Thank you."

He glances at me, and his eyes narrow, his brow furrows. "Am I allowed to ask you questions, X?"

"If you answer them yourself, sure."

"It's a deal," he says. "And you drive a hard bargain. I'm not much for talking about myself, either."

"So we're quite the closed-mouth pair, aren't we?"

He nods, laughing, and tears a piece of garlic bread off the loaf. "Guess we are." He chews, swallows, and his smile fades. "I guess I'll start with the obvious first: How is it you know so little about yourself?"

I sigh, a long breath of resignation. "I can answer that in four words: acute global retrograde amnesia."

Logan blinks as if trying to process what he's hearing. "Amnesia."

"Right." I attempt to cover my discomfort with a large mouthful of Malbec.

"Acute global retrograde amnesia," he repeats, and leans back in his chair as Gino arrives with a large bowl of salad and two plates, dishing a generous portion to each of us before vanishing once more without a word. When he's gone, Logan picks at the salad with his fork, spearing some romaine and a chunk of fresh mozzarella, his eyes on me as he does so. "Can you unpack that a bit for me?"

I take a few bites, sorting out my thoughts. "It just means I have no clue who I used to be. I suffered a severe cranial trauma, which affected my ability to recall anything about myself whatsoever. I have no memories prior to waking up in the hospital. None. That was six years ago, and I haven't recalled anything either, so the doctors say it is unlikely I ever will. Many amnesia patients experience what is called temporally graded amnesia, meaning they won't remember events nearer the trauma, but will remember pertinent information about themselves and their past farther back, childhood memories and the like. Most patients can and will experience spontaneous recovery, wherein they recall most of the forgotten information, although events immediately prior to the trauma will often still be absent. The severity of the trauma and damage to the neural pathways determines the severity and permanence of the loss of memory. In my case, the trauma was extremely severe. That I survived at all, that I woke from the coma at all, much less was able to function on anything like a normal level? It is considered an unexplainable miracle. That I escaped the accident with *only* amnesia, however severe, is a cause for celebration. Or so I was told. But the fact remains, I woke up with no memories. No knowledge of myself whatsoever."

Logan seems shaken. "Damn, X. What *happened*?"

"No one is entirely sure. I was . . . found by—by someone." I don't dare even think the name. "I was nearly dead. A mugging gone horribly wrong, it is thought. I should have died. And, I'm told, I *did* die on the operating table. But they brought me back, and I survived. I had a family, but they died and I did not. They were murdered, and I escaped, somehow. Or . . . so I'm told."

"And no one could identify you?"

I shake my head. "It seems not. I had no identification on me, and my family was dead. There was no one to identify me."

"So you woke up alone, with no knowledge of who you are?"

"Not . . . alone, no."

"We'll come back to that, as I have my suspicions." Another pause as Gino removes the half-finished bowl of salad and our plates, replacing them with small squares of lasagna. We both dig in, and after a few bites, Logan speaks again. "So you can form new memories, though, right?"

"Yes. That's the other kind of amnesia, the inability to form new memories. It's called anterograde amnesia." The lasagna is incredible, and I don't want to ruin the experience by talking, so we lapse into silence as we both eat.

"So—" Logan starts again, after we've both finished.

I speak over him. "I think it's my turn."

He shrugs. "Fair enough."

"Tell me about your childhood."

He smiles, and it seems a bit sad, to me. "Fairly typical story, really. Single mom, dad left when I was a baby. Mom worked two, sometimes three jobs just to provide a roof and something like three squares a day. She was a good woman, loved me, took care of me the best she could. Got no complaints, there. She just . . . was working a lot. Couldn't keep me under her thumb the way I needed. I skipped a lot of school. My buddy's dad ran a surf shop outside the city, right? He knew we were skipping, but he'd never graduated either, so I guess he didn't care. I don't know. He'd lend us boards and we'd surf all day. We'd only come to shore to eat a sandwich and then go back out, stay out on the waves till we were too exhausted to swim. This was how it was for Miguel and me, from like fifth grade onward. Skip school, go surf. Eventually his dad just gave us our boards, and we'd run the beaches hunting for the best waves. Sounds great, right? It was. Right up until we hit high school age. Miguel had a cousin, Javier, and he got us into smoking dope. And he also got us into helping him sell dope. Which led to being in a gang, of sorts. Me, Miguel, his cousin, a few other dudes. Lots of trouble. Quit even pretending I gave a shit about school. Mom pretended she didn't know, as long as I didn't get arrested and let her know I was alive every couple days. Just how it was, you know?"

He trails off again as Gino appears yet again, this time with plates of chicken parmesan with a side of pasta topped with a dollop of red sauce.

"So, things were . . . not good, but nothing crazy, I guess. Nobody went to jail, nobody got hurt. We smoked dope and surfed and sold a few dimes here and there. Nothing big, not enough to really call the attention of the more serious dealers, right? But then the summer before I'd have been a senior, I was seventeen, I think. Almost eighteen. Miguel's cousin got approached by a big-time dealer from down by the border, dude called himself Cervantes. Wanted Miguel and Javier to be his mules, run some product south. Big cuts, big risk. I wasn't in on it, 'cause I was white, you know? Most of the time, that didn't matter, but for this, it did. So he approached them when I wasn't around. They went with it. Ran the product, got paid out big time, figured they'd hit the jackpot, right? Yeah, that went fine for a few months, until Javier got in trouble. Got caught by a DEA border guard sting op. Javi turned snitch. Set Miguel up to take the fall. And Cervantes . . . he figured it was Miguel that was the snitch when a big shipment got intercepted and cost him a couple hundred grand. Miguel and I were surfing, like we always did early in the morning. Best waves, you know, when it's just past dawn." He ducks his head, gently swirling the dregs of his wine. "Cervantes and three of his soldiers were on shore, waiting for us. Didn't say a word, just—just lit him up. A dozen slugs to the chest. Right in front of me. That was it. No threats, no warnings, no interrogation. Didn't say shit to me, either. Like, obviously if I said anything to the cops, I'd be next. Miguel was my best friend, man. He was like family, you know? We'd been friends since third grade. *Blam-blam-blam*, dead. Right in front of me."

"My God, Logan."

He bobbles his head side-to-side. "What was I supposed to do? I knew I'd be next. Either I'd be his mule—which would land me in jail, eventually—or I'd wind up dead. Well, one day I happened to walk past an armed forces recruitment office, and this guy was standing outside smoking a cigarette, wearing a badass uniform, badges and a real medal and shit. Stopped me, asked me what I was up to. Made the army sound like a good gig. A good way out of the shit I'd found myself tangled up in. So I joined the army. And honestly, it was the best thing for me. Got shipped to Kuwait. Turned out I had a knack for engines, and they needed mechanics to fix up the trucks and tanks and shit. Ended up getting my diploma and a set of skills and some money in the bank. But then, like I told you before, when my four years were out, I ended up stuck in St. Louis, met Philip, the Blackwater guy . . . got my ass recruited again. This time, I got combat training. They put a gun in my hands, sent me to Iraq, and paid me huge amounts of money to hang my ass out the side of a helicopter. Had as much of a knack for nailing insurgents from a hundred yards away out the side of a moving helicopter as I did for cleaning sand out of piston chambers. Did that for . . . too long. Felt like a badass, you know? The regular army and Marine guys hated us, but that was just because we got paid quadruple what they made to do the same thing."

"Quadruple?"

He nods. "Hell, yeah. Easily. Danger pay, right? And I liked the danger. Didn't have anyone back home waiting for me, and I honestly didn't give a shit what happened to me."

"And then you got shot," I suggested, sensing the shape of what came next.

"And then I got shot," he agreed. "Some asshole with an AK got lucky. I mean, there was no way he could have made that shot on purpose, you know? Way too far away, moving way too fast . . . but that didn't stop him from trying. We wore bulletproof vests, of course, but there was an early-morning incident with an IED and an ambush, so we got scrambled and I forgot the vest in my rush to get on the helo. Took the two to my shoulder, no big deal, wouldn't have been life-threatening. But then he shoots again, and a round hits me down low. You saw it." He indicates his ribs, and I can see the puckered wound in my mind's eye. "Good thing I was strapped in, let's just say that. They hauled me back in, got me to a medic, shipped me stateside. That was it for me, as far as combat went. But I spent a long-ass time on my back, recuperating. Thinking. I'd narrowly avoided death twice. Cervantes should have killed me. Probably would have, eventually, if I'd stuck around. But he didn't, and I ran off with the army. So then I took the bullet to my stomach, and it nearly killed me. Nicked my lung, permanently compromised my lung capacity. Narrowly missed hitting a bunch of other organs and my spine. It was bad. Real bad. And you spend enough time horizontal, thinking about how close you came to dying, realizing you *should* be dead, you start to rethink your priorities."

"What conclusions did you come to?"

"That I had to make something of myself. I'd survived when I shouldn't have. I was alive, and I mean I guess it sounds like a cliché, but I felt like I'd been given a second chance. One thing led to another, and I ended up in Chicago, working for a flipper, a guy who buys foreclosed houses, fixes them up, and sells them at a profit. I had money, but I needed to stay busy. Learned enough to do it myself, flipping houses on my own. This was a big thing for a while, back when the real estate market was going gangbusters. I made a mint, and decided to go bigger. Bought a bar that'd gone under, owner ran out of money. Renovated it, hired some folks who knew shit about running a bar, sold it for a big profit. That earned me deeper pockets, let me take bigger risks for bigger rewards. Most of them paid off, some didn't—and every time I got a big payout, I used it to fund the next deal. Learned other skills, learned to recognize when something will pay off and when it's a bust. Got into technology development, bought some other companies . . ."

"And then you found yourself on the losing end of a bad deal."

He nodded. "Yeah. But that's a whole different story."

"And one you don't like to talk about."

"Right." He eyes me. "Back to you. How'd you end up with Caleb?"

Everything inside me freezes. I don't know how to answer. I don't know how to talk about Caleb. How to explain it.

"He was there when I had no one," I end up saying. It's true enough.

Logan nods, but it's the kind of nod that implies he realizes I'm keeping back more than I'm saying. "How about I offer up some really . . . personal information? So you see I'm for real. I just want to know. I'm not going to judge you or try to . . . I don't know. I just want to know."

"What kind of personal information?" I can't help asking.

A pause, as Gino brings yet another dish, something else kind of like lasagna, wide rolls of pasta in sheets, stuffed with ricotta and ground sausage, doused in marinara.

"Did you see the painting?" Logan asks.

"*Starry Night*," I say. "Yes, I saw it. I wondered about that."

"You know, Van Gogh only ever sold a couple paintings in his lifetime, and that was one of them. But that particular version of *Starry Night* was actually only one of dozens he did that were similar. He painted them from an asylum in France. What we'd call a psychiatric home now. It was a lunatic asylum for the wealthy. He was chronically depressed, suffered a mental break. Cut his ear off, I guess, or part of it. Admitted himself there, to Saint-Paul de Mausole. He had a whole wing to himself, and he'd sit in this room he'd made into his studio, and he'd paint the view, over and over and over. Different perspectives, trying different techniques. Day, night, close up, far off, everything. There's another one, called *Starry Night over the Rhone*. Anyway, he'd just paint the view from that room over and over again. But that one, the one we both have copies of, it's something special. He was a deeply troubled man, Van Gogh, and that painting, I guess to me it just . . . echoes things I sympathize with. That deal that went wrong . . . I ended up in prison. I don't want to go into the details, but they'd let us out into the yard during the day, so we could lift weights and all that cliché bullshit. The view from the yard, there was this hill in the distance with some trees on it, and birds would fly in from all directions. I can see it now, the grass heading off into the distance, with yellow dandelions in patches here and there. Then the hill, and the trees. I don't know what kind, oak, maybe? Thick, huge, with these massive spreading branches. And I'd be there in the yard, in the crazy fucking heat, staring at that stand of trees and the shadows they cast, daydreaming of being up there on the hill, in the shade. It was a scene I could paint from memory, even now, if I were able to draw for shit. And *Starry Night*, it's . . . there's this sense of distance, peace—I don't know, it's hard for me to put it into words. But it just reminds me of how I felt, staring out at that hill every day."

"For me, it's the view of the city from my window, at my condo. It's hard for me to go outside. You saw that. Walking here, it was the first time I can remember that I didn't feel any panic at all. But looking out, watching the people and the cars, everyone just going about their lives so easily, it just . . . sometimes I'd long for something that simple, that easy. But then—I get outside, and the noise, and the people, and everything is so big, and there's so much of everything . . ." I close my eyes, try to make sense of my own thoughts. "*Starry Night*, to me, is about how none of that matters. The stars will shine, and they'll light up the world, no matter who you are, or, in my case, who you are *not*. I mean, I woke up, and I was no one. But the city goes on. That's both comforting and scary, depending on my mood. But the stars will shine, for Van Gogh, and there will be cathedrals and cypress trees, and there will be *something* out there that's beautiful, no matter what's inside me. I don't know how to make any more sense of it. Like you said, it's hard to put into words."

"No, I get it." His hand reaches for mine, and there's a moment, then, that passes between us. An understanding. It's nebulous, but real.

But then time reasserts itself, and I can't fall back into that moment, no matter how much I wish to.

Something has shifted.

Being here, with Logan, like this . . . it's too easy. Too simple. Too *real*. I want to enjoy it, the wine and the food and the impossibly handsome man who seems to want to know me, but I can't. He wants to know about Caleb, and how do I explain that?

How do I explain that even now, Caleb is a part of me? Even now, to talk about Caleb feels like . . . sacrilege. Like betrayal. Like to put into words the wealth of what has occurred between Caleb and me would be to make less of them, to bare to the light things that should not be revealed. Not secrets, just . . . private things.

One cannot be more bare, more naked, more vulnerable than to be without identity, to be denuded of all personality, to be utterly without an identity, without a soul.

To be *no one*.

Caleb made me *someone*. And that someone is all tangled up and woven around the person that is Caleb.

"X?" Logan's voice. Quiet, but sharp.

"Yes, sorry." I try to smile at him.

"I lost you there, didn't I?"

I can only stare at him, stare into his eyes. "Can we . . . can we go, Logan? This is . . . wonderful. And maybe you can't understand this, but . . . it's *too* wonderful. Too much."

He sighs, a sad sound. "Yeah . . . no—I get it. I really do." He stands up, digs into his pocket, and tosses some money on the table.

Gino is there, dishes in hand. "No, no, you cannot go, not yet. The best is yet to come!"

Logan claps him on the shoulder. "Sorry, man. My friend isn't feeling good."

"Ah. Well, if you must go, you must go." He shrugs, as if to say *what will be, will be*.

Outside, then, Logan's hand in mine. Evening has fallen. Golden light has faded to dusk, gold melting into shadows. The magic hour has gone, and the spell seems to have snapped. I don't know why or how. But I walk, and feel ill at ease.

Instead of beauty, now I see the underbelly. The trash on the streets, the smell of Dumpsters, diesel fumes, a man's angry shouts from an open window. A curse. Glass crunching underfoot. Graffiti on the walls, ugliness marring crumbling brick.

I feel a bit dizzy from the wine, thick-headed. A headache prods at the interior of my skull.

The walk back feels like it will be endless, and my feet hurt.

When was it I woke from the bath?

How long has passed? An eternity, it feels.

Was that really all just today?

The length of the day is crashing down on me, the pressure of all I've experienced weighing heavily. Heavy food, heavy wine. Logan's mouth on mine, his body against me, his kiss. Wanting him, yet feeling as if . . . as if I shouldn't have him. As if to be with him would be . . . wrong, somehow. I can't make sense of it. To try is dizzying.

I want my own bed, my library. I want to read *Mansfield Park* and sip Earl Grey. I want to watch night fall from my window.

But I can't. I left that behind. I walked away from it.

Was that a mistake? It felt right at the time. But now? I'm not so sure. Who is Logan? A warrior. A man who has been to prison. A man who has been to war.

A man who risked much to do what he felt was freeing me.

But can he understand me, understand my situation?

"X?" Logan's voice again, concerned. "Are you okay?"

I try to nod. "It's been a long day. I'm very tired." So much left unsaid.

"Let's get you home, huh?" His arm around my waist.

Home? Where is home? What is home?

"I can't walk anymore, Logan. I just can't."

I feel him look at me. "Shit. I'm an idiot. I'm sorry. You've been through a lot today, haven't you? What was I thinking?" He lifts a hand, and like magic, a yellow taxi appears and swerves over to us.

Logan helps me in, slides after me, gives his address. The ride is short.

He pays the taxi driver. We are stopped, rows of brownstones on either side. Darkness like a blanket, pierced by lamplight. Logan's arm around my waist, helping me walk the few feet from where the taxi let us out to Logan's front door.

Will I sleep with Logan? In his bed? On a couch? A spare room?

So much of me wants to go home. This feels like an adventure, like something from a story, and I just want to return to real life. But it's not life, it's not a story, it's not a fairy tale.

What is it?

I'm very tired.

I want to go back to when I was naked in the hallway, Logan's hands on me, back to when things felt simple and possible. In that moment, everything was simple and easy. I just *wanted* him.

I still want him.

I feel safe, his arm around me like this.

But I don't know what tomorrow will be like. For that matter, I do not know what *now* will be like. I am lost and confused and homesick. This is the longest I've ever been away from my condo, away from all that is familiar.

I feel Logan tense, come to an abrupt halt. "Stay here," he whispers to me, and helps me lean against the tree.

The light shines from below, bright. I blink, and see Logan standing with his hands in fists at his sides. He is taut, coiled.

I peer into the shadows and see another shape, sitting on the steps to Logan's brownstone. A familiar shape. Familiar broad shoulders, familiar curve of jawline seen in profile, those cheek-bones, that forehead, those lips.

I step forward. "Caleb?"

"Stay there, X." Logan's voice is hard as iron. "And you stay right where you are, Caleb. Keep away from her."

"X. Let's go." That voice, deep and dark as a chasm.

I blink, sway on my feet. Logan, in front of me, acting as a human shield between Caleb and me.

Caleb, standing now, hands in pockets.

Two men; one dark, one light.

I want to run, want to climb into this tree and huddle in the nook of the branches.

Caleb takes another step closer to me, Logan blocking the way with his body.

Tension crackles.

Violence is thick in the air.

I cannot breathe, panic welling up within me, as familiar as the wrinkles on the palms of my hands.

I see eyes like midnight shadows, staring at me. Expectant. Knowing.

Seeing me, seeing *me*.

"It's time to go home, X." That voice, implacable, like darkness made flesh, like shadows that curl as sleep stakes its claim, shadows not to fear but rather shadows that lull, shadows that witness dreams and wait through the night until the sunrise.

"You don't have to go with him, X." Logan.

"You know where you belong. It's time to go." Caleb.

Where I belong? Do I know where I belong?

Caleb strides away. Toward a sleek, low, black car, Len waiting, holding the rear passenger door. Logan swivels to face me. He is not standing in my way, not preventing me. Nor is he touching me.

Caleb to my left. The condo, what I know. My library. My window.

Logan in front of me. The brownstone, Cocoa. The fantasy of normalcy.

"You are Madame X." The voice to my left, confident, calm, strong. "And you belong to me. You belong *with* me."

"But you don't *have* to, X." Logan reaches for me but doesn't touch me. Not quite. Almost, but not quite. "You don't have to. Don't you see that?"

I feel the pull. An invisible thread, ensnaring my wrist. My ankle. My waist. My throat. It isn't a scent, or a memory, or a touch. It isn't sorcery.

I lost twenty years of memory. I lost all I was. I lost me.

But now I have a past. Six years, perhaps only a fraction when compared to the totality of my life, but it is the only history I know. The library. The window. Tea. The way time passes in lulling increments, each moment ordered and known and understood.

Logan . . . he represents the unknown, a future that *could* be. A dream. A dog to nuzzle my cheek, to welcome me. Kisses in the madness of wild moments, passion that consumes. Disorder, frenzy of need, time like sand slipping through a clenched fist, so many new things.

But then there's Caleb . . . my savior, my past, and my present. I've gotten a glimpse, rare and precious, past heaven-high walls and into the inner sanctum of who the man really is.

Caleb has given me so much . . . a name, an identity, a life.

He is a mystery, and often inscrutable, but he is all I know.

I choke on my breath.

I feel my foot slide backward.

Logan's eyes distort, and his jaw clenches. He sees the infinitesimal slide of my foot, and he correctly reads the sign for what it is. "Don't, X."

"I'm sorry, Logan."

"*Don't*. You don't know what you're doing." He sounds utterly sure of this.

"I'm sorry. Thank you, Logan. So much. Thank you."

Caleb stands waiting, watching, tall and broad and clad impeccably in a tailored suit, navy with narrow pinstripes, white shirt, thin slate-gray tie. Fingers uncurl from a fist, palm lifted, hand extended. "Come now."

I cannot make myself break my gaze away from Logan's, away from the sadness, the need. He, too, sees me.

I back away. Back away.

Logan lifts his chin, jaw hardened, fists at his sides, brow furrowed. Faded jeans, a pale green henley, four buttons at the neck, each one undone, sleeves pushed up around thick, corded forearms. I see his hands—and for a moment, only those hands. They touched me, so gently. I felt a lifetime of touch in what in this moment feel like were stolen moments.

A moment is a fortieth of an hour.

How many fortieths of an hour did I steal with Logan?

They do feel stolen, indeed, but no less precious for that.

Hands, on my shoulders, pulling me back. Fingers that know me, fingers that have peeled away all my layers, night after night, and have known me in the darkness and known me in the light.

I still do not turn away, do not look away, even as I retreat into the shadows around the waiting car.

The interior is cool, and silent.

Dark.

Logan stands in a pool of pale light, framed, illuminated. He watches me and does not blink.

I watch, still, even when Len closes the door, and I must watch through tinted glass.

A low, powerful growl of the engine, and then Logan is behind me, still watching, growing smaller.

A long, deep, fraught silence, as the car returns me to the familiar glass-and-steel canyons, echoing with the ceaseless life of night in this city.

When you speak, your voice strikes chords within me, hammers on the strings of a piano. My entire being hums, and I must turn, must look. Must meet your eyes like darkness of a moonless night.

"You are Madame X, and you . . . are . . . *mine.*" Your fingers pinch my chin, tilt my head to look at you. "Say it, X."

The words feel pulled out of me, drawn out, ensnared and tangled up and plucked out of the snarl of conflict within me:

"I am Madame X, and I am yours."

SEVENTEEN

You do not speak, not until we've returned to the high-rise, to the thirteenth floor.

"Why did you leave, X?" Your voice is like thunder in the distance.

"You left first." I stand at my window, dressed still in my plain jeans, my comfortable T-shirt, cotton underwear and sports bra, my ballet flats.

"So you ran away with another man?" An accusation.

"Yes." You will not hear any denials from me.

"After all I've done for you, after all we have shared, you find it so easy to abandon me like so much trash?" You sound almost human, almost hurt.

"All we have *shared*?" I put a palm to the cool glass, finding a tiny measure of inner peace at the soothing, familiar view of the cars passing to and fro, the buildings rising black and reflecting shadows and faint light. "What do we *share*, Caleb? I am nothing but a possession to you. You use me as you see fit, and expect me to stay put and merely wait for you."

"You act as if I treat you like a slave. Like a mere . . . physical object."

"You do!" I whirl, and you're there, and my palms strike your chest, *hard*. "I am an object for your sexual needs, Caleb. Just like Rachel and the others. Make whatever excuses you wish, you cannot fool me any longer, not as you have them. They at least have the promise of finding value to someone else. Sold as so much chattel, perhaps, but at least they have a goal, a future, a promise of something *more*. I pace these rooms day after day, day after day, and yet I go nowhere. I accomplish nothing. I have no future. I am Madame X, yes. But who is that? Who *am* I? And to you, Caleb, who am I? What am I? You enjoy *fucking* me. I understand that much. But that is something you do *to* me, not *with* me. And yes, you're very, *very* good at it. I *enjoy* it. I admit that, freely. But that is not *shared*, Caleb. And when it happens, it's just you . . . *doing*. And then you're done, and you leave. You leave. You leave. You always *leave*! You're all I fucking have, and you're always leaving me!"

You are strangely silent. How did I get here, up against you? Hands pinned between our bodies, palms to your chest. Leaning against you, as if I cannot stand without you.

I am not entirely sure that isn't the truth.

You are absolutely still, your chest barely even moving with breath. Your eyes are on me, and they are blazing with heat, crackling with darkfire, as if behind those shadows within you there is an inferno, a sun, an ever-roiling supernova, but it can only be seen or felt when you deign to allow the veil guarding the world from your inner self to be swept away.

A mistake—there is motion, coming from you: Your jaw pulses furiously.

"You think"—a pause for breath—"you think all I do is *fuck* you? Did I hear you correctly?"

"Yes." I will not flinch away. Cannot. Must not. "That's all you've ever done to me: *fuck*. Base, meaningless, and empty."

"You could not be more wrong, X. Am I monogamously faithful to you, sexually? No. And I will neither explain nor apologize for that. I am who I am. I am *what* I am. But my time with you, limited as it may be, has never been . . . *base*, or *meaningless*, or *empty*." You freight those three words, my words, with such acidic venom I cannot help flinching. "So far from that, X. I am not a man to whom emotion comes easily, and that is not likely to change."

My chin lifts. "I . . . don't . . . *believe* you."

"No?" An arched eyebrow. "Allow me to show you, in that case."

Another moment that is seared into me: You, lit by the pale glow of the city, mammoth, a creature of raw sexual potency, seething, furious, your hands rising from your sides as if in slow motion, your eyes fixed on me, blinking every few fragments of a second, a slow sweep of long black lashes, and then your hands grip my shirt, lift it.

I expect you to rip my clothes from me, but you don't. You remove them, carefully.

Reverently, almost.

The bra you roll upward until my breasts spill free, and then you tug it off my head, lifting it, forcing my arms upward. My jeans you unbutton, unzip, push down, removing my panties with the denim. And just like that, within seconds, I am naked.

And then, after a taut fortieth of an hour, your eyes roaming my shape, devouring my flesh, you take a step back. Away from me. And you look at me, your eyes daring me to glance away, to break the tensile fragility of this thing between us. What it is, I don't know. I can't stop it, though. This is your sorcery. Now I feel it. Now I am lost in its spell.

As I knew I would be.

You remove your suit coat, tossing it carelessly to the floor. Then the tie, ripped off impatiently. And then the shirt, one button at a time, with dexterous fingers. And then your belt, shoes toed off, socks. Even you look momentarily awkward, removing your socks; they are impossible to take off gracefully. But then you stand in just your underwear, black fabric stretched taut over pale skin, massive frame like a mountain of muscle, all crags of hard flesh. And now . . . thumbs in the elastic, not looking away, you shove them down, and you are naked with me.

Unmarred skin, perfectly proportioned. A god made flesh.

Your erection juts hard and proud, and I quake at the flash of physical memory that assaults me, the haptic knowledge of the way your engorged member feels, driving into me, filling me, piercing me.

I shake, but I cannot flee. Cannot speak, mouth dry, unable to look away, unwilling to try, knowing it is futile.

The way you close the space between us, moving slowly, so I know your intent, you reach for me. And I expect—I don't know what. To be kissed? To be lifted and fucked right here, in this moment?

I do not expect what happens: You take me by the shoulders, and for a split second you just look at me, dark eyes blazing, jaw pulsing, a million words burning inside you, burning and always unspoken, as if they are consumed before they can reach your lips. And then you spin me, a rough, abrupt twist, and you shove me so I slam against the window, the glass cold against my naked breasts. And then you're there, behind me, trapping me, and your shaft probes between my thighs, and your breath is in my ear.

"This is *fucking* you, X." And you drive into me.

Hard, sudden, a brief stab of pain as you stretch me to aching. And then I gush, wet at the fullness of you, and I cry out, and sag, would fall but for your presence.

A thrust.

I feel it, that burn. The explosive upwelling. I tamp it down.

"Yes, Caleb. This is fucking. This is what you do to me. Just this. This is all it's ever been." My voice is strong, though I am weak.

"Look at the window, X."

I do, but instead of the city, I see us. Reflected.

You, huge behind me, pale and heavily muscled, moving, skin flexing and shifting in the light as you fuck.

Me, palms to the glass, breasts flattened, areolae dusky circles around my erect nipples, hips wide and skin dark, hair loose and wild, eyes crazed. Moving as I am fucked.

"You see how we look together?"

"I need more, Caleb." I push back into your body, into your motion, into what you are doing to me. "I need more than just this. This is all you give me, and it isn't enough."

Abruptly, I am empty, left gasping, as you rip yourself out of me. I remain collapsed against the glass, watching you in the reflection. A moment, then, of you, standing naked behind me, shaft glistening wetly with our essences, massive chest rising and falling heavily with conflicted breath. Your eyes glitter.

I am on the cusp of orgasm, shaking with it, full to choking with need for it.

"You ask the impossible of me, X."

"All I'm asking for is you." Until I say it, I never understood how true this is. It hurts to admit, the pain lancing deep through every molecule of me.

You are an enigma. You will not change, and I know this, but still I feel as if I *NEED* you and I *HATE* you for this, hate myself even more for needing you, because needing you binds me to the howling ghosts of my murdered past, binds me to the memory of waking up as no one, waking up unable to speak or to move, unable to express the utter torment of waking up lost, alone, my soul echoing with absence, my mind blank, my past erased so completely that I cannot even mourn for what I do not know I've even lost.

I NEED YOU.

Damn all the gods for burdening me with this truth, but I need you.

I don't want to need you, but I do.

And you will not, cannot give me you. I don't know why, and I do know you will never tell me.

Your eyes ever so slowly flutter closed. Your fisted hands uncurl.

You reach for me. I tremble, paralyzed in place. Gently now, more gentle than you've ever been, you turn me in place, bend at the knees, curl your hands behind my thighs and lift me easily, tug my legs around the trunk of your waist, and in the moment before impalement, you pause.

"Oh, X. You don't know what you're asking for." The growl of your voice is the implacable slide of an avalanche.

"But I ask it anyway, Caleb," I say.

And then you're in me. A slow, sweet glide. My mouth falls open, and your eyes are wide, as are mine, and your hands cup my bottom, lower me onto you. I grip your neck, gasping with the dulcet ache of you, the molasses-slow piercing, until you are seated within me and I can't even breathe for it, can only let my head hang back on my neck and whimper.

"Is this what you want, X?" you ask, and pin my spine to the glass. "Look at me, goddammit, and answer me."

I open my eyes. My upper lip is curled in a snarl of ecstasy. "Yes, Caleb. This is what I want."

But it's not. Not only this. There is so much more, but I don't have the words for it all.

Three short thrusts, my clit scraping against your hard, pumping shaft, and I come.

I collapse against your chest, feeling and smelling and tasting your sweat.

You move, carry me, still full of you; each step causes me to flinch and twitch and gasp and tingle, shooting bolts of after-spasms through me. And then you lay me down on my bed, on my back, and my legs hang off the edge. You stand between my spread-apart thighs, and you push, once.

I cry out.

You push in again, your hands gripping my hips, and I wail aloud.

You lean forward, and I feel you over me, feel your gaze. I wrap my arms around your neck, legs around your waist, and hang on. You crawl forward, drape me gently so my head is on the pillow, and now you're kneeling over me. Still in me. Aching in me. I feel you shaking with need. Your eyes remain on mine, and you wait, utterly motionless now.

I arch my back, flex my hips, and thrust against you.

You groan.

Oh, that sound. Your voice, so often silent, rumbles a sound of wordless pleasure, and I thrill to hear it.

You dip your head, and I press my breasts to your mouth.

Something wild and hotter than lightning snaps through me at the touch of your mouth on my nipple.

I come apart again like an erupting volcano, thrust against you, and now you move, move, move.

We writhe together.

Your groans become loud.

Mine turn to cries, sobs of pleasure.

Your hand cups my neck, lifts me to you; the other curls around the back of my thigh near my knee and wraps my leg around your hip, and you push into me, and we meet each other there, thrust for thrust. I look at you and see your eyes wide and surprised, see emotion bleeding out of you. It takes the slashing rawness of this moment to make you show anything, but now I see it.

You don't know how to do this.

No more than I do.

We are learning this together.

"Caleb," I whisper, and I come.

It is a detonation of bliss, everything in me flying apart, and I exhale every molecule of breath I have left as I am wrenched by the orgasm, twisted, wrung.

And then, as the climax reaches its peak, you do the unthinkable. You kiss me.

And you come, unleashing yourself within me, a hot wet gush, filling me, and you move frantically and you kiss me and grip my thigh with bruising frantic strength and your other palm grips my breast and thumbs my thickly erect nipple and I spasm with you, coming again, and now you see me, my eyes open as are yours, and this is a moment like no other, something huge and manic and terrifying and new bursting open and filling us both.

You come,

And I come,

And you kiss me,

And I kiss you,

And there is a thread between us, something real established.

Your forehead touches mine, and you are gasping for breath. Crushing me with your weight. "Jesus, X."

You try to move off me, but I cling to you.

"Don't leave, Caleb," I whisper.

"I have to—I've gotta go." You are not you anymore.

You are starting to close down. Perhaps, becoming *more* you. Or . . . less you. I don't know. Is the real you the tormented being I glimpsed trapped behind the shadowy veil of your eyes? Or is the real you the brusque, icy, efficient, impersonal creature of tailored suits and expensive cars?

I grip your wrist with one hand, lock my thighs around your waist and hook my heels around your backside, keep you firmly against me, in me, even as you soften. With my other hand, I do something I've never done before: I touch your hair. Feather my fingers through inky strands.

"If you leave now, Caleb, all of this will be for nothing. You'll undo whatever that was we just shared. *That* was sharing something. I *saw* part of you, Caleb."

"Fucking hell, X. You don't get it." A rough growl, a curse from you, so uncharacteristic.

"No, I don't. But . . . stay anyway. Relax, just for a moment."

You are tense for a moment, a sculpture of granite. And then, slowly, you melt, soften, and you dip a shoulder to the bed, twist to your back. Gradually, as if completely unsure if you're doing it right, or even *what* you're doing, you lay your head down on the pillow beside me. Drawn out of me, your manhood is slack and wet against your thigh. I feel your essence leaking out of me, but I don't dare move, don't dare to even think of it. I lie next to you, hands stuffed under the pillow, on my side, facing you.

This feels like curling up next to a lion in its cage.

You reach out a hand, and I tense, cease breathing.

But all you do is touch me, a single forefinger stroking upward from my thigh to my hip, over my waist, up my ribs, to my breast.

"You are beautiful." A murmur, as from the bottom of the turbulent dark sea.

"Thank you." I shift to the side, drape my arm behind me so your tentatively touching finger can brush from breast back down to my hip.

I dare touch your bicep. The lion twitches, and I know I could be devoured in a split second.

A game of touches, exploration of mutuality: a fingertip to my nipple, my palm sliding from knee to jagged hip bone; tracing my backside, following the curve from outer edge of hip to inner crease and up my spine, my fingers on the furrowed field of your abs.

You do not speak, and I don't dare break the magic of this. It is too fragile.

My eyes droop, weigh heavily.

Touch skates over me, hesitant and gentle and smooth and slow.

I drift, and drowse . . .

And sleep.

EIGHTEEN

wake alone.

Silence.

"Caleb?"

Nothing.

Dawn streaks through the window. I look to the left, and see that my closet door is open. The racks are bare, not even a hanger in sight.

My throat seizes. I leap out of bed, headed for my library.

It is there, intact.

I return to my bedroom, to my closet. Empty. Totally empty. Even the bureau against the far wall of the walk-in closet is empty. I have not a single stitch of clothing left to me.

Back out to the living room. The couch is gone, the coffee table, the Louis XIV armchair. The dining room table is gone.

My front door stands open.

The elevator door is open, the key in the slot inside the car.

I am utterly confused.

Back inside, to the library. There is my chair and the table in the triangle between shelves. On the table is an envelope containing a stack of hundred-dollar bills, and a note handwritten in bold, slanting letters:

MADAME X,

THIS DRESS IS THE ONE I FOUND YOU IN. IT'S YOURS, FROM BEFORE.

I LEAVE YOU THE BOOKS, BECAUSE I KNOW YOU TREASURE THEM.

THE CAMERAS AND MICROPHONES ARE OFF.

THERE WILL BE NO MORE CLIENTS.

LEAVE, IF YOU WISH; THERE IS MONEY ENOUGH IN THE ENVELOPE TO ALLOW YOU TO GO WHEREVER YOU WISH. BUT IF YOU DO CHOOSE TO LEAVE, YOU WILL BE ON YOUR OWN. I WILL NOT CHASE YOU THIS TIME.

OR, YOU MAY TAKE THE ELEVATOR UP TO THE PENTHOUSE. BUT IF YOU CHOOSE THIS, YOU LEAVE EVERYTHING IN THIS APARTMENT WHERE IT IS, AND COME TO ME AS YOU ARE NOW, NAKED, WITH ONLY THE NAME YOU CHOSE FOR YOURSELF THAT DAY IN THE MUSEUM OF MODERN ART.

~CALEB

Folded on the cushion of the chair is a dress. Deep, dark blue. Of course. A shade of blue that seems to be a defining feature in my life . . .

Caleb Indigo.

Logan's indigo eyes.

And now this dress . . .

Indigo.

Except this dress is not new. Not beautiful. It was, once, perhaps. I lift it, and I am strangled by ravaging emotion. I do not recognize this dress; it is ripped, torn. From neckline to hem, it is torn open. Ripped in half and stained with blood. There is another rip, this one on the side, low, on the right.

I touch my right hip, where there is a scar.

There is blood staining the dark blue fabric at the neckline, all over the shoulders, down the back.

Why, I don't know, but I lift it, step through the gaping hole. Fit my arms through the sleeves. Tug the ends together.

It is too small. Even undamaged, it wouldn't fit me. I am too large in the bust and backside for this dress. Too tall, as well, perhaps.

Six years.

I would have been around eighteen or nineteen when I last wore this dress.

I remove the dress; I feel as if phantoms of the past cling to my skin, seeping into me from the fabric.

The tag says *Sfera*. Even the style is strange to me. So short, coming not even to midthigh. Sleeveless, intact the neckline would have been high around my throat, but the back gapes open to mid-spine. I stare at the material clutched in my hand, a useless clue to who I used to be. An empty fragment of my past.

The girl who wore this dress from Sfera . . . who was she? What was her name? Did she have parents? A sister? What did she like to do? Did she have friends? Did she sketch hearts on notebooks? Did she have a crush on a boy? Did she speak Spanish? If she did, I have forgotten it.

This dress can tell me nothing. I cannot even wear it, and if I could, if I could sew the ends together . . . would I?

No.

So this choice of yours, Caleb?

I see through it.

It is a way of retaking what you feel I took from you last night.

Naked, hesitant, I enter the elevator, twist the key to the *PH*.

The doors close, and the car rises.

The doors open, and now I see the penthouse, whereas the last time I was here, I didn't, not really.

Expansive space, thick white carpeting, a wall of windows with a commanding view of the city. Black modern furniture. I recognize the sectional in front of the elevator as the one Caleb had me over. It is one of a set: an L-shaped couch, a modern minimalist chair, a small round silver table, and another chair, forming a small square to block off the space in front of the elevator.

In the distance, in the farthest corner of the penthouse, the kitchen, and near it a small eating nook in the corner where two walls of glass merge. You are there, sitting at the table, leaned back in a chair, elegantly casual in blue jeans and a white crew neck T-shirt. A mug in your hands, a rectangular electronic tablet on the table in front of you.

There is a place setting beside you. A saucer and a cup. A plate, with a bagel neatly presented, sliced into halves, one half laid face-down on a just-so angle atop the other. Precise, perfect.

"Come, sit." Your voice is very far away: The penthouse is enormous; it suits you exactly.

I cross the space hesitantly. If there is anyone in the buildings across the street, they can see me, and I am still naked.

You smile as I approach you, set down your mug of coffee.

You stand. Pull off your plain white T-shirt. Settle it onto my head, tug the neck opening over me, and I feed my arms through the sleeves. Clothed, somewhat, I feel more confident.

I glance at the cup of tea—I can see the tag: *Harney & Sons Earl Grey*—and the bagel, plain with light cream cheese spread thin. "You knew I'd come."

Your eyes are still impenetrable, but I am starting to see glimmers of something. Perhaps I am finally learning to read you. Or perhaps you are learning to let me.

"Of course I did," you say. "You are mine."

And this, from you, is a truth I cannot deny.

The question is: Do I want to be?

Continue reading for a sneak peek at
the second book in the Madame X trilogy . . .

MADAME X: EXPOSED

By

Jasinda Wilder

Coming soon from Berkley Books!

am drowning in an ocean of darkness. The sky is the sea, dark masses of roiling clouds like waves, spreading in every direction and weighing heavily on me like the titanic bulk of Homer's wine-dark seas. I lie on my back on the rooftop, leftover heat from the previous day still leaching out of the rough concrete and into my skin through the thin T-shirt that is all I'm wearing.

I want to see the stars, someday. I imagine them like a spray of salt on a black table cloth. Like a handful of diamonds against silk.

There are four small black speakers planted in unobtrusive locations around the rooftop, and music floats from them in serene, soothing waves.

Debussy, you said it was: *Clair de Lune.* A piano, creating a light and airy atmosphere in this lonely evening.

You've left for the evening. Business. Nothing I would enjoy, you claimed. Listen to music, drink wine, you'll be back and we'll go somewhere.

Things have changed, but then again, they haven't, really, have they?

Perhaps I doze.

I sense a presence as I wake up, but I don't open my eyes. Perhaps your business didn't take as long as you'd thought. I feel you sit beside me, and your finger touches my hair, smooths it off my forehead.

But then I smell cinnamon and cigarettes.

I crack my eyes open, and it isn't you.

"Logan." I whisper it, surprised. "How are you here?"

He shrugs. "Bribes, distraction . . . it wasn't hard."

"You shouldn't be here."

He fits a cigarette to his mouth, cups his hands around it, and I hear a scrape and a click. Flame bursts orange, briefly, and then the smell of cigarette smoke is pungent and acrid. His cheeks go concave, his chest expands, and then he blows out a white plume from his nostrils. "No, I shouldn't."

"Then why are you here?" I sit up, and I'm self-conscious of the fact that all I'm wearing is a thin short white T-shirt, and nothing else.

"I had to talk to you."

"What is there to say?"

His eyes flick shamelessly over me. A breeze kicks up, and my nipples harden, my skin pebbles. Perhaps it isn't the wind so much as Logan, though. His eyes, that strange and vivid blue, his proximity, his sudden and unexpected and inexplicable presence on this rooftop, in my life.

"There's a lot I could say, actually." His eyes certainly speak volumes.

"Then say it," I say, and it is a challenge.

Smoke curls up from the cigarette between his fingers. "Caleb, he's not who you think he is."

"And you know that, do you? Who he really is?"

"Certain things, yes." He takes a long drag on the cigarette, holds it in, blows it out through his nose again.

"You sneaked in here to tell me all of Caleb's secrets?"

He shakes his head, almost angrily, blond hair waving around his shoulders. "No, I didn't," he confesses. "You made the wrong choice. You should have stayed with me. We could have had something amazing."

"There was never a choice, Logan." It feels a little like a lie.

Another long inhalation, exhaling smoke like a dragon. "After you left with Caleb, I did some digging."

"What do you mean, digging?" I reach for the bottle of wine, which, ironically, is Malbec.

Pour some, take a sip. I need something to do with my hands, somewhere to look that isn't Logan.

"I looked around for information on you." He says it quietly, flicking his thumb across the butt of the cigarette.

"Did you find anything?" I almost don't want to ask.

A long pause, smoke rising in a thin curl, an occasional drag. I let the silence hang, let it weigh as heavily as the clouds.

"Information is power, you know." He stabs out his cigarette with a short, angry twist of his wrist. "I want to . . . to blackmail you with this, what I found out. Not tell you unless you come with me. But then I'd be no better than Caleb."

I digest what he's insinuating. "You think Caleb knows who I am and isn't telling me?"

"I think he knows more than he's told you, yes." He stands up, unfolding his lean frame, and strides away from me across the rooftop, stopping to put his hands on the waist-high wall separating him from the tumble into space. "Do you remember that day in my house, in the hallway? When I got back from walking Cocoa?"

I swallow hard. "Yes, Logan. I remember."

I remember too well. It recurs, a dream, a fantasy, memories assaulting me as I bathe, as I try to sleep, lost details of hands and mouths when I wake up.

"You were naked. Every inch of your fucking incredible skin, bare for me. I had you in my arms. I *had* you, X. I had my hands on you, had you on my lips, on my tongue. I can smell your pussy. I can still taste you, almost. But I let you go. I . . . made you walk away." He turns, glances at me, at my legs bare under the shirt. As if he can smell me, as if he can see what lies beneath the thin white cotton. "I don't think you'll ever understand how much that cost me, to walk away from you. How much self-control that took."

I shake all over. "Logan, I—"

"You would have let me. If I had pushed you up against the wall and done what I wanted to do to you . . . you would have let me. And you wouldn't have left, because you'd have wanted more."

I can't disagree. "I wasn't—"

He turns away, resumes staring out at the skyline, continuing as if I hadn't spoken. "I feel . . . haunted by that. I had you, and I let you go. I'm not haunted by the fact that you're gone, though, that I let you get away. I'm haunted by the fact that I still know it was the right thing to do. As much as I hate it, as much as it hurts, you aren't ready for me."

"What is that supposed to mean?" I stand up now, tug the hem of the shirt down so I'm almost covered. Move, so I'm standing a few feet behind him. "And I thought you said you found something out about me."

He reaches into the back pocket of his jeans, pulls out a square of folded paper. Holds it, stares at it. The wind plucks at the paper, fluttering the corners, as if it wants to rip it away, keep it from me, whatever is written there. He pivots so he faces me. Steps closer. I stop breathing. I tingle all over. My skin remembers the feel of his skin, the taste of his tongue. I shouldn't. That is not the choice I made. But . . . I can't forget it. And deep down, I don't want to.

"X, when I said there's so much I could say? I don't know how to say it all. I want to take you away, again. Run off with you, make you mine. But that wouldn't be enough for me. I'm a proud man, X. I want you to *choose* me. And I think you will, someday."

He presses his body against mine, and I feel every inch of him, hard, taut, warm. My breasts flatten against his chest, my hips bump against his. Something in me throbs, aches. Recognizes him, feels pulled by him. I forget everything, in these moments, except how utterly stolen away and carried off into the wild wind I feel with him.

The paper crinkles against my bicep as he grips me, a hand on my arm, a palm to my cheek.

No.

Don't.

"Don't, Logan," I whisper, but maybe the words are only a breath, only a sigh, only the minuscule brush of my eyelashes fluttering against my cheek, the sweep of lips against lips.

He does.

He kisses me,

and kisses me,

and kisses me.

And I don't stop him. My traitorous body wants to writhe and meld to his, wants to wrap itself around him. My hands sneak up to his hair, bury in the blond waves, and my throat utters a sigh, and maybe a moan, a slight one, a feverish, desperate one.

It is but a moment, a single moment.

A fortieth of an hour.

But it is one in which I feel utterly changed, as if some too-loose skin draped over my skeleton is snatched away and my true form is revealed, as if his touch as if his kiss as if his very presence can make me more truly *me*.

I want to weep.

I want to sag against him and beg him to keep kissing me until I cannot bear any more of the soft and tender intensity.

He backs away, wiping his wrist across his mouth, chest heaving as if desperately battling some inner demon. "Here." He hands me the square of folded paper. "It's your name."

I feel struck by lightning, wired, surging with too much of every-thing, too much heat, too much fear, too much doubt, too much need.

He puts a hand to the half wall, as if supporting himself, as if about to leap over and fly away.

"Logan . . ." I don't have anything else I can say.

"You have to decide if you want to know," he says. "Because once you know . . . you can't take it back. Once you start questioning, there's no stopping it."

"I *have* to know now, don't I?" I ask, almost angry at him. "You posed the question, and now I have to have the answer."

"True." He lets out a breath. Moves to walk past me, but stops a breath and a touch away. His indigo eyes meet mine. "You can come with me. We can leave New York." He glances up at the cloud-shrouded sky. "I can take you somewhere far away and show you the stars."

Could he have heard that wish? Can he see into my mind, read my thoughts? Sometimes I wonder if he can.

"But . . . You won't." He wipes a thumb across my lips. "Not yet, anyway."

He almost seems about to kiss me again, and I'm not entirely sure I would survive another stolen kiss, another breathless moment far too close to a man who seems to see far too much of me.

"If you ask the questions, X . . . you can't shy away from the answers when you find them."

I don't watch him leave. I can't. I won't.

I don't dare.

A long, long, painful silence, stretching like a rubber band about to snap. When I'm sure I'm alone, I finally look away from the skyline, from the dark shapes of skyscrapers and apartment blocks, away from the clouds and the dim distant lights. The rooftop is empty once more, but for me and the ghost of Logan's kiss.

I open the square of paper, unfolding it once and again.

Written there in messy male handwriting is a name.

If I could prevent myself from reading it, I almost would. But I don't.

Logan has given me my name.

I both love him for it, and hate him for it.